THE VEIL OF CORRUPTION

The Virus of Beauty Book 2

THE VEIL OF CORRUPTION

The Virus of Beauty Book 2

A Novel

C. B. Lyall

Hazel Publishing Company, LLC

ALSO BY C.B. LYALL
The Virus of Beauty - Book 1
Copyright © C. B. Lyall (2020)

Cover design by Catherine Clarke
Edited by Elizabeth Law, Sue Khodarahmi and Sara Kettler.

Ordering Information:
Quantity sales: special discounts are available on quantity purchases by corporations, associations, and others. For details, contact the publisher at the address below.

Publisher's Cataloging-in-Publication data

Lyall, C. B.
The Veil of Corruption: The Virus of Beauty Book 2
ISBN 978-1736002728 (Paperback)
ISBN 978-1736002735 (E-Book)
The main category of the book Young Adult Fiction / Fantasy / Wizards & Witches

Manufactured in the United States of America

Hazel Publishing Company, LLC

For Nick, Alex, Anthony, Gregory, and Logan.
With love.

This book could never have been written without the encouragement and support of several people. The talented writers in our writing group: Jean Huff, Gregory French, Kim Greene-Liebowitz and Brooke Lea Foster. The instructors at Sarah Lawrence College's Writing Institute: Pat Dunn, Jimin Han, and Wendy Townsend.

The professional care and attention of my editors, Elizabeth Law, Sue Khodarahmi, and Sara Kettler. e amazing cover design of Catherine Clarke

Thanks to my first readers Julia Pennock, Rosana Szabatura, Reyna Marder Gentin, Alex Borlabi, Kim Lyall, Tom Tanne and Eve Brockway. To my sons: Alex, Anthony, and Gregory, for their love and support. To my parents, Keith and Chris Browell. Finally, to my husband, Nick, for all the encouragement, belief, support and love.

And last to my golf buddies. I couldn't survive this insane life without Linda Fox, Asma Naeem, and the Ladies Wednesday Morning Group. You have my thanks and love.

Character List

<u>Hong Kong</u>
Wilf Gilvary
Myra Picton - Wilf's stepsister
Enzo Rossi - Wilf's friend
Reginald Gilvary - Wilf's father (deceased)
Yan Shuai - Wilf's mother (deceased)

<u>Witches of Mathowytch</u>
Katryna Wakefield
Ermentrude Wakefield - Katryna's mother
Degula - Head of Security, Witch Council
Akuna - Head Witch of Witch Council
Rytan - Executrix Guard
Olga - Executrix Guard

<u>Guardians of the Veil</u>
Flayver
Betrine

<u>Wizards of Kureyamage</u>
Hywel Wakefield – Katryna's father
Thiemus Picton – Myra's brother
Malik Kamder – Biome expert
Grand Wizard Verger – Head of Wizard Council
Councilman Tyrone – Member of Wizard Council
Chief Justice – Member of Wizard Council
Captain of the Wizard Guards
Jayden – Wizard Guard.

Chapter One - Wilf's Store, Hong Kong

A green fissure burst open in the gray Hong Kong sky, and a constellation of tiny black stars spilled out. Wilf pushed off the wall and stared at the witches flying in a V configuration as they weaved in between the clouds. The pit in his stomach deepened. A plague of magic was entering this world, and he felt responsible.

The downward-spiraling fighter-plane formation of brooms swept over the Wan Chai sky, above the high-rise buildings and market. Material from the witches' robes rustled and flapped overhead as they made their last approach into Tai Wan Street. They peeled off into a single file, whooshing along the dead-end street past the Hung Shing Taoist Temple, until the brooms halted a few feet above the cobblestones. With a wave of her arm, the leader signaled, and the brooms floated down until the witches' feet touched the ground. Another signal and the black brooms shrank to fit the small, cylindrical containers strapped to the riders' belts. A thunderclap sounded as the Executrix Squad, the elite guards of the Witch Council, stamped to attention. The squad moved forward. An eerie silence surrounded their marching feet as they moved towards Wilf's souvenir store, their non-reflective black uniforms absorbing the light.

Wilf leaned against the wall, merging his six-foot frame into the shadows. If only he could be like the locals who were oblivious to the steady stream of witches landing on Tai Wan Street from the Magical Realm. They typically arrived alone or in pairs when traveling by broom — he'd never seen this many arriving together. It took magical energy to navigate the Thermals, so only witches in the early stages of contagion flew. Warehouse portals transported witches who were severely affected by the Pulch Virus. Their beautiful, radiant profiles brought tears to the eyes of the magical healers, the virus having stripped the sufferers of both their magic and their facial warts. Wilf had only witnessed a handful in the latter stages who would never have their magic and ugliness restored. But at least the antidote had saved their lives.

Wilf's store was now the Witch Council's headquarters in Hong Kong. They had swooped in, taken command, and removed all the boards and advertising bills from the windows that Myra, his stepsister, had used to disguise the store as abandoned before following Ermentrude and himself to the Magical Realm. Wilf's happiness at finding a cure for the Pulch Virus — and some control over his own magic — had disappeared when he'd realized his store, his apartment, and his life had become infected with witches. When the virus was no longer a threat and the witches' realm stabilized, they would leave and Wilf would get his old life back. He pinned his hopes to that dream.

He continued to watch the progress of the Executrix Squad towards his store. He sighed, perhaps he should find out why they were here. Before he could move, the door opened and Ermentrude stepped out. Wilf had become used to the Head Witch's doughy face and the enormous wart on the end of her long, beaked nose. It was her scratchy voice, blackened fingernails, and habit of stroking the bristles on her square chin that still made him wince. The squad saluted her before entering the store. Katryna collided with the witches in her haste to catch her mother.

"Why didn't you defend Wilf?" Katryna said, rushing ahead and angling her rake-thin body to block her mother from reaching the door to the store's apartment.

Ermentrude adjusted an enormous book in her arms. "What could I have said?" She stepped around her irate daughter.

"That they were wrong. If Wilf hadn't helped, then we wouldn't have an antidote, magic, or Mathowytch. They've forgotten that without him adding his magic, the Veil would have collapsed and we'd all be standing trial before the Wizard Council."

Ermentrude turned to face her daughter. "We're all very grateful, I'm sure. Except that mist tendrils are roaming free around Mathowytch causing witches to disappear. That's not how the Veil spell worked for the past fourteen years. It changed when Wilf added his magic."

"I don't believe it," Katryna said.

"That's because the bonding ritual you and that wizard performed is ruling your logic. Annulment is the only way to stop its hold over you both." She tapped the book. "The potion in here should achieve that." Ermentrude wiggled her hand. The apartment door swung open.

Wilf beckoned Katryna over, hoping she'd know what was going on. His spirits rose with each step she took towards him. When the witches left and returned to their Realm, Katryna would remain. They would be together.

She slumped against the wall next to him, sliding her hands down the front of her jeans. She'd abandoned her usual peasant blouses and skirts during the past few days. It would help her fit in better when he introduced her to his friends.

"Why are the Executrix here?" He resisted the urge to hug her, squeezing her hand instead.

"Degula sent for them. She says they're here to keep order, but I think she enjoys having them around because they don't question her."

"Is there any news from Mathowytch?"

"The Wizard Council is demanding we take down the Veil spell. My mom thinks there will be reprisals against the Witch Council for the capture of Mathowytch. She says fourteen years of wanting revenge for stealing their city won't disappear overnight." She turned towards him. Her small, deep-set hazel eyes burned with anger.

"Hold on! Why would they do what the Wizard Council wants? The virus isn't a threat anymore," Wilf said.

"The Witch Council thinks the Veil spell is corrupt. They were discussing having access to the biome in Sha Tin." Katryna bent one knee and placed her foot against the wall. "I didn't understand, but my mom kept nodding in agreement." She pushed back and forth on her folded leg. "My mom's still upset about the whole bonding ritual." She smiled and glanced at him through her lashes.

Wilf's heart skipped a beat, and his voice trembled. "Her face when we told her."

"I've never seen my mom speechless before. It was two minutes before she drew breath," Katryna said, laughing.

Wilf grinned at the memory of Ermentrude hearing about the mating bond he and Katryna had performed. She'd gone ballistic.

"You've done what? Of all the irresponsible rituals to perform, you decided that was the best one to use?" She had been in the store when they'd told her. Wilf was glad Ermentrude's magic had diminished in the battle with Myra and Seldan. He had explained that it had seemed the best way for Katryna to no longer be under Hywel's direct control. It still made sense to him.

Ermentrude had paced the store. "We must annul it before the attraction becomes too strong." She stopped in front of him. "Until then you keep your hands and" — she glanced towards his crotch — "everything else away from my daughter."

Her words still echoed around his head occasionally. Wilf suspected she'd attached a spell to keep them there. He shuddered, thinking of how Ermentrude would react if she knew how difficult it had become for him to concentrate whenever Katryna was near.

He bumped Katryna with his elbow and nodded down the street. Two more witches landed and entered the store. He sighed, and she flexed her fingers in his.

"It's so frustrating hanging around here all day. I want to help more," Katryna said.

"I know what you mean." Wilf wanted to be out searching for Myra. It had been two days since his stepsister had escaped into the Thermals on a broom, but until they had vaccinated all the witches, no one seemed to think searching for Myra was a top priority. Ermentrude said they had advised the witches in Mathowytch to apprehend Myra on sight, and they had placed her name on a Wanted List for crimes against the Council and for the murder of Reginald, Wilf's father.

It wasn't enough. Wilf itched to be part of the search party.

He reached into his pocket for his phone, but something dug into his leg. He dropped Katryna's hand and pulled out his family's wizard journal. The sizel on the front glowed. He placed his wizard ring on the red leather cover and watched the three locks snap open. Pages fluttered as they turned until the section marked "Wizard Wilf Gilvary" appeared.

Wilf wasn't a proper wizard. He didn't even like performing magic. The spells he tried to conjure slipped around his mind, never fully forming. When they did, he could never guarantee the results. He would much rather be a Normal, a soccer-playing high school student.

He slid down to the ground and sat, resting his back

against the wall. Katryna drifted down next to him.

"The journal's written an entire section on our finding the antidote to cure the Pulch Virus," Katryna said, leaning closer to read.

He wished he felt the same excitement as she did. "There are a few lines about Ermentrude taking me to Mathowytch by broom through the Thermals. You're mentioned here, too," Wilf said, nudging her with his elbow.

Katryna turned the page. "It mentions that terrible trip through the Veil where we nearly lost you to the Guardians. Look, it even mentions this stupid bracelet." She pulled her sleeve down and flipped another page.

Wilf had hoped the bracelet would have fallen off once they reached Hong Kong, but it remained where Hywel, Katryna's father, had placed it. At least since the bonding ritual, it now bore the name Gilvary instead of Wakefield.

"I'm not sure it's recorded all the details accurately." Katryna turned over several pages. "It says you received training in the art of magic, but I've seen you trying to produce spells. It's pure luck if they perform as they should. I've seen first graders with more control."

"Ha-ha. You'd have problems, too, if they had forced you into Hywel's magic Advancer instead of the traditional way of learning, with teachers and school." Wilf eased closer until their legs were touching.

"Every time I look in a mirror, I'm reminded that I'm Hywel's daughter," Katryna said. There was no mistaking that she had Hywel's long, hooked nose.

His eyes rested on an entry about Myra, and he slammed the book shut.

Katryna laid her hand on Wilf's arm. "They'll capture her. She can't escape justice for murdering Reginald."

Wilf hugged his knees. At least Hywel was behind bars for killing his mother. He still had a hard time reconciling the stepsister he'd loved as being the murderer of their father. The battle for the store had happened two days ago, and she'd eluded capture.

Katryna put her hand under Wilf's chin and turned his face to hers. "It's no one's fault she got away."

Wilf smiled, then dropped his gaze. "I know, but I can't sit here doing nothing." He sat up straight. "Why don't we take a broom? Go after her?"

Katryna shook her head. "My mom would stop us."

He stood. "Don't reject it without even trying."

Katryna held out her hand for Wilf to pull her up. "You can't fly a broom through the Thermals."

"I've ridden through them a bunch of times," Wilf said, folding his arms. That wasn't true, and they both knew it. The route between the Realms was full of specters — lost souls who attacked travelers. Pathways opened and closed and trapped inexperienced riders inside, never finding an exit.

Katryna gave a laugh. "As a passenger. But flying a broom isn't an option for you."

"I don't see why not. If you don't want to try, I'll do it on my own."

"But it's impossible." She tried to take his arm, but he lifted it out of the way. "You seriously want to try flying a broom?"

"Yes." Wilf returned the journal to his pocket. He would rather she came with him. Katryna had spent her entire life in the Magical Realm learning to conjure spells. Magic was part of who she was, whereas he'd be happier if he never performed another spell. If only that were an option! Katryna thought he didn't practice magic enough, but that wasn't true. It didn't matter how hard he tried — some spells refused to work for him.

"Come with me," Katryna said, walking towards the apartment.

Wilf ran to catch up. She put her finger to her lips and tiptoed past the kitchen.

"Bat's blood!" Ermentrude said. Wisps of blue smoke seeped down the stairs. Wilf preferred to remain ignorant about what she was conjuring, but it likely had something to do with himself, Katryna, and the annulment of their bond. Ermentrude had made her thoughts very clear about their growing attraction for each other.

Katryna disappeared into her room and came out carrying a broom. "Here, knock yourself out, but remember I warned you. It's impossible," she said.

"What do I do?" He grabbed hold of the broom before she changed her mind. Or Ermentrude found them.

"See the broom lifting off the ground with you on it. Then feed it a slight amount of magic. Just enough to give it life, but not too much, or it'll throw you off and disappear."

"That's all? Isn't there a spell I have to chant?" he said, glancing down at the broomstick.

"No." She folded her arms and sighed. "I'd better come with you."

Wilf grabbed the broom and headed to his room with Katryna trailing behind him.

She sat in his desk chair and spun round to face the room. Wilf straddled the broom and imagined it rising from the ground as he fed it magic through his wizard ring. The handle heated, but he kept hold until his knuckles were white. He grinned and moved his feet. He'd made it a few inches off the ground.

"How are you doing that?" Katryna said, jumping to her feet.

He fed more magic to the broom and gritted his teeth when his legs burned. The broom rose until his head bumped the ceiling. He couldn't believe it: He was flying.

"The broom is smoking! Come back down," Katryna shouted.

Smoke spiraled from the end of the handle. The broom leapt forward and Wilf lost his balance, falling backwards onto his bed. His palms stung, and red welts ran across them. The broom bounced around the room, leaving scorch marks on the posters of Newcastle United Football Team, and St. James' Park Football Stadium.

He jumped up, trying to catch the broom as it came overhead, but only smacked it against the wall. It slid down. Katryna was laughing so hard, tears ran down her face. "You look ridiculous."

A blinding flash filled the room as it touched the floor. Wilf blinked until his vision cleared, then rolled to the edge of the bed and peered down. A pile of ash and a burn scar on his rug were all that remained of the broom.

Katryna blinked and rubbed her eyes. "It's alright. I never really liked that broom."

"I made it fly." He ran his fingers through his hair and winced at the pain from his palm.

She took hold of his hands. "Wow! We'd better let Mom treat these. You know wizards can't normally fly brooms."

The door creaked open. Catcus, Ermentrude's cat, entered the room and stopped when she saw Wilf. She arched her back and hissed.

"Get out," he said, throwing a pillow at the door. His wizard ring flashed, and the cat disappeared inside a cloud of pink smoke. "Oh no, not again!"

Catcus gave a piteous wail and dashed from the room. What had he done? Ermentrude would kill him if he'd hurt her cat. He ran after Catcus. This time she still had a tail — he saw the tip disappearing down the stairs. He clattered after the cat and skidded to a stop in the kitchen.

Catcus was crying at Ermentrude's feet. The witch stopped petting the frightened animal and stood up, folding her arms. "Well?"

"She startled me... I wouldn't hurt her..." Wilf spluttered out his apology. "She shouldn't be in my room."

"You think that excuses you from turning my cat into...What would you call this?" A slight wisp of smoke escaped from Ermentrude's hair bun.

Wilf took a deep breath. "Not sure," he said. Catcus had her own head and tail, but her body resembled a lizard's.

"Don't stand there. Undo it," Katryna said, pushing past him.

Ermentrude glared at her daughter. "That will produce more damage." She wiggled her fingers at the cat, and Catcus returned to normal. "Another incomplete spell. There's something wrong with you or your magic." She sat down at the round kitchen table, and the cat jumped into her lap. "What magic were you practicing?"

"Nothing," he said, pushing his burnt hands deep into his pockets and leaning against the counter.

"Wilf flew my old broom, before it dissolved into a pile of ash." Katryna said, taking her compact mirror out of her jeans pocket.

Ermentrude folded her arms. "Wizards can't fly! It's not natural to them."

"Show Mom your hands. They're badly burned."

"Wizards have to use portals. Only witches can use a broom." Ermentrude extended her hand. "Let me see."

Wilf pulled his hands out of his pockets and opened the palms.

Ermentrude wiggled her fingers and a jar floated across the room. "Put some of this on the burns. Why do you need a flying broom?" she said, looking from him to her daughter.

Katryna kept her head bent as she scrolled through the numbers on the compact's screen.

"Let me guess. You were thinking of trying to reach your stepsister in Kureyamage. The Thermals are dangerous even for a witch who knows how to navigate them." She patted his shoulder. "It's best if you leave capturing Myra to us."

Wilf glared at Ermentrude's back. There was not a chance he was leaving his stepsister's capture to anyone else.

"No one else I know is in Hong Kong," Katryna said, snapping the lid down on her mirror.

"Speak to the check-in clerks — they have lists of all arrivals," Ermentrude said, stroking Catcus.

Wilf's phone pinged, and he pulled it out of his pocket. A text from Enzo said they'd scheduled the next soccer practice for 4 p.m. He'd be able to get out of here and leave the witches and their problems behind. But he had hours until then, if he could believe the time and date his phone was displaying.

"This phone's messed up," Wilf said, thumping down at the table. His knee banged the leg, causing the porcelain mugs to rattle and slosh their contents.

"What makes you say that?" Ermentrude snatched up the papers she'd been reading.

"The date's all wrong," Wilf said.

"Are you sure?" A stripped dishtowel flew across the room and mopped up the spilled brew.

"We can't have been away for only one week," Wilf said, thumbing through his messages.

"Why ever not? One week sounds about right to me," Ermentrude said, pushing the cat off her lap and standing. "Time doesn't move the same within the Realms. One day in Hong Kong equals ten in the Magical Realm." She picked up her bag. "I'm needed down in the workshop. Katryna, are you ready?"

The young witch shrugged and blew Wilf a kiss on her way out the door. He heard her running down the stairs after Ermentrude.

He leaned back in the chair, waiting for the front door to bang closed before letting out his breath. Katryna thought she'd got him with the flying broom, but Ermentrude had said wizards used portals. That meant his father had one hidden here somewhere, and the most logical place to hide it would be... in the workshop full of witches.

Chapter Two - Wilf's Store, Hong Kong

W itches and magic surrounded Wilf as he pushed his way through the door and into the store. He'd been avoiding entering for two days, since the battle with Myra.

The store's interior had expanded to about three times its size. It had been possible before the witches arrived to touch a wall with a few steps in either direction. The store now resembled a waiting room, with benches, chairs, and stools filling the space. There were even potted leafy green plants and magazines. However, the scent of rosewood still lingered in the store's humid air. Wilf lifted his head towards a creak from the basement stairs, half expecting his father to appear.

That last morning, Reginald had been down in the workshop when Wilf came looking for his Octopus card — a card you couldn't live in Hong Kong without. He'd been inside only a few minutes before the Mages Crystal exploded, sending glass daggers around the room. They'd have impaled him if he hadn't dived into the closet. His father hadn't seen it that way. Reginald had raged and blamed Wilf for damaging the crystal. He'd even tried to stop Wilf from attending soccer practice, but Wilf had left anyway. He hadn't understood the dangers of uncontrolled magic. If only his father had explained instead of trying to bully him into learning. It was all too late now.

A dazzle of light caught Wilf's eye when he reached the middle of the store. He turned towards the alcove. His reflection stared back at him from the crystal's fractured surface. Multiple images of his gray eyes followed his progress across the store. The eyes in the broken shards seemed to accuse him of causing the crystal's destruction. Wilf glared back, but he noticed a hint of guilt reflected in his defiant look.

He would never be sure his magic hadn't been the cause. He let his black hair fall over his eyes.

Everyone seemed busy but Wilf. The forgotten head of a porcelain Happy Cat grinned up at him from a corner. A last reminder of the souvenir store. The witches had swept everything else into trash bags. He picked it up, letting his thumb stroke its smile, before dropping it into his pocket. It didn't matter which pocket he placed an item in — as long as his clothing had a pocket, the items would be at his call.

The room reminded Wilf that while he might be back in Hong Kong, where he'd wanted to be, Ermentrude and her witches had taken over his life, the store and the workshop. A long table had replaced the sales counter, and two witches checked newcomers in and out. A large crystal ball kept clouding over in-between squawking apparitions demanding attention. One of the reception witches kept glaring in his direction.

He lifted his chin and strode towards the basement workshop. He was here for a reason — to find his father's portal. Still, he paused at the top of the stairs and ran his fingers over the runes etched into the lintel surrounding the basement entrance. The stone at the center of his wizard ring remained dull. It needed no flashes of power or blood rituals to open the entrance to the workshop. It stood wide open.

A witch, staggering under the pile of books she carried, bumped into him. He stepped aside and let her through before clomping down the stairs. Katryna, Ermentrude, and Degula, the witch in charge of security, stood at the bottom directing traffic and equipment.

"What do you want?" Degula said. Malice pulsed from the muscular witch. She didn't like being in his debt. It wasn't personal, Ermentrude had explained. Degula would resent the help of any wizard in recovering the antidote formula and preventing the deaths of countless witches. She hated all wizards.

Wilf stepped off the bottom stair and gave her a large, toothy smile.

"This is my workshop. I'm here to see what you're doing with the place," he said.

"Oh, yes," Degula smirked. "I'd forgotten about the great magic you've created down here." She cackled with laughter and turned her back to him. Wilf resisted the urge to use finger gestures at her.

"You can't stand there," Ermentrude said, pushing him out of the way. "Why don't you make yourself useful and go help those witches trying to arrange the bookshelves. Or sweep the floor."

She'd begun treating him like the team's intern, trying to find him busywork at every opportunity. He should tell them all to shove it. He strode across the workshop, but Katryna followed him.

She pushed a broom at him. "Here. Until you decide what to do. Start over there where we've cleared the floor."

He snatched the broom from her.

"It can't fly, so don't even try it," she said, turning away from him.

"Is that so?" he said, catching hold of her hand and swinging her round to face him.

"I haven't tried that one, but I believe its true function is dirt removal." Katryna opened her eyes wide.

"Don't try that innocent look with me." He checked they were out of Ermentrude's sight and pulled Katryna into the corner. "You know I will imagine some way to repay you for this, don't you?"

"I'm looking forward to you trying." Katryna laughed.

"Expect the worst," he said, swinging the broom.

"What are you doing here anyway? You never come down."

"I came to find out what's happening."

"Stay clear of Degula is my advice." She headed back towards her mother and Degula.

He dragged the broom over the floor as he inched farther into the room. A few witches looked up from cataloging jars of herbs and animal parts — at least he hoped they were animal parts — before returning to work.

Wilf pushed around a small pile of dust and headed towards the back. It was inconceivable that they thought he'd come down here to sweep the floor for this bunch of crones in his own workshop. A few days ago, he'd been in the middle of a battle, blasting magic at Myra and at Wizard Hywel, Katryna's father. At least they'd captured Hywel. That was a victory.

Where would his father hide a portal? He surveyed the room. Two-thirds of the walls contained bookshelves. It could be behind one of those, he supposed. The wall to his left had a sink and pieces of equipment being used to produce the vaccine. He faced the back wall. It seemed the best place to start.

He closed his eyes and lay his ringed hand on the wall. A small vibration tingled up his arm. He moved to the right, glancing around to see if anyone was watching. This time the sensation seemed quieter. He moved back the way he'd come, gliding his hand along the wall as he went. A pulse ran up his arm. He walked a little farther and tried again. The pulse grew stronger as he approached the bookcase.

The witch he'd followed down the stairs shelved her books and edged away from him. He smiled. She fled up the stairs. He laid the broom against the wall and let his hand brush the shelves. His ring flared when his hand rested on an old volume — The History and Magic of the Mages of Mulkulth. He tried to slide it off the shelf, but it refused to move. He closed his eyes, feeling the vibration.

"What are you doing?"

Wilf's eyes sprang open. Heat rose in his cheeks. Degula stood inches from him, peering over his shoulder. How long had she been standing there watching him?

"An inventory of my dad's books. Wouldn't want them to disappear into a crate when you leave," Wilf said, letting his hand drop. He edged around Degula and collected the broom.

Degula stared at the shelf before turning to face him. "Mulkulth! Why would you be interested in ancient legends about Mages and forgotten traditional magic?"

Wilf shrugged. "I'm not. Never heard of the place before."

She gave him a sidelong stare. "It would be better if you concentrated on current magic. Then you wouldn't destroy whatever you touched. Do you require instructions on how to sweep a floor?" She wiggled her fingers. Dirt collected in a pile next to his feet. "What use are you?"

"I can read a journal and save your ugly face," he said, then bit his tongue. The last thing he needed was to antagonize Degula.

The dirt whipped up into a vortex around his feet.

Katryna rushed over to stand between him and Degula. "Why don't you return to the apartment? We can manage here." She tried to wrestle the broom out of his hands.

"It's fine," he said, glaring at Degula and tugging the broom out of Katryna's reach. "I thought you had important work to do, saving your Realm instead of watching me sweep the floor."

"A Realm you've helped to destroy with your untrained meddling," Degula said.

"Don't worry, next time I won't help at all. See how you cope then," Wilf said, waving the broom at the witch's back.

"Wilf. Leave it!" Katryna tried to snatch the broom.

"Can you believe her?" Wilf said, kicking the pile of dust.

"She's been in a nasty mood since Akuna called a meeting of the Witch Council members." Katryna wiggled her fingers. The dust settled back into a neat pile.

"She's always in a bad mood when I'm around!" Wilf flicked the broom at the dust pile. "Why has the Head Witch calling a meeting upset Degula?"

"That's what I want to find out," Katryna said, making a play for the broom again, but he placed it behind his back. She reached for it and he pulled her into him.

"Stop it. Witches are looking," Katryna said, pressing her hands against his chest.

"Let them. You don't think I'm responsible for the Realm collapsing, do you?"

Katryna held his gaze. "No! The earthquakes had begun long before you arrived. It was Hywel and the Wizard Council's fault for releasing the virus. I have my magic back because of you."

She caught hold of the broom.

He bent his head to her ear. "A kiss for the broom."

She blushed and pecked him on the cheek.

"That's not a kiss."

She smiled. "Later. Not here. Mom is glaring."

"Let her." He laughed, but handed her the broom. Resting his hand on the book, he felt the pulsing vibration. It had to be the portal. He couldn't search with the workshop crawling with witches. He needed to come back later and try to work out how to open it.

"I'll see you later," he said, leaving Katryna at the workbench.

Degula stood talking to the captain of her Executrix Squad. Her eyes followed him as he made a direct line for the stairs.

If he had found the portal, he had no intention of sharing its discovery with Degula, Ermentrude, or even Katryna. He would make the trip to Kureyamage alone and bring Myra back for justice.

Chapter Three - Wilf's Store, Hong Kong

Wilf headed back to his bedroom and collapsed into the desk chair. It had to be his father's portal he'd felt hidden down there. Myra wouldn't be safe in Kureyamage for much longer.

He allowed a tiny ball of magic to build in his hand. It glowed and sent out sparks, but made no noise. Earlier, the Executrix Squad had used sound to intimidate. When they'd snapped to attention, the street had echoed with the sound of thunder, but there had been complete silence as the squad marched. The control of senses was part of the magic. He closed his fist, letting the magic squeeze through his fingers. Instead of a ball, the magic flattened into a disk, like a Frisbee. He snapped his wrist and it disappeared. He had never thought of magic as surrounding him before. Existing in everything connected to him. He had thought he could escape, walk through a door, and exit this life. But that wasn't true. His every breath was touched with magic. There was no escaping it. To the witches, he was the deafening roar of a crowd after scoring a goal. He charged ahead, trying to bring his magic under control, but most of the time it spun away from him. No wonder the witches feared him. If he could develop a connection to his magic, then he'd know when he was using it.

He opened his palm, trying to connect with the magic again. A ball the size of a pea materialized and then fizzled out. He tried again, but this time only a wisp of smoke rose from his palm. Anger pulsed through him. It shouldn't be this difficult. Magic sparked from his fingers. He struggled to control the energy. He took several deep breaths and closed his eyes; he tried to gain control.

Suddenly adrenaline whipped through him and sweat trickled down his face. Spikes of magic flowed through him. He gulped air into his heaving lungs. It felt like he'd been sprinting the length of a soccer field, with defenders at his heels. He squeezed his eyes shut, but shrouded images with outstretched arms swirled behind his eyes. Neon lights darted around shadowy creatures while cackles and screams filled his head. What were these witches doing to him? Was Ermentrude sending him visions of the Thermals to frighten him? Why couldn't she leave him alone?

A bright pinprick of light built in his mind and he grasped the chair's arms, his fingers digging into the leather. He forced his eyes open, trying to cling to the sights and smells of his bedroom. A searing pain ran up his arm from the shooting star marking. He ground his teeth and thrust back into the chair.

Mist swirled around the room as the cackles and screams grew louder. A figure emerged, the edges of her black gown still blended into the mist.

"Who are you?" Wilf edged his chair backwards.

"I am Flayver, a guardian of the Veil."

"That's not possible." A guardian shouldn't be able to leave the border between Mathowytch and Kureyamage in the Magical Realm. But here she stood in his room. "What do you want?" Wilf braced in his chair and edged farther away.

"We're connected through magic," Flayver said, floating closer to him. The mist extended with her, keeping to the edges of her gown. Her features sharpened, but her hair and slim body remained translucent. "We have work to do. It's time."

"Did Degula send you?" Wilf wouldn't put it past her to send an apparition.

"I do not answer to that witch." Flayver placed her hands on either side of his head. Her fingers were ice, but the pain increased to a searing pulse, like the agony he'd suffered in Hywel's Advancer machine. Wilf fell forward when she released him.

As she stretched out her fingers at the mist, a tendril broke off and snaked across the floor. Wilf half stood, but the tendril weaved up his body, pushing him back, and entered the shooting star marking. He watched in horror as the end disappeared into him.

"It's done. The connection is complete." The guardian melted back into the mist.

"Wait! I don't understand." His head felt heavy, and pain throbbed across his forehead, blurring his vision.

"Soon," Flayver said, dissolving into the mist as it coiled

around her.

"I don't know what you mean," Wilf said, leaning forward and rubbing his forehead.

"I will continue alone until you are ready to join me." Flayver's voice echoed in his head.

The cackling stopped, and the sounds of Hong Kong filled his room again. His hand burned, and a ball of white energy grew in front of him. The bedroom lights flickered and buzzed. His body trembled, and the fist-sized ball of magic sizzled. It rose to hover above his head. A flash of red from the ruby in the center of his wizard ring spiked to the ball. The room filled with a blaze of color, then the ball exploded. Wilf dove to the floor, but the energy surrounded him. He covered his head with his hands. A loud crack left a buzzing in his ears. His body absorbed the magic as it pressed against his skin. Collapsing to the floor, he arched his back as pain lashed through him. He lay panting when the pain receded. The smell of sulfur filled his nostrils, and then the room plunged into darkness.

His legs shook as he hauled himself up using the bed. His desk chair still spun. It took him several breaths before he could slow his heart rate. He switched on the light and noticed that the shooting star marking had disappeared from the back of his hand. It had been there since he was thirteen. His wizard mark was gone but not his magic. That still blazed inside him.

Noise rose from the kitchen. He should tell Ermentrude or Katryna, but what would he tell them? They wouldn't believe a Veil guardian had visited and that she'd taken away his star tattoo. A guardian wasn't an actual person. It was part of a spell. It made no sense. Ermentrude would think it was his lack of control. Perhaps she was right, and he was losing his grip on reality. Flayver had said they were connected. He ran his hand through his hair. If only his father was around to explain what was happening.

A lump grew in his throat. He'd spent most of his childhood arguing with his father over magic. Reginald demanding that Wilf study and Wilf refusing. There had been two topics they never discussed: his mother's death, and why Wilf needed to learn magic. If his father had explained that magic could be dangerous, he might have been more willing to learn. Perhaps he could have been the wizard his father wanted him to be. And maybe Reginald would have watched him play soccer like the other dads. An image of his father sitting in the bleachers, or of Wilf standing next to Reginald performing magic, refused to form. Who was he fooling? He and his father had never talked or behaved like a Normal's family.

Wilf sighed. The visit from the guardian had clearly spooked him; otherwise he wouldn't be letting his thoughts run down this rabbit hole. His father had evaporated. It was too late for regrets.

He sat arguing with himself over whether to tell Ermentrude about Flayver's visit. In the end, he decided to keep the episode to himself. For now. He plodded down the stairs to the kitchen.

Katryna glanced up as he entered. "Are you all right?"

"I'm fine," he said.

Katryna sat at the table where Myra used to sit, and Ermentrude sat in his father's place, reading. She'd turned the round table yellow. Catcus greeted him in her usual manner by arching her back and hissing before scurrying under Ermentrude's chair.

Katryna wiggled her fingers and a mug of brew settled in front of him. He let the chatter between the witches filter through, blocking out his other thoughts.

Ermentrude furrowed her brow and tutted at the document.

"What are you reading?" Katryna pushed her lank hair behind her ears.

He smiled. She'd been so happy this morning when the last curl had disappeared. She'd come barreling into his room without knocking. He'd have to use the lock in the future or wear shorts to sleep in. He'd grabbed the bedsheet as the door flew open. She'd stopped at the mirror and shaken her head.

"Not a curl or a bounce," she'd said, leaning in to examine her face closely. "If only my warts would return."

He'd pushed the pillows behind him and sat up. "I think you look great." He hadn't been about to fall into the trap of calling her beautiful or ugly. That was a minefield no male should cross, especially not a wizard.

She'd turned and smiled.

"Katryna!" Ermentrude's voice had echoed around his room.

"Coming," Katryna had yelled, but she'd stopped to kiss him before she'd left. He'd tried to pull her down, but she'd danced out of his grasp and the door had closed behind her.

Ermentrude looked up from her papers. "It's a Letter of Negotiation. Degula gave it to me as we left the workshop. The

Wizard Council wants a meeting to discuss the return of Hywel to them."

"What? That's not right. We should imprison that wizard for eternity and throw away the key." Wilf banged down his mug.

"Impossible. They can't release him. He manufactured and spread the virus," Katryna said.

"Hywel will pay, but at the moment we need him. He's crucial to the successful transition we'll need to make from source magic to biome magic," Ermentrude said, keeping a finger on the word she'd been reading.

"Biome?" Katryna wrinkled her brow.

"So, now Hywel and Myra will both be free," Wilf said, balling his fists.

Ermentrude bent her head over the document. He glared at her anyway.

"What's a biome?" Katryna said.

He opened his hand and the journal flickered into appearance. "There's a mention in here." He placed the book on the table and laid his ringed finger on the red leather cover. The three locks snapped open, and the pages turned. Words appeared, and Wilf read the words out loud.

"Biomes: a complex biotic community maintained under the same climatic conditions as the Magical Realm to produce and protect magic. The following pages explain how the process works."

"There are pictures and diagrams." Wilf leaned over Katryna's shoulder and flicked over the pages. Her hair brushed his cheek and he inhaled, aware of the warmth of her body and the faint citrus fragrance that always surrounded her. The memory of this morning's kiss and her soft lips surfaced. He straightened up.

"It's a dome," she said, tracing the diagram with her finger. The journal's page rippled and sighed.

"They're about half the size of the Meeting Hall building," Ermentrude said. "But they won't be visible to Groundlings. It's in Sha Tin, near the warehouse portals."

"Groundlings?" Wilf said, looking up from the page.

"That's what some witches call Normals," Katryna said, blushing.

"They can't fly or use magic. I think it's quite an appropriate name for them," Ermentrude said, turning back to the document. "If the Magical Realm collapses, the biomes will be our only source of magic. The Councils are planning in case we need a mass evacuation to this Realm," she explained.

"Hywel can't be the only wizard with this knowledge? I don't see why we need to surrender him," Katryna said.

"Believe me, I'm the last person who wants that wizard set loose, but Hywel built the biomes. We don't have a choice. That book can't help with this."

The journal emitted a puff of smoke and slammed shut, almost trapping Wilf's fingers. The locks snapped closed, and the book jumped into his pocket.

Ermentrude shook her head. "You need to control that journal better. You should train it to obey you. But that's what comes from allowing it to become the center of attention for so long." She folded up the papers. "We must give in to their demands if we want access to magic."

"What about traveling back to the Magical Realm?" Wilf said.

Ermentrude took a deep breath. "That's another problem. Several witches have tried to return, but the Thermals are only allowing selective broom travelers."

"Wait! You mean Myra might still be in Hong Kong?" Wilf caught Katryna's quick glance in his direction but avoided her eyes.

"There's been no sighting of her," Ermentrude said, sending her empty mug to the sink. "Though she'd be able to hide since she knows the city so well."

"But we saw an entrance being created when she left." Wilf gripped the back of the chair. Was it true that his stepsister was trapped here in Hong Kong?

"That doesn't mean they allowed her safe passage." Ermentrude stood, and the papers jumped into her bag. "She could have traveled in them for a time, before they threw her out, or she might be flying around in them." She shook her head. "With the Thermals behaving this way, we'll need that biome available as soon as possible."

"Why didn't you tell me?" Wilf said. It was unbelievable. He should have been searching for Myra in the city. Instead he'd been trying to fly a broom and look for a portal he didn't need. His ruby ring flashed.

Ermentrude folded her arms. "Because I wasn't sure you could handle the news."

He thrust his hand into his pocket.

"Degula has witches searching for her. Any sighting and

we'll be the first to know." Ermentrude's bag jumped into her pocket. "Katryna, are you ready to leave?"

"Where am I going?" Katryna said, opening her eyes wide.

"With me. I'm not leaving you two alone until there's a way to release you from that bonding ritual."

Katryna blew him a kiss, which landed on his lips, before running down the stairs after Ermentrude.

Ermentrude had no right to keep Myra's whereabouts a secret from him. A shiver ran down his spine and a whiff of sulfur floated past him. He scratched the back of his right hand, where the shooting star marking had been. He, too, had secrets.

C. B. Lyall

Chapter Four - Kowloon Walled City Park, Hong Kong

Myra stared down at a folded copy of the South China newspaper. Her eyes focused on the date. It couldn't be true. The Thermals had thrown her out two days after she'd entered. She dug her fingernails into her palms, not wanting to remember that day. It was too late, and Wilf's words surfaced once more.

"I'll find you," he'd shouted as Myra ran from the store, grabbing a broom and speeding off into the sky. After the heat of battle and the exhilaration of escape, she'd welcomed the cool air on her face as she flew high above Hong Kong. With a crack of thunder, the fissure had opened into the Thermals. She'd tightened her grip on the speeding broom and sailed through the entrance, her legs and arms tingling as ribbons of neon-colored lights touched her. The broom bucked and then leapt forward. The view of Hong Kong faded, and the tight knot in her stomach unraveled when the entrance closed. She had outsmarted Wilf, Ermentrude, and Katryna. She allowed a smile to spread across her lips.

Myra veered to the right, blasting at the narrow-faced specters clawing at her leg. The broom wobbled, threatening to tip her into the abyss, but she wrestled it back under control. She had to stay focused. Icy chills ran down her legs. She needed to fly faster. Too long in the Thermals led to madness or death. She hunched lower along the broomstick to cut down resistance, and it sprang forward.

Her fingers cramped, and the biting wind numbed her face. She didn't know how much longer she could cling to the broom. A pinprick of white light appeared in the distance, and she made a steep nosedive for the growing exit. Her hair whipped across her eyes, but she didn't dare loosen her grip. The fissure opened wider, and she steered through it, letting out a whoop of joy. She had made it back to the Magical Realm. Her shoulders relaxed, and she glided the broom towards a flat, grassy area between two low-rise buildings.

When her feet touched the ground, Myra jumped off and spun around, taking in the surrounding buildings. Her vision blurred as recognition slammed her. She knew this place too well to deny that she'd landed in the Kowloon Walled City Park. She held back a roar of frustration. The broom shrank to the size of a pencil with a wiggle of her fingers, and she thrust it into a pocket. She'd been refused access to Kureyamage by the Thermals, and instead the broom had spiraled her back to Hong Kong. The irony of landing in a park that had once been a lawless city felt personal. Bulldozers had been the solution for the city three years before Hong Kong reverted to Chinese rule. They'd made a beautiful park from the territory. She'd love to wipe away her old life for a fresh one.

The thud, thud, thud of a bouncing ball filtered through her memories, and she spun around. A soccer ball rolled towards her. She pointed her fingers and the ball shriveled with a loud hiss. The small boy chasing it stopped and scooped up the deflated ball, letting out a howl of despair that Myra would have loved to echo. A release for the aching disappointment trapped deep within her. The child's mother wrapped the boy in her arms, trying to comfort him. Myra shook her head and threw the newspaper into a trash can. No one would soothe Myra's pain. It was always the same — whenever she thought she was ahead, life slapped her down.

She sighed. There was no point standing around feeling sorry for herself. She turned her back on the family scene and wandered over towards the Walled City's historical displays, the only reminders that the park had once been an ungoverned, densely populated enclave with 50,000 residents controlled by local triads. Her mind ran in circles. What was she going to do now?

Tourists jostled past her and a woman bumped into Myra. She lifted her hand. She'd love to vent some of her fury. Blast the woman across the park. Hurl her into the lake. Myra pushed through the crowd. It might boost her spirits, but it was best not to create a scene in the busy park.

She wandered along the twisting trail before collapsing onto a bench in a quieter section. All the risks she had taken and the sacrifices she had made, and where was she? Returned to the beginning. Except this was worse. Hywel was a prisoner of the

Witch Council, and Myra was a wanted felon trapped in this Realm.

She had no contact with another magical person who might help her. She took a deep breath. A black pit inside her cracked open, threatening to pull her down. She'd believed she had broken free. That she could enjoy a life of magic without reporting to Hywel. But it would never happen. Since Hywel had entered her mother's life he'd owned them, herself, and Thiemus. The pit opened wider, encouraging her to slide into its depressing depths.

An energy booster would revive her. She slipped her hand into her pocket and pulled out the red makeup bag where she kept the Enhancer Elixir. Her fingers trembled as she opened the bag. Empty! She turned the bag inside out. It wasn't possible. There should be one vial left. No! She remembered using one earlier, but there had been six only a few days ago. She stuffed the bag back into her pocket and slumped further down on the bench. Her hands trembled, and she clasped them together.

The only bright side to this complete fiasco, she thought, was that Wilf would search for her in the Magical Realm while she remained in Hong Kong. Perhaps that might buy her enough time to work out her next steps.

The compact mirror in her pocket pinged. She rummaged around until her fingers clasped its smooth surface and flipped it open. Strange runes she didn't recognize filled the screen. Someone was trying to locate her. Was she being watched? How had they discovered her?

It pinged again. She held her breath. It pinged four more times before going silent. The lid closed. Then it vibrated and pinged again. She flipped it open.

"Yes?" she said, before panic made it impossible for her to think or speak.

"Where are you?"

"Is this Thiemus?"

"Who else would it be? Stop asking stupid questions. Are you back in Kureyamage?"

"The Thermals won't let me through." Myra heard the whine in her voice and cringed. Thiemus mustn't know how vulnerable she was, otherwise he wouldn't call her. There was no sibling love between them. Never had been.

"Do you have a copy of the vaccine formula?"

"Yes." She touched her pocket and the paper gave a reassuring crinkle. She'd almost forgotten he'd be waiting for the cure. It had been days since Ermentrude had infected him. His magic must be almost depleted. She straightened up. He'd need her for his survival.

"Good. I'll meet you in Sha Tin. I don't have enough magic left to work the biomes myself and travel between Realms. Those... witches are still holding Hywel. I have to start the initiation process on the biome soon, otherwise the Council won't be able to bargain for his release."

Myra remained silent. Could she trust him? Then again, did she have a choice? It was risky. If she did what he wanted, she'd be back under his control. But, he had access to a portal. He might be her ticket back to Kureyamage. Once there, she could disappear.

"It'll take me about an hour."

"Don't be late," he said.

Her screen went blank, and she left the park. It was a 15-minute walk from Tin Kwong Road to the MTR at Lok Fu. Her mind ran over the rest of the route while she weaved past slower pedestrians.

Thiemus was a healer. Her heart pounded and she started walking faster. He must have a supply of elixir, perhaps even a whole cupboard full. She smiled and quickened her pace as the MTR sign for Entrance B came into view. Elixir for the vaccine formula would make a good trade. She charged down the steps and through the barrier.

The double doors of the train swished open, allowing the flow of passengers to enter. She let their momentum carry her along until she could grasp a handrail near the carriage's entrance. The train jerked forward and picked up speed. The darkened carriage windows reflected the bright interior lights, and Myra let her thoughts run back to the fight in the gift store, and Wilf's outraged expression.

"You killed our father?" he'd said.

"He wasn't mine," she'd replied, but that wasn't honest. She hadn't intended to kill Reginald, only stun him. She had no idea why her magic had morphed into a killing spell. He was the only father she had ever known.

From the first day she'd arrived in Hong Kong from Kureyamage to live with Reginald and Wilf, he'd supported her. It had been Reginald who had wiped away her tears when she felt like a misfit in the non-magic world. Griselda, her mother, had been too busy spying on Reginald for Hywel to offer support to Myra. On the night of her mother's marriage to Reginald, Myra had asked about her biological father. Griselda had dismissed the question with a flick of her hand. Myra had rifled through her mother's belongings looking for clues to her father's identity when Griselda had contracted the virus and left Hong Kong. He'd remained a mystery. Whoever he was, Griselda had wiped all traces of him from her life.

The train pulled into Sha Tin station. Myra paused at the exit to check the street before hailing a green taxi and diving into the backseat. It was dangerous around here. Witches might arrive via portal, and Degula, the head of Witch Security, would have sent guards to watch for her. It wouldn't be long before the Witch Council knew the Thermals were no longer allowing broom travelers through to the Magical Realm. When that happened, the search for Myra would switch to Hong Kong — and the warehouse portals in Sha Tin would be a fitting place to start.

Myra sighed as the taxi bumped along the street. She'd made a dangerous situation worse when she had teamed up with the young witch Seldan against Ermentrude and the Witch Council. Seldan had supplanted and kidnapped Ermentrude before being captured herself. The Witch Council had disbanded the militant coven, leaving Myra friendless and on the run. It might be another wrong decision to meet Thiemus, but her options were limited.

The taxi stopped on the corner and she edged out, giving the area a sweeping glance before heading down Shing Wan Road.

The place appeared deserted, but who knew what trigger spells guarded the perimeter? If only Nipits had been with her, she could have used the cat's eyes. It surprised her how much she missed him.

Stepping back against a wall, she scrunched up her eyes to change focus. Her vision cleared and an enormous dome shimmered into view at the end of the street. A swirling mist filled the interior, but the outer shielding reminded her of Hywel's Advancer. The last time she'd seen that machine, Wilf had hung suspended inside the large frosted bubble with strands of magic pulsing from his fingertips. His magical ability had advanced until he had broken the machine. She shuddered.

A blond stooped figure limped from behind the dome. Thiemus beckoned her to join him. The fool should be more cautious! They were both on the Witch Council's Wanted List.

She had no desire to stand trial alongside him and Hywel.

The dome pulsed and her breath quickened. The magic inside called to her like a giant bubble full of elixir. She stepped closer to the biome, putting out her hand.

"Don't touch it," Thiemus growled. "I've been trying to calibrate it so we can start the initiation process." He turned to her. "Where's the formula? Give it to me."

Myra took the page out of her pocket but kept it scrunched in her hand. "When we're back in Kureyamage."

"That's very trusting of you, Sister. Afraid I'll leave without you? Don't worry. Because of the virus, I need your help." He waved his withered arm at her. A gift he'd received from Hywel when their mother had failed to steal Wilf's family journal.

"Then the sooner we're back in Kureyamage, the sooner your magic will be back to full strength." She crammed the formula back into her pocket. "I'm surprised there's no outward sign you have the virus. The witches became beautiful."

Thiemus glared at her. "I've lost the extra knuckle on my wizard finger, and my tattoo has disappeared."

Myra hadn't noticed his other hand. It was true. His ring finger no longer had its extra knuckle of power. More concerning, the loss of his healer's tattoo meant he'd lost a serious amount of magic.

"So how much magic do you have?"

"I'm having to use this to boost the little I have left." Thiemus held up a vial of elixir.

Myra's fingers twitched to grab the vial and let its sweet contents coat her throat. She longed for the buzz as the drug coursed through her magical synapses. Her hands shook, and she shoved them out of view. She swallowed with each outward movement of her brother's throat as he drank the vial's contents. When he removed the vial from his mouth, she ran her tongue over her lips.

"Shall we?" he said, heading for an outbuilding the size of a tool shed. "We developed this floating portal over the past few months. It doesn't take much magic to operate it."

"It'll run on witch and wizard magic?" Myra said, stopping in front of the portal.

"As long as the operator controls it."

"But I've never used one before," she said.

Thiemus stopped and stared at her. She could almost see the cogs spinning in his mind. He shrugged. "It's easy. You'll need to learn to use it."

Myra stopped and stared at her brother's back. This wasn't the Thiemus she knew and feared. Could the virus have caused the change in him? More likely it was an act to get her to lower her guard. She would play along if it meant he'd pass on information, but he had better not rely on family loyalty.

Thiemus held the door open.

She took a deep breath before stepping inside the compact room. It reminded her of a two-seater booth from a diner. She slid along the black leather bench and Thiemus eased onto the opposite side. But instead of a table between them, a white column held a glass globe the size of a basketball. Flashes of electricity spiked within the sphere.

Myra leaned forward, watching Thiemus's every movement as he uncorked a second vial of elixir and swallowed the contents. How many vials did he have? She should demand one. After all, he needed her help.

"Myra. Are you listening?"

She pulled her gaze away from the vial to Thiemus's face and nodded.

"Place your right hand on the globe. The energy inside will link to your fingertips. The connection is a sensation like needles pricking your skin. This causes a tunnel to form between the two Realms. You'll then be able to steer the portal."

She glanced around at the four solid walls. "How will I see the route?"

Thiemus waved his withered arm at the wall on the right. "That will become transparent."

Her palm was sweaty as she spread her fingers and placed them on top of the globe. Spikes of energy stabbed her fingers.

"Ouch!" She went to pull them off the globe, but Thiemus held her hand in place.

"Keep the connection."

"Your idea of pinpricks is different than mine," she said, glaring.

He sneered. The wall vanished and a tunnel appeared.

"Feed magic into the connection as you build an image in your mind of traveling from here to Kureyamage."

"I don't know the route. I've only traveled twice, and each time I wasn't conscious." Her voice rose in panic.

"It's not an actual route, but the way you envision it," Thiemus snapped.

Had she been thinking of Hong Kong when she rode the broom? She hadn't built a route to Kureyamage, and so she'd returned?

Myra swallowed, clearing her mind and dispelling the desire to run. An image took shape in her mind. The Dragon Ride at Ocean Park. The track layout solidified. She remembered the train rocketing along rails with corkscrews and 360-degree rotations. She'd ridden it only once and it had terrified her. Shaking, she glanced at the window to her right and the track stretching skyward in a steep incline.

The portal shuddered forward with several violent shakes. A clanking sound reverberated around her, like a chain being winched up a steep slope. The portal crept upward towards an opening fissure. Neon lights flashed and fizzled out as they passed through the entrance and into the claustrophobic darkness of the Thermals.

"What have you done?" Thiemus shouted, his words echoing her panic.

The portal plunged down an invisible track, and Myra let out a piercing scream.

Chapter Five - Wilf's Store, Hong Kong

Wilf kicked a soccer ball against the wall, caught it on his foot, and flicked it onto his knee. He juggled the ball from one knee to the other. His mind roamed free from whatever problems he was trying to solve. He'd spent the last hour working on ideas to capture Myra.

A familiar whistle pierced the air. Wilf caught the ball and turned. Enzo strolled down the street. He grinned and ran to meet his friend.

"Where've you been? Coach is frantic. You've missed eight practices, and the championship's only two weeks away," Enzo said, clasping Wilf's arm in greeting.

Wilf steered Enzo away from the store. "I had to visit my stepmom. She'd become critically ill."

"I'm sorry. Are your Dad and Myra still with Griselda?" Enzo asked.

"Yes," Wilf said. He wanted to tell his best friend the truth. That he'd been to a Magical Realm full of witches and wizards, and that he had himself become a powerful wizard. About how he'd recovered the formula to stop the witches from losing their magic. But who would believe it? He wasn't sure he did, and he'd lived through it.

"Isn't practice at four?" Wilf asked.

"Didn't you get my text about meeting up before?" Enzo said.

"I've got nothing," Wilf said, pulling out his phone and scrolling.

The bell jingled from the store behind him, and Katryna crossed the street to join them.

"I want you to meet someone." Wilf caught hold of her hand. "Make yourself visible," he whispered.

Katryna wiggled her fingers.

"This is Katryna," Wilf said, holding her hand.

Enzo stepped back, his eyes widening. "Hi. Sorry. I didn't see you there."

"I was in the store," Katryna said.

Enzo glanced at the store and then offered his hand. "I'm Enzo."

She smiled and turned to Wilf. "Degula wants you in the workshop."

"What workshop?" Enzo asked.

"She means the store. We're renovating it," Wilf said. Typical, he'd been at loose ends for hours and now he was in demand. But he was not about to leave Katryna and Enzo alone. From the look on Enzo's face, he was going to try his charms on her. They didn't work on the girls at school. How would Katryna react? Enzo was the first Normal she'd met, and she didn't seem impressed. Wilf grinned and relaxed. It would be interesting to watch her response.

"Looks like I'll have to hang here for a while longer," Wilf said.

"I'll inform Coach I've found you. It'll give him some time to come up with a range of extra activities for you." Enzo paused. "Be warned, he's being more sadistic than usual since you vanished."

Wilf glanced back at the store. "I'll be there."

"You'd better be," Enzo said.

"I promise," Wilf said, pointing to his backpack. "I've my kit right here with me."

Enzo turned to leave, then stopped. "There's something wrong with this road."

"What do you mean?" Wilf watched two witches walk down the road. They parted around Enzo before entering the store.

Enzo shivered. "Didn't you see those shimmering lights?"

Wilf shook his head. "Just the heat rising from the road."

"You're probably right, but it seemed different from the usual heat haze." Enzo stared down the street, then shook his head. "See you later." He waved his hand and broke into a jog.

"What was he talking about?" Katryna asked.

Wilf put his soccer ball into his backpack and followed her to the store.

"Enzo felt those witches," he said, dropping his bag by the door. "Shouldn't they be invisible to Normals?"

"That's what Degula and Mom want to talk to you about. The magic isn't working as it should." Katryna gazed deep into his eyes as she spoke. His breath caught in his throat as she ran the tip of her tongue over her lips. They looked so moist and inviting. An overwhelming need to kiss her surged through him. He took a step closer and placed his hands on her arms.

She smiled and wrapped her arms around his waist.

"That's enough," Ermentrude said, coming up behind them. She wiggled her fingers.

A rush of power pushed him three feet from Katryna.

Ermentrude stepped into the gap and faced Wilf. She reminded him of a defense wall blocking a corner kick at goal. He shuddered.

Her jaw tightened, and her eyes held his.

"I wasn't…"

"And you won't," Ermentrude said. "You're wanted in the workshop. Why don't you lead the way?"

"I thought you'd banned me from there," he said.

"Degula is waiting. It's not an activity she's good at," Ermentrude said, nodding towards the store's door.

He hesitated for a moment. "What's this about?" Peering through the window, he saw two Executrix guards protecting the entrance to the basement workshop.

Ermentrude wiggled her fingers and the door opened. "After you."

Wilf's skin crept as he entered the store. The guards' malicious gazes drilled into him from across the room.

"Why are they standing there?" he said.

"I'd guess to make sure no one enters without permission. They rarely perform guard duty," Katryna said.

He glanced over his shoulder at her. "What do they do?"

"Last time I met a squad they were escorting your stepmother into quarantine."

"So they do Degula's dirty work," he said.

Katryna nodded.

"Well, I hope they don't stop me leaving for soccer practice," he said.

"You're going?" Katryna's tone showed that she thought he should stay here.

"Yes." He stopped and faced her. "Why?"

"You use magic…"

He took a deep breath. "You think I should let the team down."

"I wouldn't put it that way, but yes." She nodded.

"Magic is just another skill I have, like being able to see

C. B. Lyall

patterns in play. I mean, you build control over magic, so it must be a skill," he said. That's what he'd been telling himself all morning, and he'd thought it sounded convincing. Only now, when he said the words aloud, they didn't have the ring of truth he'd hoped for.

Katryna bit her lip and paused for a few moments. "Lie to yourself, but you have a better sense of fair play than that. Perhaps I should join the girls' team and use my natural magical talent as well?" She brushed past him and followed her mother to stand in the store.

He would be the bad guy no matter what he did. If he went to play soccer with the team, Katryna would think less of him. However, if he didn't play, Enzo and the team would hate him for letting them down right before the championship. Life had become so complicated. To some witches, he was a hero. To others he was the enemy, a destroyer of their world. His friends thought he was a natural soccer superstar and Katryna thought him a cheat. His shoulders slumped. The day seemed endless, and it wasn't about to get any better. He scuffed his feet along the floorboards.

"Why am I needed in the workshop?" he said.

"Degula wants us to run some tests," Ermentrude said, turning to face him.

"What? On me?" Wilf backed up a few steps.

"They placed you in Hywel's machine. We don't know what that did to you or your magic. It's a reasonable request from Degula."

Heat flared in his cheeks. "You think that's reasonable?"

"It's important we try to understand the amount and range of your... ability." Ermentrude pronounced the last word as if it offended her.

"And why does it matter?" he said.

Ermentrude stroked the bristles on her chin, and Wilf's fists clenched. It was one of her many habits that irritated him, and he was sure she did it on purpose for that very reason.

"Degula says there's a possibility that the Wizard Council is controlling you," Ermentrude said.

Katryna took a step forward. "Does she think they're trying to use him to destroy the Veil? Or spy on us?"

"It's a possibility. He's at an elementary level in his training. Anyone could control him." Ermentrude still sounded annoyed. "He has a paltry defense set up."

Wilf edged farther away. Power built inside him. He needed to escape before he blasted the place to oblivion.

"I will not allow a bunch of witches to treat me as an experiment," he said.

"Wilf, I can understand why Degula would want to test whether the Wizard Council has interfered with your magic," Katryna said, reaching for him.

"You too?" He pulled his arm away from her. "I will not allow anyone to experiment on me."

"I'd have thought you'd want to find out?" Katryna said, stepping closer.

Wilf backed away and snatched up his backpack.

"Where are you going?" Katryna asked.

"Soccer practice." He bolted through the door.

Ermentrude's cackle followed him up the street. He didn't stop running until he stood outside the Hong Kong Football Club. Katryna was right, using magic in soccer seemed like he was cheating. He shook his head. Perhaps he shouldn't be here. The problem was, he didn't know where he fit in anymore.

"Enzo told me you'd materialized." Coach stopped beside Wilf. "Well, what are you waiting for?" He took a few steps and waited.

"If you're worried about how the boys and I will react to your disappearance, don't be," Coach continued. "Enzo explained about your stepmother becoming ill and the entire family having to leave. It happens sometimes. As long as you're here for the tournament, that's what matters."

When Wilf still hesitated, Coach walked back and stood in front of him.

"I also know you've had some trouble with your father not wanting you to play soccer. It hasn't gone unnoticed that Mr. Gilvary has never been to one of your matches. Anyway, the families of the other team members will fund your travel expenses. However, I will need your father to sign the consent form. I hope that won't be a problem?"

Coach was offering him a way out. He only had to say his father wouldn't sign the form, and then Wilf could bow out without everyone blaming him. He wiped his palms on his shorts. But why shouldn't he play? The team needed him, and he needed to be part of the team.

"Thanks. That's generous of everyone," Wilf said, walking beside Coach into the club. "I'm sure the form won't be a problem."

"Great. Hurry along and get changed," Coach said,

heading for the practice ground.

As Wilf made his way to his locker, teammates thumped him on the back, shouting, "About time you remembered your way here," and "Is that the lost striker... What's his name again?" and "Hope you remember how to kick a ball!"

"You're all hilarious. I've missed you, too," he said, opening his locker and taking his kit out of his backpack.

"It's good to have you back," Enzo said, punching his arm. "See you out there."

The team filed out, leaving Wilf to put on his soccer cleats.

They were exceptional guys, and he'd never been so miserable in his life. They'd never forgive him if he didn't show up for the championship. Before, he'd been happy not knowing he used magic to win, but now that he knew, how could he play?

He tied his laces and jogged out onto the pitch. Usually he would have run out feeling proud. Now he dragged his feet. He glanced at the stands. The usual bunch of girls sat pretending not to watch the boys warming up. He glanced to the other side and saw Amy, his ex-girlfriend, sitting with her friends. Two rows below sat Katryna. What was she doing here? And why was she making herself visible to Normals?

He glanced down at his ring. It glowed. The bond. She'd used it to track him down. He ran out onto the pitch and hoped Amy wouldn't find out that Katryna was his girlfriend.

The team was doing sprints through cones and other warmups. It felt good to exercise his body again. Wilf jogged over to the goal and waited in line to take some practice shots. His ring flashed as the memory of the last time he'd stood before the net came to mind. It had been the day he'd received his father's wizard ring. The day Reginald had evaporated.

"You going to kick that ball?" Enzo shouted from behind him.

"I told you he'd forgotten how we play the game," the goalie said.

Wilf lined the shot, took two steps, then powered his foot through the ball. It spun into the top of the net.

"He's back!" Enzo thumped Wilf's back.

He returned to the line. The problem was he didn't know if he'd kicked the ball into the net, or if his magic had helped to make the shot. Next time he lined up, he tried to shoot straight for the goalie to deflect. The ball curved at the last second. Had magic moved it, or had he used spin? He wasn't sure — and if he didn't know, then how could he stop using it?

His shoulders slumped. He loved playing soccer, but magic ruined everything for him.

Coach called them into teams, putting Wilf and Enzo on opposing sides. Coach blew the whistle and Enzo passed the ball to one of his forwards. Wilf marked Enzo as he made a push to find an open space. The forward passed the ball and Wilf went to intercept. The ball spun away from him.

"What the…" he said, chasing after it.

Again he saw his opportunity, but as he approached the ball it stopped and changed direction. He glanced over at the stands. It had to be Katryna. It took all his willpower not to run over to her.

He continued to play, but was never sure if he'd connect with the ball. Sometimes he could, and other times the ball changed direction at the last minute. Katryna was having fun. The breaking point came when he charged up the field to receive a pass. He powered up to take a shot on goal. The ball rolled a few inches. The momentum took his standing leg off the ground and he fell, scraping his side on the artificial turf. Blood ran down his leg and arm. He would kill her.

"Get that taken care of," Coach said. Wilf heard the bewilderment in his voice.

He limped over to the stands.

"Are you enjoying yourself?" Wilf said, using a water bottle to wash away the blood.

"Yes. It's very interesting seeing all your friends chasing a little ball," Katryna said.

"Well, at least you're letting them kick it," he said.

"Whatever do you mean?"

"Stop interfering." Heads snapped round to stare at them as he raised his voice. He climbed up to sit next to her. "Why are you doing this?"

"So you'll know how someone could control you. I can feel you calling on magic through the bond. It's like a tingling whenever you use magic to help you," she said.

"I don't." He stared at the ground.

"Every time you go to kick the ball, there's a surge of magic."

He shook his head. This couldn't be true.

"You're telling me I have to stop playing?" His face heated. He wanted to lash out and scream.

"I'm only pointing out your use of magic. Only you can

decide whether you should play," she said.

The metal bleachers clanked and shook. Wilf caught a waft of Amy's perfume.

"You haven't introduced us to your friend," Amy said, tapping him on the shoulder.

They both turned around.

"Not now, Amy." Wilf ran out onto the field, leaving Amy and Katryna together.

Enzo ran over and slung an arm around Wilf's shoulders. "That was quite the performance out there. What's up?"

"Nothing," Wilf said.

"I see Amy's introducing herself to Katryna. That won't end well."

Wilf glanced back at the stands. He was sure Katryna could take care of herself.

Chapter Six - Wakefield Tower, Kureyamage

Myra stumbled behind Thiemus into Hywel's Tower. Broken glass crunched under her boots. Cracks ran up the walls and shredded ancestral pictures hung in broken frames. She stepped around the rubble and continued down the corridor to the kitchen. It was the first time she'd been in this room without the heat from the stove making it overwhelmingly stuffy, or the smell of cakes and cookies sweetening the place.

Thiemus threw himself into a chair at the kitchen table. Dust thick enough to write your name in covered every surface. He breathed heavily and sweat dripped down his face. His blond hair stuck up from where he'd dragged his hand through it.

Myra took the formula from her pocket and gave it to him. His hand shook as he read the ingredients.

"We have all this in the palace laboratory," he said, struggling to stand before collapsing back into the chair. "I can't stop the pain in my arm and leg any longer."

Myra's brother's face had changed as the virus ravaged him. He looked more like seventy than seventeen. Deep creases ran across his forehead and shadowy circles surrounded his sunken eyes.

"Did Hywel place you in the Advancer?" Myra asked, dusting a chair before she sat down.

"He needed a wizard to try it on. I was… available."

"I didn't know he was abusing you," Myra said. He'd been so young when their mother had left him with Hywel.

"What could you have done? Griselda gave me to him." A vein pulsed at Thiemus's temple.

"In fairness, I don't think mother had a choice."

Thiemus banged his good fist on the table. "There is always a choice. She didn't fight for me. On her visits she noticed what was happening but still left me here. I refuse to call that witch my mother."

They sat in silence. Myra recalled an image of her mother placing her on a broom before she climbed on behind, Thiemus standing like a stone statue next to Hywel as they rose into the air. Myra raised a hand to wave, but her brother hadn't looked up.

She gave herself a mental shake. Memories and recriminations would keep for later.

"I'm presuming the basement passage has collapsed, judging from the amount of debris in the entrance. Is there another way to the laboratory?"

Thiemus nodded. "There's an entrance in the courtyard. An emergency escape."

She stepped towards him. "Do you need me to help you?"

He sat back and stared at her. "Why are you doing this? What can you possibly hope to achieve?"

She looked at him. She wasn't sure herself. Thiemus had never shown her any kindness, but if she helped him, he would owe her, and with magic becoming unstable that was a nice favor to hold. There was also his supply of elixir.

"You've access to the biomes," she said. "I'll need magic, and I don't think the witches are likely to allow me any. Do you?"

Thiemus nodded, but his eyes held her gaze.

"Let's get you into the lab and produce a batch of the antidote," she said. Her hand shook as she went to reach for his arm and she pulled it back, hoping he hadn't seen the trembling. "It might be best if you take some Enhancer Elixir to help you. Do you have any left?"

"I used the last of my supply, but there should be a pouch in Hywel's desk." He gestured with his withered arm.

Myra left the kitchen and forced herself not to run to the study. She paused in the doorway. The room seemed untouched by the earthquake. Had Hywel protected it? She reached out, expecting to find a spell stopping her, but she didn't experience so much as a tingle. She raced over to the desk and pulled open all three drawers before she found a silver pouch containing four vials of elixir. Sweat beaded on her forehead and her hands twitched. She glanced over at the door before uncorking one and bringing it to her lips. The fiery liquid burned as it coated her throat. She closed her eyes, waiting for the kick to her brain and for her senses to buzz with energy. It seemed like minutes passed, though, before she felt a slight jolt. She opened her eyes and looked at the empty vial. This must be a weakened strain. She opened a second vial and swallowed its contents.

The clock's ticking increased in volume, blocking out all other sounds. Her vision snapped into its alternative focus, blearing the room. The scents of musk and damp overpowered her, and she balked. The tips of her fingers buzzed with flares of magical energy. She flipped her hands over and blue flashes escaped into the air. She'd never had a reaction like this before.

"Myra? Are you all right?" Thiemus called from the kitchen.

Myra clutched the silver pouch tightly. There were only two vials left, and she had no intention of wasting them on her brother.

"I'm having trouble locating the vials. Are you sure they're in here?" she shouted, pushing the pouch into her pocket.

Thiemus appeared at the door, leaning heavily on the frame. "They should be in the drawer."

"Perhaps Hywel took them with him when he went after Wilf?"

"It's possible…" Thiemus rubbed the back of his neck.

"Is there a supply in the workshop?"

He nodded slowly, never taking his eyes off her.

"Let's find the elixir and start a batch of vaccine. We don't want you losing more of your ability." She moved towards him, and he turned into the corridor.

She buried her hands in her pockets. The last thing she wanted was for him to see the blue glow of her fingertips in the darkened hallway.

He led the way through the kitchen, outside to the garden wall, and placed his hand on the wooden planks. A grating sound started in the wall and a doorway appeared. Myra conjured a globe, making sure she hid her hands from Thiemus, and its light floated through the opening. Thiemus limped down the stone steps into the gloomy interior. Myra followed him down the steep, slippery steps that seemed as if they were never coming to an end. Finally, her foot connected with the soft earth of the passage.

"It's at the end," he said, dragging his left leg. He kept pausing, resting against the rough stone wall to take deep breaths. They made slow progress along the corridor until he stopped and placed his hand on a ceramic tile. It moved with the pressure of his palm. A heavy, studded oak door slid open.

Myra glanced around as she entered the room. Dust danced in the dim illumination.

"Light the other globes." Thiemus moved towards the central wooden table. He placed the formula on a bookstand and limped over to the shelves, where he started taking down jars.

Myra eased her hand out of her pocket when her brother turned his back. She let out a sigh of relief. The blue flashes no longer sprang from her fingertips, but there was a bluish tinge to the ends. She lit the globes around the room with a swish of her hand.

A crash sounded behind her.

"Frog's entrails!" Thiemus yelled. A shattered jar lay at his feet, black liquid oozing across the floor. Myra wiggled her fingers at it.

"No!" he screamed.

Her magic combined with the liquid to produce a blinding flash. When she focused again a black hole swirled in the floor where the liquid had puddled.

"That was the last of the Night Blackness," he said, collapsing onto the wooden bench.

"I'm sorry. Can't we collect any more?"

"It's harvested from inside the Thermals. How do you suggest we collect some?" he said.

She shuddered at the thought of entering them again so soon. She paced the workshop. "Are there other workshops here?"

Thiemus lifted his head to stare at her. "The biomes team have the workshop next door."

"Won't they have the…" She stared at her brother.

"Night Blackness. Yes, they might."

"Why don't we go ask them?" She moved to the door.

He pressed down on the table and tried to heave himself to standing. His legs buckled before he slumped down. "I don't have the strength anymore."

"You said there was more elixir here. Why don't you take some?"

Thiemus's hand covered his nose and mouth as he watched her. He paused and then gestured at the bookcase. "Top left drawer," he said.

She pulled open the drawer and almost let a sigh escape. Racks of elixir stood in rows. She collected a vial and brought it over to him. He bit off the stopper and drank the contents in one gulp. Leaning on the table, he pulled himself up.

"Let me help you." She put his arm around her shoulder, then half dragged, half carried him from the workshop and back along the corridor.

"Here," he said.

The wall didn't seem any different from the one opposite. He laid his hand on the stones and they pushed back into another tunnel.

Myra struggled under Thiemus's weight as they slowly progressed. He stopped again, but this time at a ceramic tile with five red dots on it. He placed his hand on the tile and a doorway came into view. He knocked on the door.

The door opened with the sound of wood scraping on stone.

A wizard with black scruff covering his chin glanced up from his computer. He pushed his messy hair out of his eyes and blinked at them.

"Malik, I need your help," Thiemus said, leaning on the doorframe.

"What's wrong?" Malik rolled his chair back as Thiemus and Myra entered the workshop. "You don't look well. I heard some witches stuck you with that virus."

"I need Night Blackness. Do you have any?" Thiemus asked.

"Maybe," Malik said, heading for the shelves.

This workshop was unlike any Myra had seen before. There were computer screens on a long black table pushed against the wall. Several relay mirrors covered another wall. Racks of routers, switches and cables dominated the room.

She shivered. It was about twenty degrees cooler in here.

"It's not something we normally keep. I'm not even sure it hasn't reached its imperfect date." He picked up a jar and turned it over. "You're in luck. Still a month left."

"We're trying to make a batch of the antidote," Myra said, lowering Thiemus into a chair. "I don't suppose you'd help?"

Malik glanced from her to Thiemus. "Not really my field — potions."

Myra saw pinpricks of green and red LED lights twinkling in the darkness behind a glass door covering the entrance to an alcove.

"It's a data center," she said.

Malik grinned. "Exactly, but we still run on magic. It's more efficient using technology and magic rather than having to brew concoctions in a cauldron."

"If I gave you the formula for the vaccine, could you make a batch using your…" She waved a hand at the screens.

Malik raked the scruff on his chin. "I'm not sure. As I said, potions aren't my thing."

"But you'd try?" she asked.

"I'm not taking the risk," Thiemus interrupted. "If Malik uses the last of the Night Blackness and then can't make the vaccine, I'm done for."

"He's right," Malik said. "Look, why don't I help you back to your workshop and assist."

"That would be marvelous," Myra said.

"My pleasure." Malik winked. He helped Thiemus to his feet, and they gradually made their way down the corridor to Thiemus's workshop.

Thiemus grunted as he sat down and smoothed out the crumpled paper containing the formula. At his direction, Myra and Malik collected the remaining ingredients. Jars, vials, and bunches of herbs soon crowded the table.

Myra carried a small cauldron to the table and wiggled her fingers over the ingredients. They measured and weighed themselves before jumping in.

Malik ran his finger over the formula. "The last ingredient is the Blackness."

"Here," Myra said, handing it to him. He glanced at her blue fingertips.

Heat rose in her cheeks as Malik measured the required amount into the cauldron.

"Bring that," Thiemus said, stumbling towards the centrifuge.

Myra wiggled her fingers, and the cauldron rose into the air and followed him. She leaned over to read the formula. "There's not much left to do now but wait."

"I'll be off, since you don't need me anymore," Malik said.

"Thanks for your help," Myra said. "Perhaps we'll see you again." She cringed inside at the hopeful tone in her voice.

"I'm sure you will. Thiemus and I are working on the biomes together. In fact, we've been colleagues for some time, but he never mentioned a sister."

"I was on assignment in the Real World," Myra said.

"See you around," Malik said, closing the door behind him.

"You can count on it," Myra said.

Thiemus was busy in the corner. Myra settled down in the leather club chair next to the fireplace, stretched out her legs, and examined her hands. The blue tinge had faded from her fingertips. She wished Malik hadn't seen them. Why had she taken two vials? She knew better than that. She chewed her nail and tried to remember when she'd first used the drug. It was after Ermentrude had injured her. Hywel had given it to her before sending her through the tunnels to Mathowytch to find Wilf. She'd used the twenty vials he'd given her. It had helped her remain focused and boosted her magic. She glanced over at the drawer containing the rows of elixir. She would need to distract Thiemus if she hoped to replenish her exhausted supply. The two vials in her pocket wouldn't last long.

Myra drew up her knees and wrapped her arms around them. She'd always wanted to live in Kureyamage, surrounded by magic, and here she was. So why did she feel sad? She couldn't miss Hong Kong or Wilf. But a small voice inside her admitted that she did miss Wilf. He'd loved her when no one else had. Treated her as his sister.

A clang of metal and a muttered curse came from Thiemus.

She sat straighter in the chair. The only reason Myra had been in Hong Kong was that her mother had been on a task for the Wizard Council and had dragged her along. The only brother she had was limping around this workshop. She'd forgotten that and become sentimental about Wilf. Not any longer.

The one person she should care about was herself. Nobody else would. She moved in the chair and the vials clanged together. So what if she needed a little help sometimes? She could handle it.

Chapter Seven - Hong Kong Football Club, Hong Kong

Katryna stared out at the soccer pitch as the game restarted. Wilf had the ball. Enzo and another player chased him. She grasped her wrist as Wilf reached for his magic as he approached the goal. She didn't understand his passion for this ridiculous game, but he shouldn't be using magic. If he practiced more, he could build a barrier to prevent its use during soccer. She'd tried to tell him, but he refused to listen. She had thought her demonstration would have helped, but he seemed angry and upset.

"Who are you?"

Katryna turned to examine the girl Wilf had called Amy. She was taller than the other girls, and her long blond hair bounced in a twisted ponytail. Katryna sighed. The poor girl was beautiful. She felt sorry for her. Although it seemed strange that Amy wore a team shirt with Wilf's number and "Gilvary" written on the back. There were many strange customs here.

"Why?" Katryna said.

"I've known Wilf for an age, and he's never mentioned you."

"I'm a friend," Katryna said. She didn't see why she should explain their relationship to this Groundling.

Amy looked her up and down.

"I'm Wilf's girlfriend. I know all his friends, but I've never heard of you."

His girlfriend. Katryna didn't understand what that meant. Did that make her his witch friend?

"We haven't known each other very long," Katryna said.

Amy leaned closer. "Don't get any ideas. He's mine and I don't intend to give him up. I mean, you're quite the ugliest person I've ever seen."

"Thank you," Katryna said, but Amy had already turned to speak to a girl on her right.

"Who'd want that on their arm?" The girls giggled.

Katryna stared out at the pitch and at Wilf. She didn't understand what Amy meant, but tears pricked her eyes. Ermentrude was right, they didn't belong here. Once the Magical Realm had rebalanced, they would return to Mathowytch — Ermentrude, Wilf, and herself.

She raised her fingers, wiggled them at Amy, and smiled as a red swelling appeared on the girl's chin.

Amy winced when her fingers brushed another angry spot erupting on the tip of her nose. She gasped and held her hand over her lower face before scrambling to her feet. She clattered down the bleachers and ran into the club. Two girls ran after her.

The match ended, and Katryna watched the players head for the locker room. The bleachers shook as the spectators filed out until she was the only one left. She climbed down to the turf. She would never get used to the peculiar smells and customs of this place. If only she could take her broom and travel through the Thermals back to Mathowytch. She walked into the club. She touched her golden vein. Where was Wilf?

"Amy's hysterical. What did you do to her?" Wilf said, catching up with her. "Did you use magic on her?"

"It's called acne. I saw it advertised this morning and thought it might improve your girlfriend's looks. I doubt she can grow her own warts."

Wilf blocked Katryna's path. "She's not my girlfriend."

"Then you should tell her, because that's how she introduced herself." Katryna's vision blurred and she blinked.

"She knows. She just won't accept it," Wilf said, combing his hand through his damp hair.

What did any of this matter? "I hate this place. Let's go back to the store."

"I need to change and hang out with the team for a while." He stared at his cleats.

"Oh! Don't worry about me, I can find my own way." Through the window she noticed rain bouncing off the sidewalk. Which way led to the store? Wilf hadn't asked her to stay with him.

"Great, I'll see you back at the apartment." He walked away.

"You know, if you were in command of your magic you wouldn't call on it when you played soccer," she said to his back.

"Leave it, Katryna," he shouted over his shoulder.

She entered the revolving door and strode down the street towards Morrison Hill. Rivulets of rain ran down her back. It didn't seem worth conjuring a spell of protection.

She stopped on the corner, glancing up and down the street.

Which way? It had been easy to use the bond to find her way to the Football Club. Wilf's longing to be with his friends had overridden the bond's attraction. He'd wanted to be with the team instead of with her. And now he seemed angry with her. She'd thought she was helping him by showing him when he used magic. Tears mixed with the rain running down her face. Why was she crying? She never cried. It was being in Hong Kong, surrounded by Normals and not knowing when, or if, she would ever be able to return to Mathowytch.

Traffic whizzed past her. A taxi sped through a puddle, drenching her in muddy water.

"Wow. You're soaked!" Enzo appeared next to her, holding an umbrella.

She nodded. "And I'm lost too."

"The streets can seem the same." He stepped closer so that the umbrella covered them both. "I'm going past Wilf's place, if that helps."

"Thanks," Katryna said, shivering.

"Take my arm. We can make the lights if we run."

Run! She never ran unless she was being chased. Enzo weaved through the throng crowding the sidewalk. She tried to keep hold of his arm, but a small woman pushed her aside. When she reached the crossing, the lights had already changed.

"What happened to you?" Enzo said, leaning on the barrier.

She waved her hand at the people waiting to cross. "I'm terrible at maneuvering through this many people."

Enzo laughed. "It's a daily routine here."

"Have you always lived in Hong Kong?"

The walk signal came on and the crowd propelled her forward. Enzo took her arm and linked it through his.

"My mom's from here, but Dad is from Naples, Italy," he said, tipping the umbrella to cover her.

The crowd thinned as they continued down Queen's Road East. As they approached the lights at the Hopewell Center, Enzo reached for Katryna's hand, and they ran across the road. He halted when they reached the other side, and she bumped into him.

"Good, it's stopped. These showers are heavy but brief." Enzo let go of her hand and lowered the umbrella. "Where did you and Wilf meet? I mean, no offense, but you're not his usual type."

"Is Amy his type?" She weaved round a woman struggling to fold her umbrella.

"They were an item for a few months, but with Wilf soccer always comes first." Enzo stopped at the temple. "This is the street. The store is on the left. Are you staying there?"

Katryna nodded. "Thanks, I think I can find my way from here," she said. The gold band running up her forearm tingled.

"I don't mind walking to the door," Enzo said, smiling.

The band pulsed. This wasn't good. She needed to protect Enzo. She glanced back down the street.

"Okay," she said, increasing her pace as the store came into view. The band hadn't warned her like this since she'd arrived in the Real World. What could have caused it? An image of Enzo holding her hand surfaced. His fingers brushing the golden band.

Enzo stopped outside the store, his back to the street. "It was nice to meet you. I'm sure Wilf will be here soon."

"Sooner than you were expecting." Wilf stood inches from Enzo.

"What?" Enzo said, shaking his head. "Katryna was lost."

"And you happened to be going her way." Wilf stepped closer and glared down at his friend. "Is this the urgent appointment you had so you couldn't stay?"

"No. I've a dentist appointment. Chill. I was just helping her find the store," Enzo said, raising his hands.

Katryna clutched her burning arm.

"Wilf, you're building too much power," she said before turning to Enzo. "Thanks for bringing me here. It might be best if you leave this to me."

Enzo gawked at Wilf. "There's no need to get all possessive," he said, stepping around Wilf.

"Please," Katryna said.

"All right. I'm going." Enzo thrust his hands in his pockets and set off down the street.

Wilf stared at Katryna.

Ermentrude came running out of the store. "What's happening?"

"Jealousy. A side effect of the bond." Katryna moved closer to Wilf. "I thought you didn't want to be around me."

"I changed my mind."

"If you practiced any control, this wouldn't happen," she said, gripping her arm and wincing.

"That's not helping," Ermentrude said. Her brow furrowed.

Katryna pointed at Wilf. "He's drawing too much energy. The vein is burning up my arm. Make him stop." Pain pulsed in her neck and she moaned.

Ermentrude wiggled her fingers at Wilf.

He spun his gaze to her and raised his hand. Ermentrude flew across the road and landed in a heap next to the wall.

Katryna edged backwards and Wilf followed.

Ermentrude sent a blast of white magic at him, but he

deflected it with a flick of his hand. A witch heading into the store dropped unconscious to the ground.

"You're always trying to control me," Wilf said, advancing on Ermentrude as she struggled to stand. Black mist circled around his feet and climbed up his legs.

"This is bad," Ermentrude muttered. "Wilf, control your magic before it kills us all."

Katryna wedged herself between Wilf and her mother. She put her arms around his neck, and he wrapped his arm around her waist, pulling her tight against his body.

"Is this what you wanted Enzo to do to you?" Wilf's eyes blazed.

"I don't want anyone else." It was true she'd never felt this way about anyone before. "You know how I feel about you. Take a breath and start releasing the energy. Imagine it dissipating like early morning fog on your favorite soccer pitch," she said, kissing his cheek. Pain and longing haunted his eyes. She moved her lips to cover his. He pressed his body against hers and pointed his wizard ring at the ground. The black mist stopped swirling around his legs and receded. His body relaxed as he deepened the kiss.

The gold vein on her arm and neck pulsed in rhythm with her heart, and the pain receded. There was anger, and deep longing, in his kiss.

Ermentrude cleared her throat.

Katryna broke away and stepped out of Wilf's embrace.

"Disaster averted," Ermentrude said. "What caused all this panic?"

"Enzo held my hand with the band on it," Katryna said. "I hadn't realized it would cause so much pain."

"Why was he touching you?" Wilf's ring flashed red, threatening to reignite the jealousy that came from their bond.

"He helped me through the traffic as we crossed the road," she said, gasping. Her mind and body urged her to step back into Wilf's arms. She wanted his lips on hers.

"This is ridiculous," Ermentrude said. "We have to annul this bonding ritual. Luckily, I've found a potion that might work." She took a step towards the store.

Katryna had seen fear on her mother's face when her magic hadn't been able to subdue Wilf. Ermentrude needed to be in control of every situation. Katryna knew her mother would be relentless until she regained control, and that could be terrible for Wilf.

They returned to the workshop, where Ermentrude revealed an enormous leather book. It must have taken two or three witches to carry it from the shelves. She ran a finger down a lengthy list of ingredients. Then she walked back to the shelves and wiggled her fingers. Vials and bottles floated to the table. She opened a cupboard, pointed at a cauldron, and called the last of the ingredients across the room.

"What are you doing?" Wilf asked.

Ermentrude picked up a black silk scarf.

"Making a potion to undo the bonding ritual," Ermentrude said.

"But…" Katryna said, reaching for her mother's arm. A vial crashed to the floor.

Ermentrude shook off Katryna's hand. "I've had enough of that boy not being able to concentrate when you're around. He's always got a glazed expression on his face."

Wilf's ring flashed red, and he glared at the witch.

"See what I mean? He has enough problems controlling his magic without also having to control his hormones."

"It never occurred to you to include us in this decision? I don't think we should destroy the bond." Wilf stuffed his hands into his pockets.

The broken vial threw itself into the nearest trash can. A replacement lifted from the shelf and landed with a thump next to the cauldron.

"Right times never arrive," Ermentrude said, waving at the ingredients. A set of measuring scales appeared from the shelf beneath the table, and the first vial tipped its contents onto the dish. The scale balanced, then the dish rose above the cauldron and emptied into it. The stopper jumped back into the neck of the vial. Ingredients continued to float down and were measured.

"We've needed the bond in the past to track each other," Katryna said. "Don't you think we should keep that ability?"

"It's not worth the risk," Ermentrude said, glancing down at the book.

"What risk?" Wilf said.

Ermentrude huffed, folded her arms, and stared with enough loathing to make a toad long to be a tadpole again.

"Mom, he's right. We might need the bond," Katryna said.

The last ingredient tipped into the cauldron. A lid slammed on top and the cauldron settled onto the arm over a Bunsen burner. Flames licked the sides of the cauldron.

"We'll manage," Ermentrude said. "This entire bond thing has been a distraction to you and me. I've had to keep checking on both of you. I'd rather concern myself with the biome and the Realm's collapse than whether you two can restrain yourselves."

Wilf folded his arms. "It's a mistake."

"I don't agree," Ermentrude said, stirring the contents in the cauldron. She wiggled her fingers and a large hiss of steam rose from the pot. "That should do it." She poured the contents into two glasses. "Drink down the potion." She picked up the black scarf. "I'll wrap this around your joined hands and this ritual mess should disappear." She smiled.

"No!" Wilf said. "I'm not drinking that."

Two guards appeared behind him.

"You'll force me?" Wilf said, bracing against the table.

Ermentrude waved the guards away. "Of course not. The spell will only work with your cooperation." She gave a deep sigh. "You don't know each other. Performing the bond saved Katryna from Hywel, but now it's unnecessary because she's safe. Meanwhile, take today as an example. You were ready to fight your friend and me. The attraction will only grow stronger."

She twisted the black scarf around her hand. "Wouldn't you rather find out if you have genuine feelings for each other, rather than being pushed by magic into a relationship?"

Katryna could see the logic in her mother's argument. How did she know if she even liked Wilf?

"But…" Wilf began.

"You don't need to keep tabs on each other," Ermentrude said.

"I think Mom's right. Can you tell if our emotions are real?" Katryna said.

"No. Whenever you're around I can't think straight," Wilf said, shaking his head.

He looked so miserable Katryna wanted to take him in her arms, but she folded them around herself.

Ermentrude held out the glass to Katryna and she took it. Wilf accepted the other one and lifted it to his lips.

"Wait," shouted Ermentrude. "Hold it in your left hand. I'll bind your right to Katryna's." She picked up the scarf and wrapped it around their wrists.

His pulse beat against her skin. Sweat broke out on her forehead and she sucked in her bottom lip.

"Those that are joined shall be unjoined. A ritual not consummated shall be undone. Let the Potion of Annulment quench the fire of attraction. The longing to be one shall yield its hold and two shall walk free."

Ermentrude watched as they drank the potion. "Well, any difference?"

Wilf gazed into Katryna's eyes and smiled. A tingle rang through Katryna at the hungry look in his eyes. He rubbed his finger along her skin.

"The same," she said.

The Veil of Corruption

"Bat's blood!" Ermentrude wiggled her fingers. The scarf disappeared and the table cleared. Wilf ducked as the scales headed straight for his head.

Katryna sighed. She knew her mother wouldn't give up so easily. The sour taste of the potion coated her mouth. Perhaps the next one would taste better.

Chapter Eight - Wakefield Tower, Kureyamage

Myra stood in front of the workbench, studying Thiemus as he mixed potions. Sulfur dust burned her throat. She rubbed her eyes and glanced towards the door, but instead of following her urge to leave she began to examine the spines of several books on the shelves next to her. She selected a small book from the middle and flicked through it before putting it at the end of the row.

Thiemus paused as he poured a vivid blue liquid into the cauldron. "I've indexed those books, so put them back where they belong."

She gave a loud sigh and replaced the book. "I'm bored. You don't want my help and I'm not used to waiting around for something to happen."

"Why don't you go annoy Malik?" Thiemus grinned.

"Because I don't know him," she said, trailing her fingers along the workbench.

The wall imaging mirror pinged, and Thiemus limped over to answer it. The vaccine was restoring his magic, but his physical deformities were taking longer to mend.

Hywel appeared in the mirror. "There you are," he said.

Myra stepped around the bench, making sure Hywel couldn't see her.

"They released you?" Thiemus asked.

"The Witch Council is arranging my transportation to Sha Tin. The difference in time means I'll be there tomorrow."

"Do you want me to meet you in Hong Kong?"

"No. It's better if you stay there. You're still a wanted criminal. Have you started the collection process?"

"Last night. The tanks should be at full capacity tomorrow."

"Excellent. Advise Malik to collect me via the portal." Hywel paused. "Have you seen Myra?"

Thiemus glanced over at her and she shook her head. "I brought her back here, but I haven't seen her since."

"Make sure she doesn't leave. I may have a use for her," Hywel said.

"Very well." The screen went blank, and Thiemus hobbled back to his cauldron.

"I was hoping not to see him again," Myra said. Her hands trembled, and she stuffed them into her pockets. Her fingers wrapped around the vials of elixir.

"You'll need his protection," Thiemus said, continuing to add ingredients to the bubbling cauldron.

"I don't need anyone."

Thiemus gave a mocking laugh.

Malik nudged the door open. "Where do you want this?" He carried a computer monitor.

"Put it over there." Thiemus nodded towards the chess table.

"Hywel wants you to collect him," Thiemus said. A green cloud rose from the cauldron. His ring flashed and the cloud shaped into a string that wrapped around the inside of a jar. A stopper rose to squeeze into the top.

"Now?"

"In about three hours," Thiemus said.

"It's good that the collection stage can run on its own." Malik faced Myra. "Seems I have some free time. You want to get out of here? Take in the sights and grab a bite to eat?"

"For my sanity, go with him," Thiemus said.

"If you think you can manage without me?" she said.

"Don't hurry back," Thiemus said, grabbing a jar of purple moths.

Myra picked up her jacket and followed Malik. He snatched up a backpack as they passed his workshop. Myra blinked several times at the bright glare of the sun when they reached the top of the stairs. She paused, letting the breeze warm her.

"Come on." Malik hitched the backpack over his shoulder and led the way down the street from Hywel's Tower.

The last time she'd been in the market square, stalls had occupied the entire space. The noise of price haggling and vendors calling to customers had been energetic and fun. The aromas of herbs, fruit, meat, and baked goods had filled the air. Now the stalls filled a quarter of the square. Supplies were reduced to sparse food and potion ingredients — only the necessities to sustain life.

"Have the quakes stopped?" Myra asked. There were more piles of rubble than properties standing in the streets surrounding the square.

"No, but they're not as frequent. That's why the biome project is so important — they should allow us to rebalance the Realm."

"The biomes will collect magic from here?"

"No, the biomes create their own magic for us to use. They're self-sustaining, so we won't be reliant on this Realm's magic. That'll mean no one will draw magic from here. Once the collection system is running, there'll be a mass evacuation until we achieve the correct ratio of wizards to witches. This will give the Realm healing time. Well, that's the theory."

Malik stopped by a stall with baskets of apples and pears. He picked out two apples, pulled a handful of crystals from his pocket, and selected three hexagonal red ones. He dropped them into the stallholder's outstretched hand.

A shadow emerged from a doorway. The emaciated figure pulled at his tattered cloak with fingers that looked like talons. The wizard stepped into the light, his hands and face blue. Myra gasped as sparks of magic sizzled with each step he took.

The stallholder turned towards him. "Get away from here." He picked up a rotten apple and hurled it at the wizard. "They used to stay in the abandoned buildings near the Veil, but they've moved up here now," he said to Malik and Myra.

"I'd fear disappearing, staying that close to the Veil," Malik said.

"There's been an increase in the number of users. Supply can't meet demand anymore," the stallholder said, replenishing the fruit in the basket. "When you're that dependent on elixir and the supply diminishes, then magic leaks out. Only last week they found a young witch next to the palace. Bright blue she was. Sparks flying from her fingers and hair. Screamed her lungs out before a healer could get to her."

"Did they save her?" Myra shoved her hands into her pockets.

He looked surprised. "Course not. Once they reach that stage, there's no helping them except putting them out of their misery before they can cause any harm to anyone else." He shook his head and turned to another customer.

Myra watched the wizard disappear down an alley. She shuddered and turned her attention back to Malik. He held out an apple. "Sorry! You were telling me about the Realm being isolated," she said.

He nodded. "We'll send portals, but it will make supplying and running Kureyamage a problem."

"Who will stay here?" She tried to concentrate on what he was telling her, but her mind kept returning to the stallholder's story about the elixir addict. She resisted the urge to check her own fingers, even though she knew her fingernails were no longer blue.

"The Council will choose how many wizards and witches to

strand here to rebalance the Realm." Malik bit into his apple.

"We could be stuck here?" Myra didn't think the Wizard Council would choose her. She'd end up back in Hong Kong.

"It's possible. I'm hoping to convince Hywel that I should run the Hong Kong end of the project. I'm not being marooned here." He took another bite and walked to the edge of the market. "Your stepfather escaped to Hong Kong and got away from all the politics."

"They exiled him for working with the Witch Council. It was a punishment," Myra said. She had no desire to discuss Reginald.

"I think he arranged to leave Kureyamage. He was the smartest wizard around, I was told." Malik waved his apple at her as he spoke.

"I don't want to talk about him," Myra said. Did Malik not know her role in her stepfather's death?

He stopped and faced her. "Sorry! I forgot about you and..."

She held his gaze until he lowered it.

"Sorry," he mumbled again before setting off.

Myra considered heading back to the tower. She shrugged. There was nothing to do there. She ran to catch up with him. "Where are you going?"

He stopped and she collided with his back. A tendril of midnight-colored mist slithered out from a narrow street towards the closest stall.

"Is that from the Veil?" Myra asked.

"There've been reports of strands breaking off." Malik moved closer.

"Isn't that impossible?"

"Should be, but the spell's corrupted. Who knows what might happen?" Malik crept forward.

Myra shivered. She'd traveled through the tunnels under the Veil twice to enter Mathowytch. She had no desire to repeat that journey, ever.

The wizard behind the stall collapsed.

Malik ran forward but stopped at the edge of the stall. Myra peered at the wizard.

The midnight tendril that had wrapped itself around the wizard pulsed and squeezed. Tiny grunts and moans came from the wizard inside the mist cocoon.

"I've never seen that before." Malik's voice trembled.

"The Veil is hunting wizards?" Myra whispered.

Malik grabbed her arm and pulled her back into the shadows. The tail end of the strand slipped into an alley.

"It's leaving. It's as if it swallowed him," she said.

"We should follow it," Malik said.

"Are you mad? What if it's waiting for us?" She could hear the fear in her voice.

"Let's hope not." He stepped around her and continued towards the corner. He beckoned her to join him.

The Veil, a wall of opaque mist, blocked the end of the street and obscured the entrance to Mathowytch. A midnight-colored tendril slithered into a small opening at its base.

"The rumors are true," Malik said, wiping a bead of sweat off his forehead. "The Veil is capturing wizards." He turned back towards the market. "I think it's draining them of their magic to sustain itself."

"What? That sounds crazy. The spell has never needed outside magic from wizards before."

"The Veil is a witch spell. It doesn't have access to wizard magic, so it must seek it. Your stepbrother's actions have corrupted it," Malik said.

"You think Wilf caused this?" Myra ran to keep up with him.

"I was told he helped prop up the spell by letting the Witch Council use his magic. Seems that his act, however well-meaning, has corrupted the Veil. This news will delight the Wizard Council."

"How?" Myra was having trouble following his reasoning.

Malik stepped around a large mound of rubble. "It will give the Wizard Council a legitimate reason to demand the Witch Council dissolve the spell. And once that happens…"

Myra touched his arm. "They'll send in the wizard guards to reclaim Mathowytch."

He tossed his apple core into a trash can.

"What do you imagine the witches will do to Wilf?" Myra said.

Malik sneered. "Do you care?"

"No! He's been trying to find me," she said.

"Soon he'll be too busy trying to save his own skin to worry about you. It's fair to say that your stepbrother won't win Wizard of the Month." He caught hold of her shaking hand. "You should ease up on that elixir."

Myra rubbed her wrist as Malik walked on and entered the square. She ran to catch him. "The witches accepted Wilf's help. They're unlikely to hold him responsible."

"That's exactly what they'll do. He's the ideal scapegoat. A young, uneducated wizard would be a simple choice." Malik grinned.

Myra shook her head and maneuvered through the stalls. Could it be true that Wilf was about to become the Council's Enemy Number One?

"I'm right in thinking Wilf doesn't have full control over his magic?" Malik called after her.

Myra kept walking.

"I rest my case," he added smugly.

Wilf might be only her stepbrother, but she'd always taken care of him. He needed her. He'd gone from one disaster to another on his own. She should be glad she was free of him, after he'd aligned with the witches. She wasn't responsible if that proved to be a dire decision.

Malik's wrist mirror pinged, and he flipped it open.

"Why haven't you left yet?" Hywel shouted.

"On my way, boss." Malik smiled and closed the mirror.

"Won't that piss him off?" Myra said.

"Maybe, but he won't fire me. He needs me enough to put up with whatever I feel like dishing out."

Myra hoped Malik was right. Hywel had a long memory, and when he didn't need you anymore, he would remember every little slight you've ever given him. Her mother, Griselda, had learned that lesson the hard way.

"We'd better return to the tower." Malik leaned in and kissed her cheek. "I'm glad you came back to join us."

Myra felt the heat spreading up her neck. She prided herself on not being easy to read, but Malik was treating her like she was a novice at this game. She'd have to be more careful around him.

Picking up the pace, she jogged to catch him. The vials in her pocket clinked, and she wrapped her fingers around them. Malik seemed concerned about her habit. Which was nice, but she'd been hoping to convince him to supply her with a few vials. She couldn't keep stealing from Thiemus, but now she didn't dare risk asking Malik. He pushed open the gate to the tower and stepped back for her to enter, making a mocking bow before her.

"See you later, I hope," he said, turning towards the portal she'd traveled in with Thiemus.

She nodded. "Be careful. The Thermals are fighting back."

He'd already walked away, but he raised his hand and saluted her before opening the door and stepping inside.

The portal swayed from side to side, then vanished in a flash of green light.

Hywel would return soon.

Grasping a vial from her pocket, she uncorked it and swallowed the contents in one gulp. The rush wasn't as great as she needed, but it blocked some of the emptiness she felt. Rather than worrying about Malik, she should worry about her own reunion with Hywel. She needed his protection from the Witch Council, but that would come at a cost. How much of her soul would he demand this time?

Chapter Nine - Wilf's Store, Hong Kong

Wilf caught the ball on his foot and flicked it up to his knee.

"You were always good at ball tricks," Enzo said, thrusting his hands deep into his short's pockets.

Wilf let the ball drop to the floor and then passed it to Enzo. "Look, about before, that thing with Katryna." He took a deep breath.

"It's fine," Enzo said. "Don't sweat it." He kicked the ball at the wall, angling it back to Wilf.

"Thanks," Wilf said, kicking the ball back at the wall so it returned to Enzo.

"It's just a little weird how much you're into her. I've never seen you like this over a girl, and I mean, she's not exactly a looker," Enzo said.

Wilf turned to meet Enzo's gaze.

"How are you doing that?" Enzo said, pointing at the soccer ball floating in mid-air above Wilf's knee. "That's amazing."

Wilf concentrated on the ball and it dropped to the ground. His wizard ring flashed.

A bell sounded, and Katryna raced out of the store. "What are you doing using magic? Aren't you trying to play without it?"

Frustration bubbled through him. They had been fighting all morning. He'd run from the apartment, not wanting to remain in the same room as her. Still, his body tensed and his heart raced just looking at her.

"That's how you made the ball levitate? It's a magical illusion?" Enzo asked, doing a good fish impression as he looked between them, waiting for an answer.

"I don't want to talk about this now." Wilf glared at Katryna. Not only was she pointing out his failings — yet again — but she was yelling about magic in front of Enzo.

Katryna's eyes flashed with anger and her cheeks flushed. She placed her hands on her hips and leaned towards him in the way

Ermentrude did. "You still want to be a Groundling, don't you?"

"No," Wilf said. A breeze blew down the street and he caught a slight scent of citrus.

"When are you going to accept you're a wizard?" She stepped closer to him. "You should be practicing your magic, not playing ball with your friend."

The citrus aroma circulated around them. He balled his fists to prevent himself from placing them on her arms.

"We've been through this. I play in the championship and also help with capturing you know who." Wilf gave a pointed look over at Enzo. He'd rather not have this conversation in front of him. He wanted to smooth her hair from her face. He shook his head. Where had that thought come from? "Go back inside with the others. Leave us alone."

"Wait." Enzo's brow furrowed. "You're saying he's a wizard? Pointy hat? Beard?"

"How can you put soccer before magic and your Realm?" Katryna said, poking Wilf in the chest.

"Stop doing that," he said, batting her hand away as he fought the urge to hold on to it.

"Magic? There's another realm?" Enzo said.

With a wiggle of her fingers, the soccer ball gave out a long hiss and deflated at Wilf's feet. She crossed her arms. "Go on, inflate it."

"Shit! You just… with your fingers." Enzo edged away.

Wilf bit the inside of his cheek. Power surged through him. He'd controlled it until Katryna had come out here behaving like she was captain of Team Wilf. He had no intention of performing magic in front of Enzo.

"It's a trick ball. Katryna likes to show off sometimes," Wilf said, glaring at her. He took several deep breaths, but it was no use. Energy pulsed through him. The ruby ring flashed and the ball inflated.

Why did she have to interfere? It was the bond linking them. They were both finding it harder to resist. Perhaps Ermentrude was right and it was time to annul the ritual. Wilf knew that Ermentrude's failure last time had only spurred her on. Not that he'd ever say that to her face.

"Eh! I don't know how you did that, but that's enough air," Enzo said, retreating several more steps.

The ball continued to inflate. Sweat trickled down Wilf's face as he struggled to gain control. He balled his fist, but the ring burned into the palm of his hand. He moved away from the ball as the rubber thinned. "Katryna, help!"

She gave a huff and a wiggle of her fingers. Air rushed out of the ball with a loud hiss. "Magic is what you should practice, not children's games."

"You're both magicians?" Enzo said.

Wilf's face burned. "No," he said.

"I'm a witch," Katryna said, covering the tip of the golden vein protruding from her sleeve.

"That would explain the… wart." Enzo sidled up to Wilf. "Is she for real? Are you under her spell?"

"You might say that," Wilf said. Although not in the way his best friend meant.

"Funny! But you don't get me that easily. Seriously, what's the trick?" Enzo shook his head and punched Wilf's arm.

"It's true," Katryna said. "Wilf is a wizard, I'm a witch, and magic is real. Unfortunately, Wilf needs to practice his magic so he can control it better and not use it to play soccer."

"Katryna…" Wilf pleaded.

Enzo ran his hands through his hair and edged a few steps away from Katryna. "Come on. I've known Wilf since kindergarten. He's no wizard." He paused. "Are you?"

"Yes, I am." Wilf sounded defeated even to his own ears. He saw the direction this conversation was heading. It was like a runaway striker towards an open goal. "Everything Katryna has said is true."

"You use magic to play soccer?" A deep flush rose in Enzo's cheeks and his brow creased.

"I try not to." Wilf stared at the ground.

"What does that mean?" Enzo stood inches from Wilf.

"I refused to use magic, so I thought I wasn't. However, it seems because I didn't have any control, the magic was deciding for me. Now…"

"Yeah!" Enzo punched Wilf in the shoulder.

He rocked backwards. "I'm learning to control it."

"Like when that ball almost exploded and you needed her to help. That kind of control?" Enzo threw his hands up in the air. "Wow! That explains the times when I've thought the ball changed direction. I'd put it down to divots in the pitch, but it was you controlling it." He thrust his face forward. "We thought you were this fantastic striker. The team admired your skill, and in reality, you were just a low-level cheat."

"It's not like that, believe me. I'd give up magic in a heartbeat." Wilf tried to grab hold of Enzo's flailing arm.

"Sure you would." Enzo said, pushing him off.

"Magic is part of me. I have no control." The words sounded weak, but what other argument did he have? He tried to put his hand on Enzo's shoulder, but his friend distanced himself further.

"I can vouch for that, but that's because he doesn't practice," Katryna said.

"Piss off," Wilf said, wishing he could magic her away. "Enzo…"

"Mates don't keep secrets from each other, and they don't cheat." Enzo shook his fist at Wilf. "If you're really a wizard and don't want everyone to know your secret, stay away from the club and the championship. We don't need your magic to win." He waved his hand towards the store. "Stay with your own kind, Wizard Wilf."

He turned and ran down Tai Wang Street.

"Wait!" Wilf yelled after him but didn't pursue him. "Happy now?" He turned to face Katryna.

"It's not my fault. You brought this on yourself." She marched past him and into the apartment.

Wilf ran after her and caught her outside her bedroom. "Are you pleased with the effect your display of magic had on Enzo?"

She turned so her face was inches away from his. "My magic! You'd already used it in front of him. That's why I came outside."

"I'm sick of you trying to control me." Still, his nose filled with the citrus fragrance of her. He could almost taste the peppermint of her breath. He shook his head, trying to get rid of the emotions her closeness aroused in him. He needed to focus on his anger, not the warmth of her body.

"I am not controlling you." She placed her hands on his chest.

Katryna's hazel eyes glistened and her pupils dilated. His attention dropped to her lips as she moistened them with the tip of her tongue.

"Yes, you are," he said, slipping his arms around her waist and jerking her to him. She gasped, and he pressed his body against hers. He bent his head and nuzzled her neck. She groaned, and he brushed her cheek with his lips. His mouth covered hers and he kissed her. He didn't have the strength to fight how much he wanted her.

She answered him with parted lips. He licked along her upper lip and teeth. Teasing and tempting her. He stepped one leg between hers, urging her backwards into her room. Moving together, they never broke contact with their lips until they bumped into the bed. With a wiggle of her fingers, the door closed with a click.

His fingers trembled as he lifted the hem of her T-shirt and slid his hand onto her warm stomach. She wrapped her arms around his neck, and the golden vein on her arm pulsed in rhythm with his pounding heart. His body trembled as his hand traveled up her back. He found it impossible to think of anything but the growing need to possess her, be part of her. Her hands traveled under his shirt and he held his breath. His heart pounded against his chest. Her fingers traced his waistband. He groaned when her hand slid lower and brushed against his…

With a crunch, his head bounced off the wall as he hurtled across the room. His vision swam, and he rubbed his head.

"I can't turn my back on you two for one moment," Ermentrude said. Her eyes blazed and a cloud of smoke rose from her hair bun.

She must have placed a warning spell on Katryna's bedroom. It explained how she'd known where they were. He eased himself up against the wall.

"There's a new potion waiting downstairs in the kitchen. And given this little performance, this one better work," Ermentrude said.

Katryna crossed the room. Wilf went to follow her, but Ermentrude stepped in front of him. He grinned at her, behind her back.

"Don't think I didn't see that," Ermentrude said, glancing back at him. "Wizards! Nothing but trouble."

They descended the stairs to the kitchen. A small cauldron sat in the middle of the table, the black silk scarf beside it. Ermentrude took two glasses from the shelf and filled them with black liquid from the cauldron. She placed a glass in front of Katryna and gave the other to Wilf.

"Clasp your hands together so that Wilf's ringed finger is on your pulse." Ermentrude said.

"I know," Katryna said.

The scarf rose from the table and wrapped around their clasped hands, binding them together. Wilf rubbed the skin of Katryna's wrist and she glanced up at him and smiled. Slight shock waves ran up his arm.

"Drink it," Ermentrude commanded.

Katryna looked at him, and he shrugged his shoulders. There was no point in fighting Ermentrude once she'd decided on a course of action.

"This is a mistake," he said. He couldn't get rid of a nagging doubt in the back of his mind.

"Drink," Ermentrude said.

He raised the glass to his lips and drank. The liquid had a peculiar consistency that reminded him of thick pea soup. It ran down his throat rather than him swallowing it, but it also seemed to fizz on his tongue. He banged the drained glass back on the table.

"Good," Ermentrude said once Katryna had finished hers. She placed her fingers over their bound hands and repeated the words from the last attempt.

"Those that are joined shall be unjoined. A ritual not consummated shall be undone. Let the Potion of Annulment quench the fire of attraction. The longing to be one shall yield its hold and two shall walk free."

A cold sensation started in Wilf's stomach and spread throughout his body. He could see his ring pulsing through the black silk. The golden vein on Katryna's arm glowed. On top of the scarf, a spark grew to the size of a golf ball. It circled their hands counterclockwise, moving faster and faster, then shot up to the ceiling and exploded, raining gray cinders over them. As they touched the scarf, it dissolved.

Katryna let go of Wilf's hand as if his touch scalded her skin.

"Well?" Ermentrude asked. "Still want to rip each other's clothes off?"

Katryna's face turned bright pink, and she shook her head.

"Wilf?" Ermentrude said, smirking.

He held her gaze but shook his head.

"Excellent," Ermentrude said, wiggling her fingers at the cauldron. It flew across the room and clattered into the sink. "I feel safe leaving the two of you alone now." She walked over to the door. "Except that Degula wanted to see you, Katryna." She stepped to the side to allow Katryna to go ahead.

Wilf collapsed into a chair when the front door slammed shut. He reached for the bond, his attachment to Katryna. Nothing! It felt as if a part of him was missing. He'd lost his best friend and his girlfriend within a matter of hours. This day couldn't possibly get any worse.

Chapter Ten - Sha Tin, Hong Kong

Katryna trailed down Shing Wan Road behind Degula. She paused once to alter her vision, and the gigantic shimmering dome of the biome came into view. It glowed and pulsed like a living entity. The surging energy inside sang to her.

"Does the magic call to you?" Degula asked.

"So much power," Katryna said. "It makes me want to dive into it, to try to claim and control it, even though I know it would destroy me to hold that amount of magic."

Degula's eyes shone. "You are so unique to possess both magics. No one has possessed that ability since ancient times."

Katryna didn't want to be different. She loved being a witch. She glanced down at her deformed right ring finger with its extra knuckle. When she made a fist, her fingertip now disappeared into her palm. She never called on the wizard magic Wilf had accidentally given to her.

A small wooden building appeared next to the biome and a young wizard stepped out. He pushed his hair out of his eyes and walked towards them.

"Excellent timing, Malik," Degula said.

"Is this Hywel's daughter?" he said, stopping in front of Katryna. Degula nodded.

Malik grabbed Katryna by the arm. "Your daddy will be so happy to see you again." He snapped magic-dampening handcuffs on her.

"Hywel's obsessed with reuniting with you," Degula said, wrinkling her nose.

"I think it passed that stage a long time ago. Hywel sees it as his duty to protect her from the corrupting influence of your Witch Council," Malik said, tightening his hold on Katryna.

Katryna jerked her arm, but Malik's viselike grip held. He dragged her towards the sentry box. She gave a sudden twist and kick, and Malik swore as she escaped his grasp. She charged down the road. If she could reach the corner…

Her knees buckled and her shoulder took the full force of her fall. She tried to move but was powerless.

"Get her!" Degula said, lowering her arm.

Malik picked up Katryna and threw her over his shoulder. He kicked open the portal's door and dropped her onto a bench. The sound of marching boots stopped with a stomp to attention. Malik stepped outside, leaving the door ajar.

"Here are the release papers for the prisoner Wizard Hywel Wakefield, ma'am," a voice said. Katryna heard the rustling of papers followed by Degula's dismissal of the squad. The sound of marching feet faded.

"Very efficient," Hywel said, grasping the edge of the door. Dirt smeared his clothes, and his hair needed washing and combing. Large bruises circled his eyes.

"Not so fast," Degula said. "I'm coming with you."

"That wasn't part of our bargain," Hywel said. "You're needed here to monitor Ermentrude and send me reports on the Witch Council."

Degula gave a bark of laughter. "I'm supposed to arrange your freedom, hand over your daughter, and then trust you to fulfill your part of our arrangement?"

"I have no reason to cross you," Hywel said, folding his arms. "You'll have full access to the witch magic from the biome in the next day or two."

"And the other?"

"As soon as I discover how it's possible to possess both forms of magic, I will inform you. The delay results from the time my release took." Hywel's ring flashed and the dirt disappeared from his clothes.

Degula gave a huff.

"May I leave?" Hywel asked, brushing his hand down the front of his jacket.

Malik stepped into the portal, reached over, and pushed Katryna into the corner before squeezing in next to her.

Hywel sat opposite them as the door closed. "What's wrong with Katryna?

"Degula did it, not me," Malik said, raising his hands. "Your daughter wasn't too happy about taking this trip."

Hywel grabbed her arm and pushed up her sleeve to expose the golden vein. His ring flared and the handcuffs disappeared. He twisted the bracelet around her wrist. "This has my name on it again, not Wilf's."

Katryna wanted to rip her arm out of Hywel's grasp, but she

couldn't move. She wanted to scream, shout, and break the globe, but she sat slumped against the arm of the bench. Ermentrude's potion had worked. Her bond with Wilf was broken, and they were no longer connected. She was again a possession of her father's.

A piece of her was missing. At first it had been annoying to feel the connection with Wilf, but she'd grown used to knowing he was there — reassurance that she was not alone. Now, with the bond's dissolution, no one could find her.

"I presume Ermentrude broke the bond. She has done me a huge favor." A smile slithered across his lips.

Malik leaned forward and placed his hand on the glass globe. The electrical spikes inside the sphere aligned to connect with his fingers. The amber stone at the center of his wizard ring flashed. "Ready?" he asked.

Hywel dropped Katryna's arm and leaned back on his bench. He nodded at Malik. The wall beside Katryna changed into a window. The portal gave a shudder and leapt forward onto an unfurling ribbon of neon light.

Tingling spread through Katryna's fingers and toes as she regained control of her body. She gave a grunt when Malik's elbow struck her side as he maneuvered the craft. A jagged boulder landed on the track, and Malik swished his hand. The portal jerked to the right, missing a collision by millimeters.

"I'm not sure how much longer travel between the Realms will be possible," Malik said, trying to stop the sphere from rocking on top of the column and breaking contact with his fingers.

"That's why we need Katryna." Hywel steepled his fingers and continued to regard her. "Although you're quite the puzzle, daughter," he said.

"My help? Is that why you kidnapped me?" Her voice came out in a rasp.

"I haven't. I've only arranged for you to return home where you belong. You should be grateful," Hywel said. "I will turn you into our Realm's savior. You should be happy to help."

"What are you talking about?" A sinking sensation grew in the pit of her stomach. She was about to become her father's newest project.

"Both magics in one person. There hasn't been a record of someone with your ability, or something similar, since the days of Mulkulth. It should be impossible. But here you sit," Hywel said in a hushed voice. "Amazing! The power a wizard could yield with that capability." He tapped his fingers against his chin.

"Toad's innards!" Sweat trickled down from Malik's forehead. His fingertips were white from the amount of pressure needed to maintain contact with the sphere.

The portal hurled towards the end of the track.

"The door isn't opening!" he shouted.

Hywel turned his head and regarded the track. The grain pattern of the wooden door became visible as the portal sped closer. They'd be smashed against it, left to float in the Thermals with no possibility of escape.

Hywel raised his hand. His wizard ring's black stone flashed and the door swung inward, then slammed shut behind them as the portal jerked to a stop.

Malik broke his connection with the sphere and stood, flexing his hand. "That was exhilarating."

Hywel stood when Malik opened the portal's door. "After you, my dear."

Katryna took a deep breath and stepped from the portal. She was back in Hywel's Tower. Rubble littered the ground where the east wing had been.

"What are you doing here?" Myra stepped out from the entrance's shadow.

"So you did make it back to Kureyamage," Katryna said, watching Nipits jump from the bushes. The cat sauntered over to Myra and purred as he wrapped himself around her legs.

"My daughter is where she belongs," Hywel said, entering the tower. "Malik, escort Katryna to the workshops. Put her in room four."

Malik took a step towards Katryna, but she sent a blast of magic to push him away.

"I'm not one of your experiments!"

Hywel's brow furrowed. "I've had a rather trying time in that other Realm, and I don't have time for teenage whims. You will go where and when I tell you."

Katryna sent a blast of magic at her father, but he blocked it. He fired back at her, but she'd stepped behind the portal. She heard footsteps on the gravel to her right and assumed it was Malik. She edged to her left and sent a blast at the column next to the entrance. Hywel stumbled backwards into the tower. The door to the street was four or five steps away. She made a dash for it, sending a bolt of magic to her right and another to her left.

A fizzing missile hit her in the back and she collapsed.

Malik yanked Katryna up by her elbow.

"Nice try," he said, leading her into the tower, down the corridor and through the kitchen. Katryna stumbled down the stairs and Malik caught her as she tripped over loose rocks. Myra and Nipits trailed behind.

"What does he want with her?" Myra asked.

"I'm just the errand boy around here," Malik said, giving Katryna a tug when she slowed down.

"I don't believe that," Myra said.

"It doesn't do to ask too many questions. If Hywel wants you to know, I'm sure he'll tell you."

Myra nodded and continued to follow them.

"Stop pulling me," Katryna said when she tripped for the umpteenth time.

"Then walk faster. I've more important tasks to attend to than being the delivery guy," Malik said, giving an extra jerk on Katryna's arm. "Myra, as you're insisting on coming along, please light a few more globes?"

"Sure." Myra wiggled her fingers, and the corridor shimmered in a murky yellow glow. "There's a problem with the light."

"There's a problem with the magic," Malik said. "I'll check the flow as soon as I've dumped this freak."

Katryna's vision swam as tears threatened to spill. She'd dreamed of returning to the Magical Realm, but not like this — as a prisoner of her father's. She edged past an enormous boulder and her hand grazed the wall. The golden vein in her arm pulsed. If only she could contact Wilf or her mother and explain that Hywel had kidnapped her. She'd have to accept that she was on her own. Hywel would never let her leave.

Malik had called her a freak of magic. That's what she was. Neither a witch nor a wizard. An anomaly for her father to experiment on. Delivered by that traitor, Degula.

"Ouch," she said, banging her knee on a piece of wood sticking out of the wall. She bent to rub the injury, but Malik pulled her.

"You'll have all the time you need to sit when I get you to room four. So quit pausing every two steps," he said.

Katryna bit her lower lip as pain shot up her leg. She might be helpless, but they were offering her time to think, create an escape plan. She'd no intention of spending the rest of her life being her father's science project.

Chapter Eleven - Wilf's Store, Hong Kong

Ermentrude exited the store. "There you are," she said.

"What do you want with me? Where's Katryna?" Wilf asked, twisting the wizard ring around his finger.

"She left with Degula." Ermentrude avoided looking at him.

"To go where?"

"I don't see why that's any of your concern." Ermentrude glanced down the street. "I wanted to catch you before you ran off to play with your friends."

Wilf stopped fiddling with his ring. "I'm not going to soccer."

"Hmm. So you're busy feeling sorry for yourself," Ermentrude said, pursing her lips. "Well, you can stop that — there isn't time for self-pity. Come with me." She turned and walked into the store. "Now!" she said, popping her head around the door to glare at him.

His feet dragged, but he followed her inside. He knew that look. She would find him busywork. At least it wouldn't be to clean his room or take out the trash. She might watch over him while he studied from magic workbooks. He hoped not, but the way his day was progressing the task would be terrible and boring.

Ermentrude avoided answering any of the questions flung at her from the witches around the room and disappeared into the workshop. Wilf thumped down the stairs behind her. When he reached the bottom, the room hushed, and all the witches turned to stare at him.

"What?" he said, his face burning. He was counting the

days until they were all gone.

Ermentrude glanced around, acknowledging the room's vibe for the first time. "Pay them no attention," she said.

That was easy for her to say. She didn't have eyes following her as she walked across the workshop. Whispered conversations buzzed around him as he trailed behind her. He could sense an increase in the wave of animosity directed at him. What had happened?

"Has there been any word from Akuna?" Ermentrude addressed a witch at the far end of the wooden table, sitting with her hand on a glass globe.

She shook her head but stopped as the interior of the globe clouded with blue mist. The mirror and the back wall flickered. The thin, bony face of the Head Witch from the Witch Council filled the mirror's surface.

"Is Degula there?" Akuna asked.

"She and Katryna have gone to Sha Tin to make sure Hywel is dispatched back to Kureyamage," Ermentrude said, stepping up to the mirror.

"You released him?" Wilf said. The witches gasped and shuffled away. What did they imagine Wilf would do? Lose it and destroy them all? They had no faith in his ability to control his magic.

"At least that is one of the Wizard Council's demands met," Akuna said. The image pulled back so they could see the Head Witch sitting at her desk. A painting of a witch flying through the Thermals filled the wall behind her.

"How many demands have you and the Council agreed to?" Wilf asked.

Ermentrude tutted at the interruption.

"Three." Akuna wrung her hands and then dropped them to the desk. "That's what I'm trying to discuss with Ermentrude, if you could stop interrupting."

Wilf squared his shoulders.

"We are to take down the Veil…"

A louder gasp filled the room, and all attention turned to the Head Witch's image.

"What else do we have to give them? Not the entire Council, I hope," Ermentrude said.

"No. We're allowed to disband, but first the Council must sign an agreement," Akuna said.

"What have you negotiated?" Ermentrude said, leaning on the table.

"This isn't the place. I'll have a copy of the transcript dispatched to you." She waved a hand at someone out of the mirror's view.

Akuna cleared her throat. "We're also to hand over Wilf."

"I'm not one of your belongings. I'm staying right here in Hong Kong." Wilf moved to stand in front of the mirror. The Wizard Council had wanted him under their control since they knew of his existence. He should have guessed that would be one of their demands.

"Why do they want him?" Ermentrude asked, folding her arms.

"The corruption is spreading. The Council suggests that once Wilf completes his training in Kureyamage, he'll be able to help cleanse the magic. We can't supply enough biome magic for the entire community. We need to rebalance the Realm. Until then we'll only have limited access to magic," Akuna said.

Conversations broke out around the room.

"How is a semi-trained wizard of any use?" Ermentrude huffed.

"He created the corruption," Akuna said.

"We know nothing of the sort. It's a theory that is being bandied about as if it were a prediction coming to fruition," Ermentrude said, refolding her arms.

"The Veil spell worked without fault before Wilf added his magic. It's now rogue and attacking wizards and witches. A guardian named Flayver is wandering outside the spell and terrorizing the populace," Akuna said.

"Have you started dismantling the Veil spell?" Ermentrude's face lost all its color.

Akuna wrung her hands again, seemed to notice, and clasped them together.

"There's a problem. We've discovered two guardians within the spell. Betrine, the original spell guardian, she's cooperative and obeys the spell's parameters to protect Mathowytch from any wizard trying to enter. Flayver is battling for supremacy and is unresponsive to any requests."

"You mean you've lost control of the spell?" Ermentrude said, knitting her brows.

"The situation is being dealt with." Akuna's bangles jangled as she pushed an imaginary loose hair back into her tight gray bun. "In the meantime, it would be best to return that young wizard to Mathowytch."

"I'm not putting a foot back in that Realm," Wilf said, thrusting his hands into his pockets.

"Why don't you leave this with me?" Ermentrude asked.

Akuna turned away for a few moments. "Very well, but it's becoming difficult transitioning between the Realms. This can't wait too long."

"Very well." Ermentrude nodded, and the screen went blank.

"I'm not going," Wilf said.

The Executrix guards stamped their feet and moved to block the stairs.

Ermentrude stroked the hairs on her chin.

"Did you hear me?" Wilf said.

"It's difficult not to," Ermentrude said. "I would appreciate a little quiet."

A witch dropped a cauldron into the metal sink. A hiss and then a cloud of green smoke rose into the air.

"Perhaps this isn't the best place for me to think. Come on, let's go upstairs to the apartment." Ermentrude walked over to the witch monitoring the communications globe. "When Degula and my daughter return, ask them to join us." The witch nodded.

Ermentrude started climbing the stairs.

Wilf bit his tongue to stop the bitter words in his head from escaping. He couldn't help thinking Ermentrude treated him like a trained mascot. But the atmosphere in the workshop didn't invite him to stay. He stomped after her.

Ermentrude paced the kitchen as the tea kettle flew over to the faucet and filled with water, then alighted on its stand and clicked on. Steam soon spiraled from its spout and a mug leapt from the cupboard and rattled down next to it. A handful of herbs filled the mug. But the kettle, instead of pouring water into the mug, flew across the room and began emptying into the sink.

Ermentrude grabbed hold of the kettle and walked it back to fill her mug. Wilf pulled out a chair, sat down, and leaned back, waiting for her to speak. It didn't matter to him what she said — he wasn't ever going back to the Magical Realm.

Ermentrude clearly knew what he was thinking. "You must go," she said, sitting down with the steaming cup of brew in her hand.

"No, I must not," he said, banging his chair legs back down. "This isn't my fault or my fight. You needed me to get into the journal and give you the vaccine formula. I've learned how to control my magic enough so I'm no longer dangerous. I'm done."

"Is that right?" Ermentrude said, peering over the rim of her mug.

"Soon all the witches will have received the vaccine and you won't need my father's workshop anymore. Another couple of weeks and this will be a witch-free zone," Wilf said.

Ermentrude gave a hollow laugh. "You're living in a fantasy world if you're assuming they'll allow you to roam free. That Advancer of Hywel's has made you a powerful wizard. The Council will want to hold you. They'll need to make sure you don't draw too much magic, which will soon be a rare commodity."

"They can't hold me forever," he said, leaning on the table.

Ermentrude took a long drink of brew. "Who mentioned forever?"

Steps sounded on the stairs leading from the street. "Ermentrude, I'm so sorry," Degula said, as she entered the kitchen.

"What's happened? Where's Katryna?" Ermentrude said, jumping up.

Degula wiggled her fingers. A glass leapt from the cupboard and filled with water as the witch collapsed onto a chair. She took a long drink before placing the glass on the table.

Ermentrude's face darkened. "What has happened to my daughter?"

"It's my fault. I underestimated the depth of his feelings. If for one moment I'd imagined she was in danger, I would never have taken her with me." Degula wrapped her fingers around the glass and took another sip. She tilted the glass only enough so her eyes never left Ermentrude's.

"Stop talking around the details and tell me what happened to Katryna," Ermentrude said. She wiggled her fingers, and the glass disappeared from Degula's hand.

Degula's eyes flashed, but she placed her hands on the edge of the table. "Hywel took her with him."

Ermentrude rounded the table and stood a few feet from Degula. "To Kureyamage? How could you allow that to happen?"

"I tried to stop him, but his technician overpowered me. He had a portal and they disappeared," Degula said.

"Where were the guards?"

"They'd left, having handed Hywel over. I didn't expect him to make a move to reclaim her."

"You dismissed the squad? Why would you do that?"

Wilf swallowed as a thick silence lowered through the room. The clock's tick disappeared and the rumble of traffic from outside faded.

"They were no longer needed. Katryna and I should have been able to handle Hywel, but…"

"You couldn't." Ermentrude held Degula's gaze.

"I admit I underestimated Hywel's desire for his daughter's return. I assumed he would be content with being released. It was an oversight on my part. I love Katryna as a daughter, you know that," Degula said, placing her hands in her lap.

Wilf eased all four legs of his chair down on the floor, trying not to make a sound. He'd no wish to remind either witch he was still in the room.

Ermentrude let silence descend on the room for several heartbeats. "Let me see if I understand. Hywel arrived escorted by a squad of guards, which you dismissed. Then Hywel's assistant overpowered you and Katryna. He captured my daughter and took her into a portal bound for Kureyamage with Hywel. Then you returned here, unharmed. Is that a good summation?"

Degula gave a brief nod and went to speak, but Ermentrude held up her hand. "Don't say another word."

Degula stood and faced Ermentrude. Wilf expected to see the air fizz between them. Degula broke their stare first. She turned towards Wilf and looked him up and down.

"It would have been better if I'd taken the boy with me, although his assassination might provide a better result." Degula faced him. "Do you know that the general feeling is that your evaporation would help to cleanse the corruption?" She sneered.

"I'd heard that suggestion, but as a scientist you know that isn't a plausible solution," Ermentrude said.

"You're both ridiculous!" Wilf jumped to his feet so fast his chair bounced to the floor.

"For once I agree with you," Ermentrude said. Her bag appeared on the table. "We need to leave now."

"Okay," he said. He didn't want to return to Kureyamage, but he wouldn't leave Katryna in the hands of Hywel. He also had no intention of being handed over to the Wizard Council like a trophy to the winning side.

"You can't take him. We need to do a formal handover. If you take him and he's captured, we'll have no negotiating position," Degula said.

"I thought you wanted his assassination? Now you want to use him for surrender negotiations?" Ermentrude stood toe to toe with the other witch. "Hywel has kidnapped my daughter. I need to know who is involved. Believe me, this won't go unpunished. Wilf will help me retrieve Katryna, and then he will help deal with the Veil guardians."

Degula took a sharp intake of breath. "It's a mistake," she said before heading for the door.

Wilf listened for the crash of the front door before he turned to Ermentrude. "Why would Hywel take Katryna?"

"You can ask him that just before I blast him into oblivion." Ermentrude wiggled her fingers and items floated across the room and into her bag. "Pack fast, or you'll be leaving as you are. Degula will have gone for reinforcements."

Wilf ran to his bedroom, picked up his backpack, and pushed a few T-shirts, shorts, and underwear into it. He opened a drawer and stopped. Hywel taking Katryna must have something to do with magic becoming rare. She held both kinds of magic. Was he hoping to use her to rebalance the Realm? Did he think he could give every wizard and witch the same ability? Wilf grabbed a sweatshirt and pushed it into the backpack as he ran from the room.

Katryna could use both kinds of magic because of him. He'd shared his ability with her. The Veil spell became corrupt because he had allowed the Witch Council access to his magic. Maybe all of this was his fault.

"I'm ready," he said, rushing into the kitchen.

Ermentrude's jacket held out its arms for her. "Good."

"Before we go, I want it agreed that I'll help you find Katryna and try to clean the Veil spell, but I won't let you hand me over to the Wizard Council." Wilf's backpack shrank to the size of a pack of gum and jumped into his pocket.

Ermentrude led him out of the kitchen. "I've no intention of handing you over," she said. Her broom jumped into her hand as she stepped into the street.

"We're going by broom, but I thought the Thermals weren't letting anyone through that way?" Wilf said, standing next to her.

"They're not," Ermentrude said, mounting the broom. "But I'm not anyone."

Degula ran from the store, guards at her heels. "Stop! Guards, secure that wizard."

Wilf jumped on behind Ermentrude. The broom lifted from the ground.

"Ermentrude, you can't risk using the Thermals. They're not safe," Degula shouted.

"Think of it as putting your theory to work. If we evaporate, you'll find out if Wilf's magic returning to the Source is the solution," Ermentrude said, kicking downward with her left heel as if pressing on an accelerator. A yell of exasperation came from Degula as the broom sped through the opening fissure and into the Thermals.

Wilf gulped as the rift closed behind them. He grasped the broomstick as a neon path materialized. Ermentrude guided the broom onto the pathway. It bucked three times and then leapt forward. This was a suicide mission. The first gray specter appeared and Ermentrude blasted it without hesitation.

The broom tipped to the right and Wilf clung to it until his fingers cramped. A trio of phantoms with streaming hair and tattered clothing attacked from the left. Ermentrude put the broom into a nosedive as Wilf sent a blast of white magic at the attackers.

The broom leveled out along the neon pathway and a white exit appeared on the horizon. Wilf glanced around, looking for the next attack. He almost missed the two specters materializing on the right.

"Wilf, now would be an excellent time to add more speed to this old broom," Ermentrude shouted over her shoulder.

He reached back and touched the bristles with his wizard ring. The broom bucked and Wilf's knuckles whitened with his increased grip on the handle. A flash of purple stars emanated from the broom bristles as it rocketed along the pathway. A piercing screech came from one of the pursuers. Ermentrude leaned forward until her nose was almost on the handle. Wilf turned his face to the right, away from Ermentrude's back, as he streamlined his body. The pathway became a blur as they bore down towards the exit. Wilf tried to lift his head, but pressure forced him to remain glued to Ermentrude's back.

"Bat's blood!" Ermentrude said, raising her hand and sending a blast of red magic at the exit. A hole appeared seconds before the broom would have smashed into it.

Wilf pushed himself back up to a sitting position. The broom hovered over a landing site. They'd made it.

"I didn't think we'd get through," he said.

Ermentrude wiggled her fingers and the broom disappeared, letting Wilf collapse on the ground.

"Don't sit there. We need to make it into the city before the watchers attack," Ermentrude said, heading through a gap in the trees.

Wilf jumped to his feet and ran after her. Recognition of the route flittered through his memory as they rushed along the trail. He remembered the path from his first trip to Mathowytch.

Growls and the snapping of branches followed them as they jumped over the stile and continued down the trail. When they reached the wooden fencing, Ermentrude placed her hand on the panel and a card reader appeared. A howl sent shivers down Wilf's back. The watchers were closing in.

Ermentrude slid her card into the reader, but a large red 'X' flashed onto the screen. "That's ridiculous," she said.

A snarl and a growl emanated from the bushes, and two watchers, cats the size of horses, stalked around the corner. Wilf turned to face them.

"Bat's blood!" Ermentrude said, raising her fingers. "I hate to hurt them. They do such an excellent job of protecting the landing site."

"I think it's a case of them or us. Appealing to their inner kitten adorability won't work," Wilf said.

Ermentrude sniggered. "We don't breed them that way." She

blasted the ground in front of the lead watcher and it growled.

"I think that's pissed it off," Wilf said. The second watcher sprang at Wilf, and he blasted it mid-air.

"I hope that was a stun-blast," Ermentrude said.

"Of course," Wilf said, hoping it was true. He'd meant to use stun but wasn't at all sure what magic he'd produced. All he knew was that he wasn't being mauled to death.

Ermentrude gave him a withering look before turning back to the reader. She pushed her card into it and gave it an extra push. Runes appeared on the display and she entered a sequence. A door materialized in the fence and creaked open. "About time," she said, entering the tunnel.

Wilf squeezed through the door before the entrance disappeared. He jogged after Ermentrude. An icy shiver ran through him. He was back in Mathowytch, a city where witches hated one thing more than anything else — wizards.

Chapter Twelve - Wakefield Tower, Kureyamage

Malik stopped outside workshop number three. "Wait for me here. I want to show you something," he said.

Myra leaned against the wall while Malik pulled Katryna further along the corridor. He placed a hand on the plaque and the door swung open. Then he and Katryna entered.

"Nipits, go see," Myra said. The cat bounded after them, keeping to the shadows until he reached the door and peered into the room. Myra altered her vision to gaze through the cat's eyes.

Malik wrapped a ribbon of magic around Katryna. Nipits backed away from the door and returned to Myra. She bent and stroked the cat. "Wait in the shadows," she said.

"Finished," Malik said, strolling along the corridor. "Here, take a peek at this." He placed his hand on the number plaque and the door swished open. Stale air, dust, and a floral scent, like bluebells, greeted them.

He held out his arm. "You first."

Myra stepped into the workshop, and the light changed to a rosy glow. A dresser held jars, boxes, herbs, and vials. She sauntered over to the shelves laden with books and scrolls full of old and new magic that she hadn't tried and some that she hadn't even known existed. She ran her fingers over the square wooden table in the center of the room. Scratches and deep grooves from centuries of cutting and mixing covered its surface.

Malik tripped as he entered the room. His ring flashed and a flame lit the kindling in the iron-trimmed fireplace. Warmth permeated the chilly room.

"Is this yours?" Myra asked, smiling at him.

"Mine? No, it was my mother's. She was one of the leading potion makers for the Council. I'm more into the newer forms of tech magic. That's why I've been working on the biomes for a decade or two."

"Your mother's so lucky. This place is amazing."

Malik surveyed the room. "I suppose so, but she evaporated several years ago."

"I'm so sorry," Myra said. The difficulty of expressing the right words about someone's loss always made her uncomfortable. Until Reginald had evaporated. Then she had grieved and missed him. The apartment and store were empty without his quick footsteps. The shock that she had caused his death still haunted her. She dug her nails into her palms. This wasn't the place to allow her guilt to surface.

"Thanks, but it's been a while." He stroked the back of a leather chair beside the fireplace. "I used to love visiting her and watching her when I was young."

"You still miss her," Myra said, coming to sit next to him.

"I don't think you ever get over losing a parent." He sat staring into the flames.

Unless you had a mother like Griselda. Then all you felt was relief that she was no longer alive. She hadn't been a loving mother. Myra pushed her memories away and wandered over to the shelves. She examined the rows of jars. Spidery handwriting on each label described its contents and the preservation date. This looked like a labor of love. It was a world so different from Myra's. No running and hiding, or being threatened. Time to brew potions, read, and… Who was she kidding? She'd find it boring within a week.

"Why don't you use it?" Malik said, brushing his hand over her shoulder and down her arm. He touched the back of her hand before stepping aside.

"What?" Had she heard him correctly? Was he offering her a workshop?

"The workshop is closed up and collecting dust. I'm sure Mom would have loved a witch of your caliber to use it." Malik smiled.

She wasn't sure his mother would approve of her taking over the workshop, but Myra wouldn't refuse his offer. It would be a place to escape and experiment with her own spells. She turned to him and knew she had a foolish grin plastered on her face. "You mean it?"

"I wouldn't have offered otherwise," he said.

She threw her arms around his neck and leaned in to kiss his cheek, but he turned his head. Their lips met. She pulled back, but he held her and deepened the kiss. His arms circled her waist, pulling her closer. Warmth spread through her.

Malik lifted his head. "I've wanted to kiss you for a while. I hope that's okay." Malik's smile creased the corners of his eyes.

"Yes." But she dropped her arms, confusion rippling through her. She didn't understand why Malik would do this for her, or why he was attracted to her. She'd always kept her distance, not wanting to get involved. This wasn't the time to lower her guard.

He must want something. There had to be an ulterior motive. No one handed over a workshop without wanting something in return. But with this space she'd have her own place where she could make — the ends of her nerves tingled with the thought — elixir. Produce her own supply. No more stealing from Thiemus. She'd been running a risk that her brother wouldn't notice his supply was dwindling.

"Hey, I've been told I'm an excellent kisser, but are you still with me?" Malik squeezed her against him.

Myra gave herself a mental shake. "Oh, you have, have you?"

Malik grinned and angled his head. His wrist mirror pinged, and he dropped his arms.

"Get to my workshop now!" Hywel's voice pierced the room and Myra's happiness drained away.

"On my way," Malik said.

"Bring Myra with you," Hywel said. The mirror went blank.

Malik caught her hand and pressed his lips to her palm. A shiver ran through her and she caught her breath. A strange desire to place her fingers in his silky hair rose in her. She bit her bottom lip and pulled her hand from his grasp.

"Isn't it nice being needed?" Malik grinned.

"I'd rather live without Hywel's attention," Myra said, walking towards the corridor.

"You must set a code on the panel." Malik held the door open.

Myra was confused. "How?"

Malik shook his head. "I keep forgetting you're not used to this world." He stopped next to the panel and placed his palm on it. The panel illuminated. He tapped the center with his ring and the panel slid aside, revealing a row of five cubes. Each had a different rune on it. "Select a code."

Myra moved the cubes and then stepped back.

"Close the panel," he said. Then he placed his ring back on the panel and tapped it twice. "Place your fingertips on the panel," he said.

The panel warmed under her fingers. There was a ripple along the surface of the panel and then it went blank.

"That's it," Malik said. "The next time you use this panel, it will allow you access."

"Awesome," she said.

"We'd better go. You can conjure me up a coffee sometime when you get settled."

"The pleasure would be mine," she said. But she worried she was smiling way too much. She'd have to be careful around Malik. He had a way of disarming her that couldn't be in her best interest.

They sped down the corridor, each trying to outpace the other. They arrived at Hywel's workshop panting and laughing. The door flung open.

Hywel's furrowed brow and the thin line of his lips sobered them.

"Good of you both to join us," Hywel said. "Malik, take your station and begin the algorithm for the collection routines. Monitor each tank and check that the biome's source hasn't become compromised."

Malik sat in front of a terminal, a panel slid back, and a track pad appeared. He placed his hand on the pad and the amber stone at the center of his ring pulsed. His fingertips glowed as the screen flickered to life. After a couple of minutes, he looked up. "Collection algorithm has started."

"Excellent," Hywel said. "Keep monitoring until we're at ten percent, and then you can leave it to run alone for the next few hours. I want you back at that desk before the last program starts."

Malik nodded but kept his focus on the screen.

Hywel turned to Myra. "You've a relationship with my daughter, therefore you can assist me. Come." He moved towards the door.

Myra hesitated. She didn't think she had any influence with Katryna given that the last time they'd met Myra had been attacking her.

"That wasn't a request," Hywel said.

Myra's shoulders slumped as she followed the wizard to room four.

A cell occupied the corner of the workshop. Katryna sat hunched on a bench spinning a red-stoned wizard ring around her finger. Myra recognized it as the room where Wilf had destroyed the Advancer machine. It reminded her of a medical procedure room she'd seen in movies.

Thiemus moved a cart containing probes into the cell.

"What do you want to test first?" Thiemus asked.

"Isolating her witch magic," Hywel said. "If we can disable that, she will only be able to use the new magic Wilf gave her. Let's see if it's true wizard magic."

Myra watched as Thiemus attached probes to Katryna's fingers and then her forehead. He kept his head at a slight angle, not looking at her, when he attached one to the back of her neck. Katryna's eyes sent daggers at all of them, but she didn't so much as twitch.

Hywel tapped a few keys on the keyboard sitting on the cart. The screen on the far wall lit up and charts sprang to life.

"I didn't know you could monitor magic like a heartbeat," Myra said, studying the screen.

"It took us a while to determine how to tap into the right part of the brain, but we can now isolate the lobe associated with magic. As you saw with Wilf, we can even enhance a wizard or witch well beyond their natural ability." Hywel continued to tap the keys, and a line on the chart dropped in value. "Constraint spell released." Hywel extended his finger and the ring's black stone flashed.

Thiemus moved over to a second terminal. He punched the keys and the screen split into two windows. One continued to show the charts, but the other revealed a large dial running in hundredths from one to fifty.

"Good," Hywel said. "Let's see if we can control her magic."

Thiemus turned the dial and light sprang from Katryna's fingertips. The light hit the plexiglass surrounding her and fizzled across the surface.

"Excellent! The containment spell works well," Hywel said, smiling.

"The vaccine has restored her witch magic," Thiemus said, his shoulders relaxing.

Myra nodded. It would comfort Thiemus to know that the vaccine would return his own powers soon.

"Have you identified the receptors?" Hywel asked.

"Identified and clamped," Thiemus said.

"Try her magic once more with the clamp in place," Hywel said.

Again Katryna's fingers extended, but this time no light appeared from the tips.

"Clamp secured in place," Thiemus said.

"Proceed to the next phase." Hywel paced in front of Katryna's cell.

A second dial appeared in a half-screen window, this time with black lettering. Katryna's ringed finger extended, the golden vein pulsed, and the ring's stone blazed before a blast of red light shot from her fingertip. Myra gasped and took a step backwards.

The blast hit the glass, and a bubble spread across the cell's surface. The acrylic resin glowed red and then darkened. A scorch mark expanded over the surface as the resin melted.

"Cut the power! Cut the power!" Hywel shouted, waving furiously at Thiemus.

The dial dropped to zero.

Katryna glared at Hywel. Sweat glistened on her forehead and her breath came in rapid pants, as if she'd been running for a long time up a steep incline.

"I think we can say we've tapped into the wizard side of her power," Hywel said, pacing. "The cell should have held. It's designed to stop wizard and witch magic from escaping." He stopped to look at the scorch mark. "How could it penetrate the spell?"

"I'll reinforce the containment spell before we continue," Thiemus said, punching keys on the keyboard. Myra had the distinct impression he was avoiding looking at Katryna.

Hywel's brow creased as he continued to stare at his daughter.

"Don't you think you should at least offer her a drink of water?" Myra said. It was unbelievable, Hywel appeared lost in the experiment and had forgotten that Katryna was a person.

"What?" Hywel blinked. His wizard ring flared. A glass appeared and hovered in the air.

"She'll need the ability to move," Myra said, then bit her lower lip. She shouldn't draw attention to herself, but Katryna looked lost and alone. She liked the young witch. Myra's eyes dropped to the bracelet. It didn't have Gilvary on it. They had broken their bond, Wilf and her. No wonder Katryna looked frightened. Did Ermentrude know Hywel had taken her back to Kureyamage?

Hywel's ring flashed again. Katryna took the glass and drank. Then the glass disappeared from her hand and materialized seconds later in front of Myra. She caught hold of it as it dropped. "I think you'd better reinforce your containment cell soon," she said.

Thiemus's ring flared and the scorch mark disappeared. A second flash from his ring and Katryna collapsed onto the bench.

"Incredible," Hywel said. He peered at the screen over Thiemus's shoulder. "Leave the monitors running for the next few hours. Myra, come with me," Hywel said, heading for the door.

Myra peered over at Thiemus, but he kept his head lowered over the keyboard. So they were going to leave Katryna there? She followed Hywel like the lapdog she felt herself becoming. Her shoulders drooped. This would be her life if she wasn't careful, Hywel expecting her to wait on him at all times. Her resentment bubbled, but she continued along the corridor behind the wizard. She was better than this. There was no way she'd be Hywel's henchman for the rest of her life. Malik was cute, and she'd have liked to develop their friendship further, but not at the expense of her freedom.

The workshop would enable her to make a batch of elixir. She didn't need to hang around Thiemus any longer. They had taught her how to use the portal, and at the first opportunity she would make a run for it. She'd always wanted to visit New York or London. Now she had the knowledge and transportation. She could follow Hywel for a while, knowing escape was within her grasp.

Chapter Thirteen - The City of Mathowytch

Wilf climbed the steps up into Mathowytch, the city the Witch Council had stolen from the wizards. "Won't the alarms sound as soon as I leave the tunnel?"

The last time he'd entered Mathowytch was after his escape from Hywel, and the warning spells had detected his wizard magic immediately. Then witches were glad he had arrived, as he'd brought the formula for the vaccine they desperately needed, but this time they saw him as an enemy.

Ermentrude stopped. "We don't have an option, but we're only passing through on our way to Kureyamage."

"No worries then. I'll leave the explanations up to you." He closed his eyes and took several deep breaths before stepping into the street. Sirens blared from several rooftops. "There goes the element of surprise," he said, wiping his sweating palms on his shorts.

Ermentrude pulled him into the shadow of the closest building. "This way," she said, ducking down the next alley. She came to a halt outside a colossal building with a metal door. Her jeweled hat pin appeared with a wiggle of her fingers. Wilf placed his hands behind his back. Last time she produced the eight-inch-long pin, she used it to draw blood from his finger so they could enter his father's basement. He wouldn't be a donor again.

"Don't we need to reach the border and enter the Veil there?" Wilf asked.

Ermentrude inserted the pin's tip into a keyhole and touched the emerald on the end. A pulse of magic lit the pin. With a click, a small recessed panel came into view. A set of three carved runes popped out.

"Why are you messing around here? I thought we were here to rescue Katryna," he said.

C. B. Lyall

Ermentrude pressed each one in sequence, but the door remained closed. She stepped back and rubbed her chin. "The border guard won't give us access. Yes, we're here to collect Katryna, and I'm trying to open this door because we need to get inside. The problem is, my magic isn't working," she said.

A chill crept into the air, and mist flowed into the alley. It reminded Wilf of the morning fog around The Peak in Hong Kong during the rainy season. The mist became a wall and then rolled forward in a gigantic wave, barreling towards them.

"What?" He spun around to see Ermentrude glaring at him.

"Focus," she said, trying to block his view. "Place your ringed finger on the runes and see what they tell you."

"Me?" He kept his eyes focused on the fast-approaching wave.

"We don't have time for explanations," Ermentrude retorted.

Wilf placed his finger on each rune, but it wasn't until he touched the last one that his ring flared.

"Have you seen the mist?" Wilf asked.

"Stay focused on the job at hand and add a tiny amount of magic to it," Ermentrude said.

Wilf's heart raced. A tiny amount of magic! She didn't know what she was asking. He let magic flow into the rune until it turned red.

"Quicker," Ermentrude said.

He touched the first rune, which turned yellow. The third turned blue when he touched it. There was a loud scraping noise, and the door swung open. As soon as the gap was wide enough, Ermentrude hurried through.

"Come along," she said, catching hold of his sleeve and pulling him through.

"What the…" A sucking sound sealed the door behind him. "Stop pulling me around," he said.

"You wouldn't enjoy being trapped in that mist. I suspect it's neither inviting nor friendly," Ermentrude replied curtly. She produced a light globe. "Don't move." A vortex spun ten steps from them. "This isn't what I expected."

"We're stuck, aren't we?" His eyes followed the hypnotic spirals of color that filled the passage. It reminded him of a toy he'd once received in a birthday party gift bag. There had been strings connected on either side of a multicolored disk. When you pulled on the strings, the disc spun, producing an illusion of the colors moving inward making a spiral. He'd thought it a lame gift, but on this scale it was both fascinating and terrifying.

Ermentrude twirled the hairs on her chin, never taking her eyes off the vortex.

"I'm not going in there!" It was difficult to pull his vision away.

"I've seen something like it before, although I've never traveled in one." Ermentrude stepped forward.

Ribbons of color spiraled downwards into the vortex's depths. Wilf backed away until he bumped into the door.

"We don't have a choice. It's moving closer," Ermentrude said, squaring her shoulders.

"This is madness!"

"We should try to keep contact with each other," Ermentrude said, searching in her pocket.

Wilf looked at her other hand with its black fingernails and shuddered. There was no way he'd enter that vortex holding Ermentrude's hand.

She pulled a cord out of her jacket pocket and wiggled her fingers. The cord looped around Wilf's wrist and then her own. "Let's hope this is sturdy enough," she said, stepping forward to meet the vortex and dragging Wilf behind her.

Light engulfed him. He had a strange sensation of tiny pinpricks of energy charging through his body. He stumbled along a path of red light. "Does it matter which path we choose?"

Ermentrude turned to face him. "You might have a point. Purple was the color of the talisman when we crossed through the Veil. I think for safety we should follow that pathway," she said, stepping off the red and pulling him along with her.

Spikes of energy pulsed, pushing him on. He passed through the white space until his feet touched the purple light. It washed around his feet like a gentle stream.

Ermentrude took two steps, but a shadow rose from the ground. The shape morphed into a woman. Long raven hair flowed down her back, and a high-collared black gown cascaded from her neck to the ground. Her eyes were white orbs with no pupils. Outstretched arms reached for them until she stopped several feet away, hovering above the path.

"Flayver," Wilf whispered.

Ermentrude glanced at him before turning to the guardian.

"I'm pleased you have returned," Flayver said. High-pitched cackles echoed around the surrounding walls.

"How is this possible?" Ermentrude said, blocking Flayver from reaching Wilf.

"Wilf joined me to the Source. It was time," Flayver said.

"You are giving Wilf credit for the expansion of your role?" Ermentrude said.

"Wilf set me free," Flayver said. Spikes of energy buzzed from her fingertips. "The time is now."

"You've been killing wizards," Ermentrude said. "Is that what it's time for?"

Flayver gave another high-pitched cackle. "Not dead. Changed."

Wilf pulled on the cord tying him to Ermentrude.

"What?" Ermentrude said.

"The vortex, it's spinning faster." His stomach churned as the colors merged.

"Do you mean us harm?" Ermentrude asked, glancing from him back to the guardian.

"I require Wilf. We have work to complete," Flayver said, edging closer.

"I have no intention of handing Wilf over to you." Ermentrude raised her hand.

The guardian gave a frenzied laugh. Her eyes changed to black. "You dare threaten me in my world?"

Wilf didn't think it was smart either. The last outcome he wanted was for the guardian to attack Ermentrude. He tried to step forward, but the cord fizzed and tightened. There must be something he could do. He lifted his ringed hand to point at Flayver. "We could combine an attack," he said to Ermentrude.

She glanced at him, but didn't lower her hand.

Flayver's laughter halted. "We are joined. You cannot harm me."

"What do you mean we're joined?" Wilf asked.

"The Realm is dying. You and the young witch hold the key," Flayver said.

"Katryna? What do you know of my daughter?" Ermentrude advanced on the guardian.

"She's in the Realm, but not whole." Flayver turned her head slightly, as if listening to someone. "We must travel," she said, moving back into the vortex. "Come!"

"Just a moment. Is she hurt?" Ermentrude sounded alarmed.

"A surge of power is approaching. You will not survive." Flayver kept moving away from them.

"That doesn't sound good," Wilf said, racing ahead of Ermentrude. He'd narrowly missed being zapped by a power surge before when he first entered the Veil.

"It could be a trap," Ermentrude said. "She's already told us she wants you."

Wilf tugged on the rope. "We can't stay here, you said so yourself. The only way I see is forward."

"I hate going into situations I can't control," Ermentrude said, walking faster.

The air thickened into a yellow fog. Wilf tasted sulfur. A crack of thunder echoed off the walls of the vortex. Gusts of hot, dry wind wrapped around them, but they staggered forward. Strands of

Ermentrude's hair sprang free from her tight bun and whipped across Wilf's face. He hunched forward and pushed into the gale, wobbling when gusts threatened to knock him off his feet. He scrunched his eyes as grit like sand hit his face.

Ermentrude struggled at his side, unable to make any headway. Her knees buckled, but he caught her by the elbow. His chest felt tight and breathing became more and more difficult. Ermentrude coughed and gasped. He looked down at his feet to make sure they were staying on the purple path, and when he glanced up bile rose in his throat. The vortex spun faster as they walked its walls.

Flayver vanished. One minute the guardian was waving them to follow her, and the next there were only the spinning walls. She'd tricked them into following her, Wilf thought. A cold, clammy hand touched his cheek, and he jumped.

"This way." Flayver's icy breath blew across his burning ear. She was beckoning him to follow her off the purple path.

"What are you doing?" Ermentrude tugged at his arm.

"Flayver wants us to follow her," Wilf said, pushing against the wind.

"I don't trust her," Ermentrude said, but he forced her off the path.

Flayver pushed at the vortex's wall, and a doorway appeared. She stepped through and held it open for Wilf and Ermentrude.

Wilf blinked rapidly. The bright lights of the vortex had disappeared. Now they were inside a tunnel with walls of gray mist. Dim light shimmered across the surface, and shadows moved within.

"We're inside the original Veil," Ermentrude whispered, brushing the loose strands of hair from her eyes.

"Yes. This is where I exist." Flayver floated several inches above the ground. Tendrils of mist broke free to touch her and then scurry away through the tunnel.

"But how do we enter Kureyamage?" Wilf asked.

Flayver placed a talisman over his head. "A path will appear, but the city isn't welcoming. You should stay here with me."

"I have a daughter to rescue," Ermentrude said, her voice taking on its usual no-nonsense tone.

"Beware of my sister, Betrine. She is a false guardian," Flayver said, fading into the wall. A pathway appeared before Wilf.

Cackles and screams filled the air. Mist continued to peel away, but now the tendrils slithered towards Wilf and Ermentrude.

"I can see why both Councils want this spell taken down,"

Ermentrude said, staring at the spot where Flayver had disappeared. "Although I can't see Flayver allowing that." She wiggled her fingers, and the cord disappeared from her and Wilf's wrists. "There's no point standing around here. Nothing good will come of that." She took a step on the path and screamed as a tendril of Veil struck her hand.

"Ermentrude!" Wilf grabbed her around the shoulders and pulled her back.

"My hand," she said. Two puncture wounds oozed black liquid. Veins spread under the surface of her skin. "I can't feel my magic. It's gone."

"Oops." Flayver's voice filled the corridor, and cackling laughter echoed around them.

"Your talisman is no longer purple, it's blue!" Wilf warned Ermentrude.

"The spell attacked me, but I helped build it." She cradled her hand. "How can it be hostile to me?"

"Flayver isn't witch magic," Wilf said.

The black veins were spreading over the surface of Ermentrude's arm.

"This is bad." Wilf moved to step forward.

"No!" Ermentrude grabbed his sleeve.

"I have to try. Otherwise we'll remain inside this spell forever." He took a deep breath and crept forward. His heartbeat echoed in his ears. He watched the walls on either side, waiting for an attack.

Ermentrude fell in behind him, cradling her useless hand.

Wilf jumped and power surged through him as a hand protruded through the wall. He grabbed Ermentrude's arm and his ring flashed.

Specters repeated Ermentrude's screams from within the wall. She held out her injured hand. The black veins now pulsed with a golden light that spread up her arm and neck and then disappeared beneath her hair.

"How could you do this to me?" Hatred burned in her eyes. "You've made me a wizard!"

Chapter Fourteen - Wakefield Tower,
Kureyamage

Myra placed her hand on the plaque and the door creaked open. She entered the workshop alone for the first time — her workshop. She couldn't stop the grin spreading across her face. She let her fingers walk along the volumes on the bookshelves. Next, she opened the cupboards, admiring the arrangement of cauldrons, mixing bowls, and knives. A slim volume's red cover caught her eye, and she pulled it from the shelf. It looked new and unused. She opened it and the spine creaked. The title page read, "Everyday Spells for the Busy Witch or Wizard." She leafed through the book until she came to the contents page.

A bubble of excitement rippled through her. It listed a spell for Enhancer Elixir. She flipped the pages until she came to the spell, then set the book on a stand. She collected a cauldron and placed it on the workbench. She perused the list of ingredients. What if she didn't have all she needed here? A trip to the market was impossible. She had been told not to leave. Besides, there was no guarantee that the market had what she needed. She shifted her weight from one foot to the other, and wrapped her arms around her middle. She had to hold it together.

She opened the cupboards and a row of small drawers in the center of the dresser to collect the ingredients and send them to the workbench. Her hands shook, and two jars landed on the small table next to the fireplace instead of the workbench. She retrieved them, shaking her head. A cold sweat covered her body by the time she checked off the ingredients in the book. She was missing one. Her head throbbed.

Malik entered carrying two vials. "You'll need this," he said, placing one on the table. He pushed his hair out of his eyes and waved the other vial in front of her. She opened her mouth to speak, but he pressed it in her hand.

"You'll only lie and say you're not trying to make a batch of elixir, and we both know that's not true." He took her right hand in his and then dropped it. "You're a bit of a mess."

Her hair felt greasy when she pushed the shoulder-length strands behind her ears. She examined her dirty, broken fingernails. It had been days since she'd showered. Had she been too busy following Hywel around to care about her appearance? Her cheeks flushed.

Malik turned her to face him. "I like you. You're smart and attractive, even without warts." She went to turn her head, but he took hold of her chin and made her face him. "I know you've had a terrible time working for Hywel, but this isn't the solution to anything." He flicked a hand towards the ingredients. "I'll help you make a batch of elixir, but only this once. You need to find another way."

She sighed. Another wizard was trying to control her.

"I mean it," he said, directing the ingredients into the cauldron. "This stuff will kill you."

"I promise. I won't take another batch."

Malik held her gaze for a moment and huffed. "Sure you won't."

"I mean it." She drank from the vial he'd brought her.

"Whatever. I'll believe it more when you haven't needed a vial for a week, then a month, and finally a year or two," Malik said. His ring flashed and the cauldron flew across the room and settled in the fireplace. A spark ignited the logs, and the aroma of wood smoke floated around the room.

Myra watched the cauldron as the elixir's effects warmed her body. The trembling in her hands ceased. Let him try to dominate her? She didn't need him or any other wizard telling her how to live her life. He thought her an elixir addict, but she could give it up anytime. If she wanted.

"It needs to simmer for an hour." Malik took her by the shoulders. His fingers dug into her flesh and she winced. "Don't take any until it's fully cooked and then has cooled for ten hours."

She turned to the cauldron again.

He shook her. "Are you listening?"

"Yes. I won't touch it until it's prepared. I'm not an idiot." She pushed him away.

"You're an addict. Much the same thing in my book," Malik said, releasing her. He took a step back. "I can work in here. Why don't you take a rest, eat something, have a shower?"

Heat rose in her face. Was this the payment for giving her a workshop? Malik thought he had the right to dictate to her?

He placed a kiss on her forehead before pushing her towards the door. "Go! Bring me something to eat when you come back. I need to check on some magic data. See how it progresses."

She hesitated. He was lucky. She didn't feel like arguing. After all, he was tending to the potion for her. But he could get his own lunch. She left the room without a backward glance and hurried along the corridor to the tower.

Climbing over the debris in the yard, she entered the kitchen, ran through the entrance, and up the stairs to her room. She closed the door behind her and leaned back on it. She took a deep breath and tried to slow her heartbeat, but she couldn't control it. She stripped, grabbed a towel, and headed into the shower.

Water cascaded over her and she let it bounce off the back of her head. The water turned lukewarm as she lathered up, and by the time she stepped out of the shower, her teeth were chattering.

Thiemus was heading towards his room as she stepped into the corridor.

"There's no hot water," she said.

Thiemus turned to look at her. "That's ridiculous."

"I took a shower, and the water turned cold," Myra said.

"It's controlled by magic so it's not possible. You must have turned the faucet," Thiemus said, heading to his room.

"Why would I make it up?" Myra pulled the towel tighter around her shivering body.

He sighed and turned to the stairs. "I'd better tell Hywel."

Myra dressed, then headed to the kitchen. She gave the room a cursory glance. Dirty dishes were piled high in the sink. Muddy footprints covered the floor, and a gray layer of grime covered every surface. Stains and hardened spills decorated the kitchen table. The housekeeper had disappeared days before Myra arrived. She opened the fridge. There was very little in it. Thiemus and Malik had been living here by themselves, and food shopping hadn't occurred to them.

She grabbed a loaf of bread and checked it for mold before picking up the mayonnaise and cheese. The sandwich tasted dry even with mayo oozing from the sides. She ate several bites and threw the rest away before heading back to the workshop. Malik wasn't there, but his laptop lay open on the bench.

The cauldron sat on the bench. A skin had formed over the contents. She picked up a wooden spoon and stirred it. A puff of steam rose into the air. She glanced at the door. She could skim a measure from the top. It would cool quicker that way, she thought. She wiggled her fingers at a small bowl, but nothing happened. Her brow creased, but she collected the bowl herself and poured a tiny amount of the elixir into it. Then she dipped the tip of her finger into the bowl to test how hot it was. It didn't burn, but it wasn't cool. She should leave the elixir until the next day, but wasn't everything better when fresh? Bread, cookies, pies. The aftertaste of her dry sandwich lingered. Liquid would soften the lump in her throat. She stirred the elixir again and licked her lips. The fragrance of honey and vanilla wafted from the bowl. What harm could there be in a tiny sip? A warning bell sounded in the back of her mind, but she smothered it and lifted the bowl to her lips.

She swirled the elixir around in her mouth, savoring its sweetness. It was the first time she'd noticed its flavor before. Added to the usual vanilla and honey were summer berries. She drank another mouthful, smacking her lips. Raspberries and blackberries, she thought. Her favorites. She returned the bowl to the workbench and waited for the rush. Her brow creased. How much had she taken? One vial, perhaps two. She lifted her hands and examined her fingernails. They hadn't turned blue, and no flashes escaped from them.

Pain shot through her stomach and she doubled over. Her fingertips throbbed and burned. She screamed and extended her fingers as fire shot from the tips. The parchments on the bookshelves burst into flames. She staggered towards the sink, but the sharp pain in her stomach creased her. She sank to her knees. Crackles, heat, and smoke filled the room. She abandoned any hope of saving the room, and crawled for the door, panting in between spasms.

The door burst open and Malik came running in.

"You idiot!"

She continued to crawl. He ran past her towards the sink. She heard the swoosh of water as a wave rose up from the sink and drenched the fire on the bookcase.

"I told you to wait," Malik said, lifting her up.

"I'm sorry," she said, burying her face in his shoulder. Another pain shot through her and she gasped.

"You read the recipe. It said to stand for ten hours. What possessed you to drink it?" Malik set her down on a bench.

"It was cool. You said I couldn't take it until it cooled." She moaned and her stomach twisted again.

Malik raised his hand. She flinched, but he stroked the hair from her forehead, and she released the breath she'd held. Why had she reacted as if he would hit her? Her body trembled.

"It's my fault. I shouldn't have left it. An addict like you can't be trusted." He shook his head. "I'd better fetch Thiemus. He should be able to help."

"No," she said, trying to grab hold of his arm, but Malik ran from the room. Her fingers glowed blue and pulsed.

The sound of pounding feet came from the corridor. "What have you done?" Thiemus said, towering over her.

"She took some elixir compound before it fully matured," Malik said.

"You were making a batch? After you've seen what it's doing to her?"

"What else should I have done? You weren't doing anything to help."

Thiemus laid his hands on Myra's forehead. "I've been monitoring her use and reducing the potency of the batch she's been stealing from."

"Your actions were making her take the drug more often," Malik said, flapping his arms.

"And you thought the right approach was to give her access to her own workshop?" Thiemus knocked Malik out of his way and picked up Myra.

If she'd had the strength, she would have objected. "Did you also give her the potion's instructions? I can't believe your mother would have Healer's books. You're pathetic," Thiemus said. Myra wasn't sure if he was addressing her or Malik.

Her brother put her down in a chair, and she raised her head to see Katryna watching them. Her body shook and she hugged herself. At least her blue fingers were no longer pulsing.

Thiemus's ring flashed, and a cauldron settled on the bench in front of him. "I'll make you a powder to control the effects, but this won't be easy."

"When has it ever been?" Myra said.

"Stop with the self-pity. You brought this on yourself. No one made you take the elixir." Thiemus made quick jerks with his hand and ingredients flew to him. He began grinding them.

Myra slumped in the chair, waiting for the next stomach spasm to hit. She bit the inside of her cheek. The tang of her own blood filled her mouth. The searing pain ripped through her body again. She collapsed, panting and nauseous.

Thiemus added water to the ground ingredients in the cauldron and then waved it over to the fireplace. Steam rose and the fire hissed.

He laid his hand back on her forehead, and she began to feel the knots release in her stomach.

She opened her eyes to see Thiemus standing over her. She put a hand on her brother's arm. "Don't tell Hywel," she said.

"He knows you've been stealing elixir," Thiemus said. His ring flashed and the cauldron rested on a trivet waiting on the workbench. He poured some liquid into a glass and held it out to her. "Drink this. I'll put the rest in a flask. You must take some every hour until the spasms stop."

Myra picked up the glass, expecting heat to rise from the

liquid, but it had cooled. She drank.

"Take her to her room," Thiemus said to Malik, without turning to look at him.

"Sure," Malik said, stepping over to help Myra to her feet. She staggered into the corridor. He picked her up in his arms and carried her. "I thought I was helping you," he said.

"You were. This is my fault. I'm sorry. I'm so sorry," Myra said, laying her head on his shoulder. It felt good to be in his arms, especially now that the pain in her stomach was easing.

He kissed the top of her head, and she looked up at him. His face was full of concern and she had the unusual urge to comfort him. She hoped Thiemus wouldn't mention Malik's involvement to Hywel. She didn't need that guilt on her shoulders. "I'm sorry," she said, again.

Thiemus could be right. This was her fault. Her life was chaos. The only bright point was her friendship with Malik, and she'd messed that up. Her head ached. She wasn't capable of dealing with this now. Her eyes fluttered closed. A small sigh escaped from her lips and she sank into oblivion.

Chapter Fifteen - Wakefield Tower, Kureyamage

Katryna's vision blurred when she lifted her head. She cradled her forehead and took in the room. Thiemus sat hunched over a terminal, his fingers pounding the keyboard. Her head throbbed and she squinted. Her vision kept shifting in and out of focus. She flexed her fingers, then wiggled them. Nothing happened. It felt like Hywel had placed a wall between her and her magic. The new wizard ring weighed down her right hand. She balled her fist, hating its symbolism of her as a freak. A... What was she? She couldn't call herself a wizard because she was also a witch. How was it possible to hold both magics? Wilf had given her access to magic when she was suffering from the virus. Then the vaccine had restored her witch magic, and she hadn't considered how different she was, not until now.

She pointed her ring finger and concentrated. Sparks flashed from her fingertip. They bounced off the invisible barrier surrounding her.

Thiemus raised his head and walked over.

"How are you?" he said.

"I'm your lab rat. How do you think I am?" she said, folding her arms.

"Would you like some water? Or something to eat?" Thiemus said, blushing. "I can go to the kitchen. See what we have."

Katryna shook her head. Thiemus pretending to care wouldn't fool her.

"Do you hold both magics separately?" he asked, staring at the ground.

She winced. "Do you imagine that because you're not controlling me with your machine we can have a cozy chat and I'll give you all the answers you want? You're insane."

"I'm sorry it has to be this way. We're fighting for the Realm's survival. Don't you understand, you'll be our savior if we can all develop your ability and learn to hold both magics. You would ensure that the Realm never suffered another imbalance in magic."

"So not a lab rat, but a sacrificial lamb," she said, and sneered.

Malik burst into the room. "Have you seen Hywel?"

Thiemus spun around. "What do you want?"

"There's a problem," Malik said, rushing over to the communication mirror and swiping its surface. A list of runes appeared. He selected one and placed his ringed finger on it.

Hywel appeared on the mirror's surface. "Malik!"

"The biome's magic has been corrupted. I've no idea how it happened," he said, pushing his hair out of his eyes.

"Calm down and explain," Hywel said.

"Witch and wizard magic are combining. The biome magic will be unusable. If it reaches the collection tanks…"

"Stop the feed," Hywel said. The mirror went blank. Malik rushed over to a terminal and punched the keys.

"This shouldn't be possible," Hywel said, panting. His face was bright red and glistening.

"I know. The conditions within the biomes haven't changed," Malik said. A screen full of dials appeared in front of him.

"Did the corruption spread from here?" Thiemus asked, coming to stand next to Malik.

"What do you mean?" Hywel said, his attention turning from the terminal towards Thiemus.

"If the biome is a replica of this Realm and our magic is behaving strangely, perhaps the Source was corrupt when we set the biome up," Thiemus said.

"Is that possible? I thought it was a stand-alone system?" Hywel grabbed hold of Malik's shoulder.

Malik shrugged him off. "It's supposed to be. I don't understand how the Source combined with the biome magic."

"And has it?" Hywel leaned over Malik to stare at the terminal. The younger wizard drew the keyboard closer to him and punched a few keys. The screen changed to charts, then they disappeared.

"Malik?" Hywel said, exasperation entering his voice.

"I'm…" The screen flickered several times and then blackened. Malik's face lost all its color. "All the biome's magic has corrupted into a combined magic."

"The Source?" Hywel spun Malik's chair around to face him.

"I'd need to collect test samples."

"If the magic of the Source has become combined, what does that mean?" Thiemus asked.

"That the magic in this Realm will be inaccessible to all except" — Malik stared wide-eyed at Katryna — "probably Katryna, if her magic develops into a combination."

"We need to know how she holds both magics. It's possible they are already combined." Hywel shook his head. "But this morning we successfully blocked them separately, didn't we?"

Katryna edged back to the wall. She didn't like the look in her father's eyes. She had seen it before, when he'd captured Ermentrude. The bracelet clanged against the bench and she twisted the red lettering out of sight. If only her mother hadn't dissolved her bond to Wilf. It would have given her a flicker of hope that they'd find her.

"Thiemus, attach the electrodes to Katryna again. We need Wilf here. I want to know how he transferred power." Hywel paced the room. "It had to result from placing him in the Advancer. If only he hadn't destroyed the machine!" He pulled down on the collar of his robe.

"I've stopped the feed," Malik said. "We'll have a riot on our hands when the lack of magic affects everyone."

"How is any of this possible?" Hywel collapsed into the nearest chair. "The Witch Council might have caused this sabotage, I suppose. I've been told the Veil spell has gone rogue and started killing wizards."

"From what I've been able to piece together, they're as baffled as we are. They're claiming that the corruption results from Wilf's interference with the Veil spell," Malik said, leaning forward. "That spell was the first case of magic combining."

Hywel steepled his fingers and rested his chin on them.

Katryna slid back to her bench. Why were they discussing all this in front of her? Weren't they worried she'd tell the Witch Council? Unless they thought she wouldn't survive their testing.

"I'll let the Council know, but they'll be unhappy," Hywel said. "I'll also find out what is holding up Wilf's transfer. Sounds as if he's responsible, regardless of whether it was deliberate." He walked towards the door and then stopped. "Thiemus, continue to monitor Katryna's magic. See if the corruption affects her. If you see any changes let me know immediately."

Thiemus pointed and his wizard ring flashed as the electrodes lifted from the sides of the bench and attached themselves to Katryna's temples and arms. Thiemus kept his head bent, not meeting Katryna's eyes. "I'm sorry," he whispered.

Malik stared at her, and a slight grin grew as he regarded Thiemus's actions. He thumped Thiemus on the back as he crossed the room. "You'd better not let Hywel know you've got a thing for his daughter."

Thiemus glared at Malik, who laughed. "I'll be in my

workshop if I'm needed. Play nicely, Thiemus," he shouted over his shoulder as he left the room.

Thiemus's face turned bright red. His ring flashed and a light globe exploded.

Katryna watched as Thiemus limped over to a terminal. Was it possible that Thiemus liked her? No! But he did look embarrassed by Malik's teasing. She wanted to cling to this spark of hope. If he was attracted, maybe she could use that. She sighed. If they wanted to see how she used magic, then she'd use it as little as possible. But she'd spent her entire life using magic. It was as natural to use it as breathing.

What would he try next? She felt like a caged animal expecting the next experiment. They'd cut away the sleeve from her T-shirt, exposing her arm, and she turned her arm from side to side, examining the golden vein running up to her neck. She hated the marking. She'd noticed other witches staring at it and gossiping. They'd become quiet as she walked past them in the store or workshop. She'd overheard one witch say she didn't want to recover from the virus if it meant she would be contaminated with wizard magic and belong nowhere.

Thiemus pointed his ringed finger and a small cauldron floated over to the bench next to him. He waved his fingers towards the shelves and several vials flew across the room to him. He turned his back, obscuring her view, but his shoulders and arms moved as if he was creating a potion. His magic seemed restored and working normally.

Her stomach rumbled and fluttered. How was it possible to be hungry and nervous simultaneously? If Thiemus brought her something, would she dare eat it? She didn't trust the wizard not to add whatever he was mixing in that cauldron to her food. She had to escape from this cage.

"Thiemus, I need to use the restroom," she shouted.

He twisted his head towards her.

"When the guard returns he'll take you," he said, turning back to his potion preparations.

"I can't wait," she said, moving closer to the walls of the cage. The electrodes pulled at her temple. "I have to go now."

Thiemus tipped two more ingredients into the cauldron and set it over a small flame before heading over. He waved his ringed finger. The electrodes retracted from her neck and arm. A small opening appeared in the cell wall, large enough for her to squeeze through.

"Thank you," she said. She smiled. If Thiemus had a thing for her…

"Be quick," he said, pushing her towards a door between two bookcases.

She took a few quick steps to stop herself from falling and

grabbed the doorframe. Her legs shook as she entered the compact room and leaned against the locked door. She took a few deep breaths to slow her racing heart. So much for Thiemus liking her. He seemed as thuggish as usual. She might be outside the cell now, but she still couldn't think of how to escape.

A loud rapping on the door made her gasp.

Katryna hurriedly used the toilet and flushed. She couldn't think or stall any longer. She washed and dried her hands before opening the door.

Thiemus grabbed her by the arm and pulled her across the room, back towards the cage.

"There's no need to be so rough," she said, glancing around desperately trying to find something to stop him from placing her back in the cell.

"I should trust you? Your mother gave me the virus, and you escaped. I'm not being punished for you again," Thiemus said.

She built power in her fist. It wasn't the full power she was used to generating. She still couldn't access her witch magic, and her wizard magic fought her for control. She raised her ringed hand and blasted him.

He fell backwards, dragging her with him. She struggled to pry open his fingers as they dug into the flesh of her arm. She bit his hand.

"You bitch!" Thiemus yelled, releasing her.

She crawled away from him until she could use the table to help her stand. Her legs shook. She was so weak without her witch magic. The wizard magic was taking more energy from her to control. Her wizard ring flared. Thiemus let out a grunt as he collapsed unconscious on the floor.

Katryna could see his chest rising and falling. He wasn't dead. Now she understood how Wilf struggled to control his magic. She ran from the room.

"Where do you think you're going?" The guard stood blocking the corridor. He raised his hand, but a tendril of mist appeared and darted for his leg. It coiled around him, spiraling up his body until it reached his neck and pulled taut. The guard grabbed at the tendril. His face turned deep red, and his eyes bulged as he struggled. He dropped to the ground and writhed around, his hand tearing at the choking strand.

A scream rose in Katryna's throat, but only a whimper escaped. Would she be next?

The guard stopped struggling, and the tendril broke away from him, leaving a misty choker around his neck. The tendril slithered towards Katryna. She scanned the corridor, but there seemed to be no way out.

The tendril condensed into the form of Flayver. "Hush. I am here to rescue you."

Katryna took a step backwards, bumping against the wall. "Did my mother send you?"

Flayver floated over to the stand next to Katryna. Mist flowed from her fingertips, touching the door and spreading across its surface. Flayver jerked her hands, and the strands released from her fingers. The mist melted into the door and it swung shut.

"I came to set you free. Shall we go?"

"Where are we going?"

"To join Wilf and Ermentrude," Flayver said, gliding away from the door.

Katryna ran to catch her. "Are they here in Kureyamage?"

"You ask a lot of questions. It is better if you follow me now instead of wasting time," Flayver said, glancing towards the corridor.

Katryna staggered as her witch magic came flooding back to her. She clutched her head when a violent, shearing pain shot across her forehead.

Flayver grabbed hold of Katryna's arm and dragged her along. "We don't have time to stop."

"My head," she gasped.

"Try not to access any magic," Flayver said, sending out two tendrils of mist like hounds looking for the scent of prey.

She floated along the corridor, and Katryna had to jog to keep from stumbling and falling.

"Don't worry," Flayver said. "You will have full access to magic soon."

"What do you mean?" How was a guardian outside the Veil spell? Another wave of pain shot across her forehead, darkening her vision. She tripped, but Flayver caught her in a web of mist before she hit the ground.

"Once you are safe in the Veil, you will understand," Flayver said, lifting her arm at the foot of the stairs. She rose, bringing Katryna with her. The guardian paused at the top and surveyed the route ahead. Katryna felt a ripple through the web that surrounded her. Flayver gave a brief nod before moving to the kitchen wall.

As they watched, Malik strolled out of the kitchen door and began moving towards the steps. The tendrils of mist floated into the shadows along the wall. The tips seemed to sense the air, like the tongue of a viper preparing to strike.

His wrist mirror pinged. "Hywel, I'm on my way. Do you want me to start the next phase of testing on Katryna?" He continued to the top of the stairs, conjured a globe and ran down.

Flayver's brow wrinkled and her black irises clouded. She shook her head before moving towards the tower. They passed through the kitchen and entrance without incident and into the courtyard.

A yowl of rage and a blur of fur came from the shrubbery as Nipits leapt through Flayver. The cat spun in midair and landed facing them. He hissed, back arched. Flayver raised her hand and a tendril detached, forming into an arrow shape that flew for Nipits. The cat jumped to the side, gave another hiss, and darted for the tower.

"It'll sound the alarm," Katryna said.

"Come," Flayver said, flying for the gate to the street. "I must return to the Veil. I can only roam outside for a limited amount of time."

"And you're taking me to be with Mom and Wilf?"

Flayver turned. "That is what I told you. If you don't believe me, then stay here." The net disappeared from Katryna and reabsorbed into Flayver's outstretched hand.

"I'm sorry," Katryna said, running to catch Flayver as she headed down the hill.

The mist retracted into a cloak around the guardian. Flayver pulled a black hood over her head when they reached the market square. Katryna kept a step behind as they crossed into the narrow streets and alleys beyond. Flayver moved along the shadowed side of the street as they once again picked up the pace. Katryna sidestepped pieces of masonry, some large enough to block the sidewalk. Flayver floated over them, and soon the gap between Katryna and the guardian was half a street. Katryna would have used magic, but she remembered Flayver's warning. She scrambled over a large column that lay across the road.

"Flayver," she called. "Wait!"

The guardian hovered in the air until Katryna caught up to her. Flayver's shape eroded the closer they came to the Veil. The edges of her cloak and gown grew wispier. "Hurry," Flayver shouted. "I cannot hold this form much longer."

Katryna stumbled over a heap of rubble and only just caught sight of the strands of mist as they disappeared around a corner. She rushed after Flayver. The opaque barrier shimmered in front of her. Flayver's arm was extending from the Veil, beckoning her to follow. She hesitated and peered over her shoulder at the sound of running feet.

"Stop!" Malik shouted.

"No way!" Katryna held out her hand. Flayver grabbed hold and yanked her inside the Veil spell.

Chapter Sixteen - Wakefield Tower, Kureyamage

Myra lay on the bed and turned her face to the wall. How could she be so stupid? What was happening to her? She'd never take the drug again. She was so much better than this. Her arms wrapped around her body. Who was she trying to fool? Everybody else knew she was addicted. An addict. Worse, she wasn't even clever enough to make her own batch of elixir and not kill herself. A pathetic little nobody. That's who she was. A piece of trash that Hywel sent on errands when he had no one else. The lowest of the low.

A scratching sound and a meow sent shivers through her. She clambered off the bed and opened the door. Nipits sat in the entrance, his head tilted to one side.

"What do you want?" Myra said, wiping her eyes.

Nipits placed his paw on her leg.

"You want me to go now?"

The cat dug a claw into her leg.

"Ouch," Myra said, squatting down and placing her hand on Nipits's head. "If it's that urgent, you'd better show me." Like watching a movie playing inside her head, Myra saw Katryna running through the street gate.

"How'd she escape?" Myra wobbled as she stood and reached for her compact mirror. She flipped it open and pinged Thiemus. Nothing. She tried Malik.

"Hywel will go ballistic," Malik said. Something heavy hit the stone floor and his image disappeared for a second. "Snails' entrails!" He reappeared. "Try to find Thiemus. I'll head down the hill and try to catch her."

The mirror darkened and Myra slid it into her pocket.

"Where's Thiemus?" she asked Nipits.

The cat bounded off down the corridor. "Not so fast," Myra said. Her head felt two sizes too big and heavy for her neck. She needed to kick her habit. The effect might be wonderful when she first took it, but the downsides were becoming more frequent.

Nipits raced through the tower and down the stairs. The guard lay on the floor outside the workshop. She bent down, but he seemed to be breathing. She tried the door, but it remained locked. Banging on it, she winced at the echo in her head.

The door flew open and she looked into the furious face of her brother. "Where is she?" he said.

"Katryna's escaped."

"Why didn't you stop her?" His mouth was a thin, angry line.

"Malik is rushing down the hill to track her. I thought you might want to be informed." She turned to leave, but he grabbed her arm. His fingers squeezed deep into her flesh.

"Did you let her go?"

"Take your hand off me. I wasn't the one looking after her," Myra said.

Thiemus pointed at the guard. "Was that your work? Are you playing games again?"

"I was in my room. Nipits came to tell me." Thiemus shoved her as he released her. She braced against the wall before her head struck it.

"This is the last time I play messenger for you," Myra said.

Thiemus went back into the workshop.

She leaned against the wall and let her heartbeat return to normal before she pushed off and entered her own workshop. The smell of burned paper assailed her as she settled into the armchair. Nipits jumped onto the other, clawing at the cushion, then settled down.

"What do you think you're doing?" Myra flicked her hand. "Back to your post."

Nipits stretched before jumping down to the floor. He stretched again in front of her, and she resisted the temptation to help him across the room with the tip of her boot.

"Thank you for the warning," she said. He glanced over his shoulder and tipped his head before springing into the corridor and out of sight. She smiled, glad the cat, at least, didn't judge her. She rubbed the back of her neck and leaned back in the chair. Where could Katryna be going? The young witch couldn't make it back to Mathowytch with wizard magic as her only power source. Myra's brain was foggy from the drug. She wouldn't learn anything sitting here. She groaned internally, realizing she'd have to go back to Hywel's workshop and listen. That would be dangerous, and she'd end up involved somehow. She shrugged — there wasn't an alternative. Sighing, she crossed the room and strolled down the corridor. Outside the workshop, Myra sidled along the wall and stopped in the shadow. Hywel stood next to the prone body of the guard.

"Is he dead?" Hywel said.

Thiemus placed his ringed hand on the guard's throat and closed his eyes. The amber stone of his ring flashed. "No. He's breathing. The mist choked him until he fell unconscious."

The guard coughed and tried to sit up.

"What happened?" Hywel asked.

The guard tried to speak but could make only a gurgling sound. His eyes filled with tears and he grabbed at his neck.

"I don't think he'll be able to speak for a while," Thiemus said, producing a cup and offering it to the guard. "Sip this."

The guard's face twisted with pain as he forced down a swallow of the liquid.

Hywel stepped into the workshop, and Thiemus followed. Myra slid in after them. Hywel, his forehead furrowed, examined the corner containing Katryna's prison cell.

Malik burst into the room. "She's gone into the Veil with a guardian."

Hywel spun around. "That's impossible."

"I agree it should be, but I saw her go," Malik said. His hair dripped and he pushed the wet strands from his forehead. He nodded towards the corridor. "How's the guard?"

"He'll live," Thiemus said.

"You feeling better?" Malik said, coming to stand next to Myra in the shadows.

She nodded. What must he think of her? And why was she asking herself that question and worried about the answer?

"Myra can go after her," Thiemus said.

"What?" Myra dug her fingernails into her palm when Hywel turned to look at her.

"Stop lurking in the shadows. I'm aware of your presence as soon as you enter the room," Hywel said, steepling his fingers. "It's not a terrible idea to send Myra after Katryna."

"You want me to enter that crazy spell?" she said. "If it took Katryna, I doubt it will let me find her."

"It won't allow a wizard," Thiemus said. "We need to know about her magic. Don't you understand that this Realm is dying, the biomes have corrupted and—"

"That's enough," Hywel said, sending a blast of magic to silence Thiemus. He continued to look at Myra over his fingertips. "How will you cope without a supply of elixir?"

She clasped her hands behind her back and squeezed. She would not let him bait her into a reply. She waited. The only sound was the bubbling of a cauldron, the occasional hiss from the fire when the liquid splashed over, and the rasping sound of the guard's breathing.

"Nothing to say?" Hywel said, a smile spreading across his thin lips. "Has the drug affected your ability to be of any use to me?"

"It's a big ask to expect her to walk into the Veil," Malik said, stepping closer to her.

Hywel's voice took on a dangerously low tone. "Do you imagine yourself her hero? From what I've heard, it was you that almost caused her evaporation."

Malik opened his mouth to speak, but Hywel cut him off. "I don't care what the two of you get up to, as long as it doesn't interfere with my plans. This episode with brewing elixir could have caused me to have to amend my current strategy. Myra, if you must indulge in your disgusting habit, then at least continue to steal from your brother's supply. If you both want to start a relationship, remember my wishes take precedence over anything else. Is that understood?"

Malik went to speak, but Hywel held up his hand again to stop him. "I require nothing but a yes answer."

"Yes," Malik said, and nudged Myra. She nodded.

Hywel raised an eyebrow.

"Yes," she said.

"Very well," Hywel said. "Malik, you are to continue monitoring the Source. Myra, with me." He strode from the room and she trudged after him. He stopped in the corridor and grabbed her shoulders. "You belong to me until I say otherwise and don't forget it. You're nothing without me. By the way, I have instructed Thiemus to wean you off your disgusting habit." He released her and wiped his hands. "I have a task for you. The papers are in my office."

She didn't have the energy to fight. Whenever she tried to assert herself, she only made a bigger mess and her life became worse. A clink of glass on glass sounded from her pocket and she dug deep into it. Her fingers encircled two vials. They hadn't been there before. She glared at the wizard's back. He'd put them there to control her. She stroked the smooth glass. No! She wouldn't give Hywel the satisfaction of seeing her popping the cork and swallowing the sweet elixir. Her mouth salivated. She snatched her hand out of the pocket. She should smash the vials on the floor. That would show him, and she would do it, but he was sending her into the Veil. She might need the extra strength to fight a guardian. She'd keep them as a safety measure.

Hywel stepped across the library and sat at his desk to pull open a drawer.

"Here," he said, pushing a pass her way. "This will give you authority to move around Kureyamage without a wizard's protection." He leered at her. "It's no guarantee given the current loathing of Mathowytch witches. There have been some instances of brutality. Although I'm sure you can take care of yourself."

She reached for the pass and stuffed it into her jacket pocket. "If the spell is devouring citizens, then it may object to being dissipated. Won't it fight back?"

"That is a possibility, I suppose." Hywel reached for the communication mirror and selected a contact from the list of symbols and runes. A wizard in uniform appeared in the mirror.

"Commander," Hywel said. "I've a disturbing report that a tendril from the Veil spell has broken off and is now roaming the city."

"We have had several reports of sightings," the Commander said. "I have patrols combing the surrounding area."

"Let me know as soon as it is sighted," Hywel said.

There was a brief silence before the Commander spoke.

"I'm sorry, sir, but you are no longer on my list to report to. It might be a mistake. I need to confirm with the Council."

Hywel's face turned deep purple and veins protruded from his neck. "Do what you must." He ran his ringed finger over the mirror and disconnected the call. "Imbecile."

Myra stopped inches from the door. "What if the Veil refuses me entrance?"

"Don't you still have the talisman I gave you?"

She pulled it from under her shirt.

"Then there should be no problem." Hywel picked up a scroll and unrolled it. He looked up. "Why are you still here? And take the cat with you," he added. "I don't need a spy lurking around my garden."

Myra left the tower but stopped by the fountain. "Nipits," she called.

The cat bounded from a gap between two holly bushes. "Seems we've overstayed our welcome," she told it. "We're heading for the Veil."

The cat backed up.

"You don't have a choice. Hywel wants you out, too."

Nipits shook his head but came to stand next to her.

"Come on," she said, lifting her hood.

Nipits kept close to her as she made her way down the hill and through the market square. A handful of stalls were bunched together in a corner. Since the attack, stallholders had been reluctant to set up their businesses here. Most had moved down to the port and sold from barrows along the seafront.

Myra traveled along the backstreets, trying to avoid the major areas where the guards patrolled. Her breath hitched as she turned the corner and saw the Veil. It pulsed liked a heartbeat. Ribbons of colored lights flashed across its surface. Nipits touched her legs and meowed.

"I know," she said. "I don't want to either, but we don't have a choice." She placed her hand in her pocket and the vials of elixir gave a reassuring click. "If we find Katryna we can either give her back to Hywel or we can make a deal with the witches. Perhaps get them to take me off their Wanted List. What do you think?"

Nipits gave her a sidelong look.

"I know it's a long shot. Do you have any bright ideas?"

Nipits brushed her leg.

"Didn't think so," she said.

"Hold it right there!" A deep voice shouted.

Myra turned to see a patrol making its way along the street towards her. Where had they come from? She was losing her touch. It was a full patrol, with clinking metal buttons and steel-tipped boots.

"Time to leave," she said, making a fireball of magic in her fist. She hurled it at the patrol and sped for the Veil. An opening appeared, and she raced towards it. Branches of mist stretched along the road surrounding her. She produced a protective shield to defend against the magic spells the patrol was casting. Her lungs burst, but the rush of adrenaline increased her speed. Nipits ran beside her. She could see the entrance widening to let her in. A tendril of the spell wrapped around her waist, picked her up, and threw her. She landed with a crash inside the Veil.

"Nipits!" she yelled. There was a piteous cry from outside the spell as the walls drew together, cutting her off from the patrol and the cat.

"No!" She struggled to her feet and tried to push through the growing wall. "Let him in," she screamed, but the walls knitted together, all sound from Kureyamage deadened. She could no longer see the city or hear Nipits's cries.

Myra stepped back from the mist-covered walls. Her heart raced. A tunnel formed and a guardian dressed all in white walked towards her. Myra took several deep breaths and slid her hand into her pocket, caressing the vials.

"Welcome, daughter of Mathowytch. My name is Betrine. I am the true guardian of the Veil."

"What do you mean?" Myra asked.

"I am pure witch magic, and I will lead you to the city of witches unharmed."

"I'm here for the other witch you let in — Katryna. Ermentrude's daughter."

Betrine's eyes turned red. "She is an abomination. I did not allow her into the spell."

"Then who did?"

"Flayver. She has turned against the natural order. She will destroy this Realm. It can't continue." Whispers came through the Veil's walls, echoing Betrine's words.

"Well, I'm sorry you're having sister issues, but I'm here to take Katryna back with me outside the spell. Point me in the general direction and I'll leave you to sort out your guardian problems."

Betrine shook her head. "You are a witch. You can't enter that side of the spell and survive."

Myra sighed. Another obstacle in her way. Her life had become one of servitude and goals she couldn't accomplish, all based on problems caused by Wilf.

Chapter Seventeen - Inside the Veil, Mathowytch

Cackles and hisses sounded from the other side of the tunnel walls. Ermentrude strolled on ahead of Wilf. Silence rolled off her, accusingly. It wasn't his fault. He hadn't pulsed magic on purpose.

"Look, I'm sorry," Wilf said, drawing next to her. She increased her steps, and he hung back.

The walls of the Veil tunnel thickened and pressed in on them, narrowing the path. They descended a sharp incline, and when they rounded a corner, they had to climb a steep hill.

"Does it seem like we're walking in circles?" he said. The witch turned to face him.

"I know it wasn't your fault," she said, cradling her arm. "It's a shock." She took in a deep breath. "I think we're being denied access to Kureyamage."

Wilf glanced around, taking in the trail's walls sparkling with quartz and the sound of babbling water. "We're heading for the cave."

"What?" Ermentrude wrinkled her brow.

"The last time the Veil trapped Katryna and me inside, we wandered around and then a path led us down to this cave containing the quarantined witches. I recognize the path." He started walking faster.

"You don't know that," Ermentrude said, stumbling behind him.

"I'm sure of it," he said, turning another corner. The path descended again and the sound of rushing water filled the air. "Can you hear that? It's the waterfall." He jogged ahead.

"Wilf, wait! It could be a trap."

The ceiling tapered down and he stooped to get through, crawling the last few feet. He brushed dirt from his hands. A cave and lake lay below them.

"You were right," Ermentrude said.

"Don't sound so surprised." He carefully maneuvered around an enormous boulder. A stone pathway led down to the sandy beach of the lake, where a lone figure sat on a large rock by the shore. "I think that's…"

"Katryna!" Ermentrude shouted.

The figure stood up and came running towards them. Ermentrude held out her arms and Katryna ran into them. Then she hugged Wilf. Tears flowed down her cheeks.

"Good to see you." Wilf's face flushed and his broad smile matched Katryna's. He kept his fingers interlaced with hers.

"How did you get here?" Ermentrude said.

"Flayver rescued me and then led me here to wait for you," Katryna said, dropping Wilf's hand. "What about you?"

"Flayver arranged for us to meet you here," Ermentrude said.

"I thought Hywel took you?" Wilf said.

"He held me in a workshop under his tower until Flayver's arrival."

"She can travel that far outside her spell?" Ermentrude asked, marveling.

"She visited me in Hong Kong," Wilf answered.

Katryna and Ermentrude both stared at him.

"I know I should have told you sooner, but I didn't believe it had happened." If he hadn't met the guardian again, he still wouldn't have believed it was true.

Katryna linked her arm through her mother's.

"Ouch!" Ermentrude pulled away. "I had a minor accident on the way here," she said, eyeing Wilf. "I'm sure it will heal, eventually." She pushed up her sleeve to reveal the golden vein.

"He's made you a wizard, too! Oh, Mom, I'm sorry." Katryna put her arm around Ermentrude's shoulders.

"I didn't do it on purpose," Wilf defended himself.

"That's the trouble. You've no control over that magic and we have to suffer for it. When will you learn?" Katryna said, placing her hands on her hips.

"Hey, I didn't want to come here, but you needed rescuing," Wilf said.

"Do I look like I need you to help me?" Katryna asked.

"Yes. Otherwise you wouldn't be sitting on a rock underneath the Veil." Wilf was irritated. What gave her the right to yell at him? He hadn't wanted to return to this Realm. She should be grateful instead of shouting because of a minor accident. He folded his arms and glared at Katryna. He should leave them both here, and he would, too, if he knew how to get back to Hong Kong.

Ermentrude cleared her throat. "When you two have finished

saying hello, I'd like to know how you entered Mathowytch the last time you were here."

"We went up that path, through the magical wards and gates. It leads to the Witch Council's Hall." Katryna pointed to a perpendicular path leading up the right side of the cave. The roof had collapsed at the top. "We could try blasting it with magic."

"If we blast it, the rest of the roof could collapse," Ermentrude said. She wiggled her fingers. Nothing happened. "We need more light."

The ring on Katryna's finger flashed. A globe appeared in her hand.

"You've learned to use wizard magic!" Wilf said.

"Someone has to." She sent the globe spinning into the air. It floated above their heads. Katryna pointed at it and the light intensified.

"What's that way?" Ermentrude gestured towards a path leading to the left.

"Kureyamage," Katryna and Wilf said together.

Ermentrude's knees buckled, and she sat down on the nearest boulder, staring into the rippling water of the lake.

"Mom?" Katryna squatted down beside her and placed a hand on her mother's knee.

"I'll be fine. My energy levels are low, that's all."

"I think we have to try blasting through to Mathowytch. We can't stay here," Wilf said, holding his hand out to Katryna. "Want to try it together again?"

Katryna sighed and took his hand. "Let's hope it works. Last time we had the bond to help us."

Her boots crunched on the gravel path behind him as he climbed.

"You want to take the lead again?" he said, stopping several feet from the collapsed roof.

"I didn't want to tell Mom, but my magic seems strange," Katryna said.

"Strange?"

"Hywel isolated both the magics and made me use them separately. Now I can't identify them. They feel mixed. I'm not sure how much control I have. A light globe is simple magic." She pointed at the pile of rubble. "This is tricky."

Wilf ran his fingers through his hair. "You've been using magic all your life. You've got this."

Katryna frowned. What did she expect him to do? His knowledge of magic wouldn't fill a water bottle.

"Let's go," he said, squeezing her fingers.

She shook her head but squeezed back. She extended her ringed finger to the boulders and dirt blocking the path. Her ring glowed and the golden vein on her arm pulsed. Wilf, watching her, pushed magic through his ringed hand to add to hers.

A stream of red light shot from the end of Katryna's finger. It spread across the surface of the tunnel blockage. Heat radiated off the rocks, and they both stepped back.

"Less magic," Katryna whispered. A wisp of smoke spiraled from her fingertip.

"I'm trying," Wilf said, struggling to control the flow. He could feel power building, wanting to release. He tried visualizing a dam holding it back.

Katryna loosened her fingers in his grasp, but he couldn't let go. His fingers were curled around hers. "Let go," she said. Her fingers looked crushed in his hand.

"I can't," he gasped. Sweat ran down the sides of his face. A humming sound came from the rocks and they pulsed.

"This isn't good," she said, backing away and dragging him with her.

"You think?" A scraping sound made him turn his head, then Ermentrude hit him with a blast of magic. His vision blurred, and he sank to his knees.

"Seems my magic has returned," Ermentrude remarked.

Wilf's arms lifted as he floated away and then toppled behind a large boulder. Ermentrude and Katryna crouched on either side, covering their heads. The humming noise increased to a screeching wail, and then there was a deafening boom. Rocks and dirt flew, covering the cavern's floor. Steam hissed from the debris landing in the lake.

Katryna helped Wilf to his knees. He rubbed his head and glared at Ermentrude.

"No need to thank me," she said, standing and shaking out her skirt.

"You hit me over the head," he said, resting against the boulder.

"What are you complaining about? It worked. Come on, the tunnel is clear," Ermentrude said, starting up the path.

Wilf suspected Ermentrude had dealt him that blow as retribution instead of attempting to save him. His legs buckled as he stood and he retched. The walls of the cave blurred and lights flickered before his eyes.

"You used too much energy," Katryna said, coming to help him. "You need to eat and rest."

"He isn't the only one. We can do that when we reach Mathowytch," Ermentrude shouted, continuing up the slope to the tunnel's entrance. "Come on, don't dawdle."

Wilf blew out a breath. He could strangle that old crone if he had any strength to spare. He struggled up the incline behind Katryna. She kept glancing back at him to check that he was following. Where else would he go? He negotiated through the glowing rocks that ringed the tunnel's entrance. Katryna sent a wave of magic to push the smaller remaining ones out of the path.

He stumbled and cursed, but kept shuffling along. Ermentrude had found her stride and was marching ahead without a backward glance. A corner in the trail hid her and Katryna from view. He reached inside himself trying to find the bond with Katryna. He'd become so used to the feeling of being connected. A flutter of Katryna's heartbeat echoed for a second and then died away, causing him to miss his next step. He glanced up but couldn't see either witch, and dread coursed through him. Where had they gone? What would he do if Flayver appeared? He was too weak to resist her.

He rounded the corner. Katryna stood leaning against the wall.

"Sorry! Mom gets single-minded when she's on a mission or injured. Right now it's both." She linked arms with him. Together they struggled along the path until they met Ermentrude at the buckled metal door blocking the way into Mathowytch. They'd repaired the hole he'd made with a temporary sheet of steel. Katryna braced and her ring flashed. She grunted and pushed against the door. Her ring flashed and a thin stream of magic expanded across the surface.

"I can't make it work," Katryna said, dropping her hand.

Wilf closed his eyes and lifted his hand. He blasted the door with a stream of red magic. The steel bubbled and dripped until the temporary panel collapsed. His hand fell and he staggered. He'd rebuilt the wall, controlling the surging magic inside him. He was as exhausted as if he'd played a full soccer match. The edges around the broken panel cooled with a loud hiss. Squeezing through into the Witch Council's meeting hall, he waited for Katryna and Ermentrude to join him.

Dust covered the blue-tiled floor. Artwork hung at angles or had fallen to the ground. Chunks of masonry, glass, and broken furniture littered the rooms. Ear-splitting alarm bells rang.

"Seems the wizard detection system is still functional." Dizziness clouded Wilf's vision, forcing him to stop several times.

Ermentrude marched down the stairs to the Head Witch's office. "Akuna will silence that noise."

Guards from the Executrix Squad rushed to the bottom of

C. B. Lyall

the staircase to greet them. "Good. You can take us to Akuna. I'm Ermentrude Wakefield."

A sergeant stepped forward. "Where did you come from?"

"I'm not here to answer your questions." Ermentrude straightened her spine and met the sergeant's stare. "Now, escort us to the Head Witch's office."

The guard hesitated and then nodded to his four colleagues. "Don't let them out of your sight."

The two guards saluted and then surrounded Ermentrude, Katryna, and Wilf. They motioned for them to move down the corridor to the left. Wilf remembered that the office had a pair of impressive wooden doors with the carved images of witches in swirling cloaks. When they reached the end of the corridor, he saw that only one door remained. The other had a split running down the middle, with only half its carving and hinges remaining.

They stepped inside what once had seemed to him an inner sanctum of dark wooden panels and deep-piled carpet. Sections of the paneling were now missing. Stains, burns, and dirt covered the carpet. The red-eyed witch sat at a small desk with her hand on a large crystal ball clouded with swirling mist.

The door behind the reception witch opened.

"Ermentrude. You've brought Wilf. Thank the moon and stars," Akuna said. If it was possible, the witch looked even more cadaverous. Her birdlike fingers waved at the guards outside her office. "You can take him to the holding cell."

"Wait a minute!" Wilf backed further into the Head Witch's office.

"There's some mistake. Mom, tell them," Katryna said, blocking the guards from reaching Wilf.

Ermentrude wiggled her fingers and the doors to Akuna's office slammed shut. The guards took a step towards Ermentrude, but she slammed them back into the wall. They slid to the ground.

"I'm sorry, Akuna, for the misunderstanding, but you see I didn't bring Wilf with me so you could hand him over to the Wizard Council," Ermentrude said.

"Have you gone mad?" Akuna glared at Ermentrude. Her hand slid under her desk.

"Don't press that." Ermentrude blasted the Head Witch until she collapsed back into her chair. "If your intention is to confine everyone in the room who possesses wizard magic, then you would have to include me, and I've no intention of spending a night in the cells." Ermentrude pushed up her sleeve to reveal the golden vein pulsing up her arm.

Akuna's eyes went wide. "You're contaminated."

"Katryna, take a pair of shackles from the guards and secure

Akuna's wrists behind the chair," Ermentrude said, walking around the desk. She opened the top drawer. "Wilf, use something to block the door."

Wilf grabbed the other set of handcuffs and placed them around the two door handles. He then moved the credenza in front of the door.

A shelf slid out from the desk drawer. Ermentrude tapped the surface and a screen with runes illuminated. She typed out a sequence. The silk hanging on the wall next to Akuna rippled.

"You and Katryna can go, but leave Wilf," Akuna instructed. "The Wizard Council won't give us access to the biome unless we hand him over."

Ermentrude looked down at the Head Witch. "You think once the Wizard Council has control of all the magic, they'll share it? With the witches of this Council or anyone else who is a Mathowytch witch? I doubt it. The biome can't support the entire Realm's population. My bet is the Wizard Council will use this chance to rid themselves of us. They'll say it's part of rebalancing the Realm."

"Degula has guarantees," Akuna said.

Ermentrude pushed aside the silk hanging to reveal an elevator door.

"Degula gave me to Hywel," Katryna said. "How's that for a guarantee?" The doors to Akuna's office rattled.

"Time to go," Wilf said, collecting fruit from a bowl on top of the credenza.

Ermentrude placed her hand on the panel next to the elevator and the door opened. Wilf and Katryna entered as the pounding on the doors increased.

"You're wrong. Degula wouldn't work with that wizard," Akuna shouted, straining on her restraints and inching her chair around the desk.

"I'm not willing to sacrifice our witch community on fake promises," Ermentrude said, sending a bolt of energy to knock Akuna's chair over. She stepped into the elevator and pushed the button. The doors closed as the door to Akuna's office shattered.

Chapter Eighteen - Witch Council Meeting Hall, Mathowytch

Katryna's ears popped with the speed of the elevator's descent.

"Can they override the elevator from Akuna's office?" Wilf handed Katryna a banana.

"No, but they'll alert the guards on the lower floors," Ermentrude said, accepting an apple.

"How far underground will we be?" Wilf asked, taking a bite of another banana.

"Five floors," Ermentrude said, turning to Katryna. "It was Degula who handed you over to Hywel?"

Katryna nodded. Shock etched across her mother's face.

"I had my suspicions, of course, but you never want to imagine a friend can change so much. Degula was a founding member of our coven, along with myself and Akuna. Degula had the strongest beliefs in our equality and freedom. Still, I suppose it's the fear of losing magic that caused her to change."

"You think she sold us out so the Wizard Council will give her access to the biome?" Katryna asked.

The elevator shuddered to a stop.

"Degula is a powerful witch. It seems she might do anything to keep her magic." Ermentrude raised her hand as the doors opened. She ushered them out. "Hold the door," she said to Wilf.

Ermentrude stepped back inside the elevator for a few seconds before reappearing. "You can let go. I've switched it off. No one else can use it." She peered into the corridor. "Come on. This way."

"Where are we going?" Katryna jogged trying to keep pace with her mother.

"There's a tunnel down here," Ermentrude replied, passing a row of cells.

"Have you used it before?" Wilf asked.

"No. Degula ran operations down here," Ermentrude said.

"Stop!" Two guards from the Executrix Squad stepped out of a cell and blocked the tunnel.

"I told you Katryna would need our help," one guard said, grinning.

"You don't recognize us, do you?" The other took off her cap. "It's us, Olga and Rytan."

"How…?" Katryna smiled, embracing her two friends. They'd returned to Mathowytch after receiving the antidote, and that was the last time she'd seen them. Both no longer had pretty faces; instead they possessed an impressive collection of warts. Katryna ran a hand over her nose, hoping she'd also regrown some warts, but felt only smooth skin.

"We're on guard duty down here," Rytan said. "Olga heard about a wizard and witches entering the building from the cave entrance, and we thought it had to be you. Then the alarms sounded, and we knew Wilf was here." Rytan punched Wilf affectionately in the arm. "Then someone used the Head Witch's private elevator and we heard orders being barked to capture the wizard. We figured you'd be heading this way."

Katryna was relieved that the two witches who had helped in her escape from quarantine were safe and well.

"This is a very nice reunion; however, I think we should put some distance between us and the Council Hall before more guards arrive," Ermentrude said.

Wilf shook hands with Rytan and Olga. "Good to see you're both recovered."

"You're looking for the tunnel?" Olga asked.

"This way," Rytan said, leading them further along the corridor. "It's how we transport prisoners no one will miss."

"What do you mean?" Ermentrude asked.

"Security sometimes needs to trade a prisoner or two with the Wizard Council. This tunnel exits in a building a block away," Olga said.

"Degula's been sending witches to Kureyamage?" Ermentrude said.

"They're transported by portal to Hong Kong and exchanged there. Been going on for years. Wizards needed witches to bond with and create the next generation," Rytan said.

"But that's not right," Katryna said.

Rytan shrugged.

"We should move faster and debate ethics later," Wilf said, peering back along the corridor.

The passage ended in a brick wall. Rytan wiggled her fingers, then pushed her hand on the bricks. "That's strange. The entrance should open." She tried again, but the wall remained shut.

"Let Wilf add some magic to you," Katryna said.

Rytan looked hesitant but allowed Wilf to place his arm on her shoulder. "Don't you go adding wizard magic permanently." She wiggled her fingers again with the aid of Wilf, then pushed against the wall. An entrance swung open and she stepped aside, shaking her head. Wilf stepped through, followed by Ermentrude and Katryna.

"That was weird. You should be fine now," Rytan said.

Katryna grabbed both her friends' hands. "Thank you so much."

"It's the least we could do after you saved us," Olga said.

"You'd better knock us out so it looks like we didn't help you," Rytan said.

Ermentrude nodded, raised her hand, and with a swift wiggle blasted both guards. They collapsed to the floor. She stepped into the tunnel and the door clanged shut. Katryna and Wilf produced globes. Light twinkled from the quartz embedded in the rock walls. Footprints crisscrossed the dirt floor. The globes bounced along the path in front of them. Wilf kicked a stone and it rattled off the wall and down the path.

"That should announce us to anyone listening," Ermentrude said, pushing past Wilf.

He shrugged his shoulders. "How long is she going to be grouchy about having wizard magic?"

"For quite some time, I should expect," Katryna said, running to catch up with her mother.

Wilf scuffed his feet and followed.

The air had a stale taste to it, and each step caused dust to catch in Katryna's throat and nose. She held the tip of her nose, trying to stop a sneeze, but it was impossible. The noise echoed off the walls. "I'm sorry," she said when Ermentrude turned to glare at her.

The inclining path seemed to have no end, and as Katryna trudged along she couldn't help letting her mind wander over the conversations she'd heard. Akuna would have handed over Wilf to the Wizard Council. And she had agreed with the wizards' plot to take down the Veil. What would become of the witches who lived in Mathowytch? She couldn't imagine them submitting once again to Wizard Council authority.

Ermentrude and Katryna wiggled their fingers at the bottom of a flight of vertical steps. Their feet stayed firmly planted on the ground.

"It's not working," Katryna said, glancing up at the steps disappearing into the dark.

"The tunnels must be warded against magic usage. We'll have to climb," Ermentrude said.

Wilf charged ahead, leaving the two witches panting. Katryna's thoughts returned to Akuna. Her mother had said their coven wouldn't have access to the biome. Was that the punishment they would receive for the years they'd kept Mathowytch out of wizard rule? Katryna shuddered. The Wizard Council had convicted Ermentrude of treason. They wouldn't revoke that decision.

"Ouch. Watch where you're going," Ermentrude said, rubbing her ankle.

"Sorry." Katryna hadn't noticed that her mother had stopped. She took several deep breaths and wiped away the sweat running down her face. It didn't help that Wilf sat in a squat at the top of the stairs, grinning. If she'd had energy to spare, she would have pushed him over.

"It seems we've reached the end of the path. I don't suppose your friends told you how to open this brick wall?" Ermentrude mopped her face with the handkerchief she'd produced from her pocket.

Katryna shook her head.

"Let's hope it doesn't need a special code." Ermentrude placed her hand on the wall and pushed. The bricks groaned, and a portion of the wall shuddered and slid open. "The security around here is severely deficient."

Ermentrude stepped through the entrance and an alarm sounded.

"You were saying," Katryna said, advancing into a small, empty, windowless room. Another door stood ajar, and they crossed to it. A scraping noise sounded as the brick panel slid back into place.

Wilf peered around the door's edge. "There are two guards coming this way. Ermentrude, you pull the door open. Katryna and I will blast the guards."

Ermentrude shook her head. "Given how you perform magic, it would be better if Katryna and I do the blasting."

Wilf chewed his cheek and nodded. He grasped hold of the door's handle.

"Now," Ermentrude said.

He wrenched the door open. The two witches sent streams of white energy into the room. Chairs clattered against the wall. Bright light and the buzz of energy filled the room, then silence. The guards lay unconscious on the ground.

Wilf pushed past Katryna and raced to the next door. Footsteps pounded from beyond the room. He pulled open the door and sent a blast of magic into the corridor. There was a blinding light and the air filled with smoke.

Ermentrude pulled him to one side. "More control," she

muttered. "Katryna, clear away this mess so we can see what the boy has done."

Katryna's ring flashed and the smoke rose to the ceiling and dissipated. Two other guards lay on the ground. She rushed forward and checked their pulses. "They're okay."

"Lucky," Ermentrude said, stepping over them. "Come on." A staircase led up to the next floor and the main door. They creeped through the door and out onto Main Street.

Ermentrude gasped as she took in the scene in front of them. Destroyed buildings stood on either side of the street, surrounded by piles of rubble, glass, and broken furniture.

"Where do we go now?" Katryna asked. "We're not welcome in Mathowytch, and I don't want to go back to Kureyamage."

Ermentrude stroked the bristles on her chin.

"We can't stay here," Wilf said, striding down the cleared path.

Katryna walked in a daze. She was tired and hungry, and she couldn't believe the surrounding destruction. Mathowytch had been an amazing city full of glass, metal skyscrapers, and green spaces. Now it looked like a war zone. She bumped into Wilf, who had halted at the corner of the road.

"What?" she said, moving around him so she could see what had caused him to stop.

A gray fog covered every building, lamppost, and a public garden on their right. It rippled and crept forward. The Veil was continuing its expansion over Mathowytch.

"That's not right," Katryna said.

"It's moving," Wilf said.

"Mathowytch will soon disappear inside the Veil," Ermentrude said.

"But why?" Katryna asked, staring at her mother.

"Its purpose was to protect Mathowytch from the wizards. Flayver must have decided the best way to do that is to take it into the Veil spell's protection."

"Is that possible?" Wilf said.

"It would seem so." Ermentrude pointed at a wave of mist rolling forward. "I've no desire to reenter that spell until we know what's going on. We need to reach our home."

"But won't they search there first?" Katryna asked.

"Probably, but it's our best option," Ermentrude said, searching in her pocket. "Let's get a move on. The more time we stand out here, the more likely we'll be caught." She pulled a set of keys out of her pocket. "Good, I thought I'd returned these in here."

She set off across the road. Wilf shrugged and gestured for Katryna to go ahead.

"You'll cause a panic when witches see there's a wizard running around Mathowytch!" Katryna tried to stop him.

"They'll be more anxious about the Veil expanding and destroying Mathowytch to notice one wizard," he said.

"Our luck hasn't been too good, but I hope you're right. I wouldn't want to see a panicked group of witches ready to blast you."

"Neither would I," Wilf said. "I'll keep my head down and you can guide me."

"Oh, yeah, that should work. No one will freak over a six-foot wizard looking at the ground." She took his arm. "Come on."

Chapter Nineteen - Inside the Veil, Mathowytch

Myra stumbled along a path through the misty walls of the Veil. Betrine floated in front of her. It seemed like they'd been walking for hours. Myra didn't remember it taking so long to pass between Kureyamage and Mathowytch. Betrine could have been walking in circles. The mist thinned, and she saw buildings through the walls. Shadows moved across the windows. Trees and street signs appeared.

"Why can I see buildings inside the Veil?" Myra asked.

"It is Flayver. She is expanding the spell to protect the Realm, and the Veil is covering more buildings now. Flayver's logic and her magic are both corrupt," Betrine replied.

"She can do that?" Myra's voice shook. If the guardians had become so powerful they could enshroud the entire Realm, then what would happen to witches and wizards trapped inside?

"Flayver has linked with the Source. Magic is changing." Betrine pushed through strands of mist that spat at her like serpents. "She is trying to destroy me. My territory is shrinking." She stopped and tilted her head as if listening.

All Myra could hear were the cackles and screams she'd heard the last time she was trapped inside this damned spell. What could frighten a guardian?

"I'm the true guardian. I protect witches — that is my purpose. I have allowed no wizard access through the Veil. What is my reward? The destruction of myself and this spell. But Flayver's power is increasing. She can wander throughout the Realm." Betrine glided further along the path and turned the corner.

Black mist slithered behind them, closing off the path. A breeze of icy air wrapped around Myra and she pulled her jacket tighter. She ran to catch up to the guardian, but a thick fog blocked the way in front of Betrine.

"I can no longer go this way." Betrine turned from side to side.

"What am I to do if I can no longer reach Mathowytch? Beware of Flayver, Myra. She will destroy this Realm." She pushed past Myra.

"Hey, where are you going?" Myra called after the guardian, but Betrine continued to float away. "You can't abandon me here!"

"Save yourself!" Betrine's wail was piercing. She merged with a wall of white mist and vanished.

Myra glanced at the blocked path in front of her. Mist appeared on the path behind her and edged closer. Strands peeled from the surrounding walls and pressed her nearer to the thick wall. She stepped slowly away from the advancing tendrils. She'd seen them attack the stallholder in the market and swallow him. Her hand brushed the damp cold of the mist as she retreated. She snatched her hand back and risked a glance at the swirling mist. A strand detached from the wall and circled around her ankle. She tugged with her leg, but it held her fast. Another icy tendril coiled around her wrist. She jerked her arm, but more strands detached from the walls to bind her other wrist, ankle, and body. She writhed at the strands securing her.

Flayver stepped out of the fog, her black hair and gown billowing out behind her. "What have you caught for me?" Flayver asked the mist.

She wiggled her fingers and Myra, still secured, floated towards her. "I've seen you before."

Myra shook her head.

"You've entered my territory without permission." Flayver spread her fingers and ran her hand above Myra's head. "I recognize your magic. It's different from the other witches. You haven't been part of this Realm for long." Flayver tilted her head to one side, studying Myra. "I know! You were here with Katryna and Wilf."

Myra groaned, and the tendrils tightened.

"Careful. We don't want to harm her," Flayver said, and the bindings loosened a fraction. "They didn't mention you were here."

"I lost them. I'm trying to find them," Myra said.

"They went into Mathowytch," Flayver said. "Perhaps I should keep you here?"

"They are expecting me. I'm helping them," Myra said, pulling at her bindings.

Flayver moved closer and lifted Myra's chin. "You are part of them?"

Myra blinked. Was Flayver offering to let her go?

"Yes. Wilf is my brother," Myra said, nodding her head.

Flayver floated around Myra, scrutinizing her. "But you're not like them. Your magic needs correcting."

Myra tried to shake her head. "I'm fine." Flayver was part of the corruption, but was she suggesting Myra join her? "Thanks, but if you allow me passage to Mathowytch, I'll find Wilf. I'm happy with this old magic. I need nothing new." Myra twisted her wrists.

Flayver leaned forward so her face was directly in front of Myra's. "No new magic." She placed her palms against Myra's head and pressed. Myra squirmed, but the tendrils tightened until she gasped for breath.

"Why are you struggling? It is my purpose to help the Source restore balance to the magic," Flayver said. Moans came from inside the walls.

A vibration filled Myra's head. Her vision doubled and blurred. A searing pain ran across her temples. The tendrils released, and she fell to the ground.

"There," Flayver said, floating above Myra. "You are whole again."

Myra rolled to her side and tried to stand.

"Careful." Flayver giggled. "You have been a long time unbalanced. It will be difficult for you to connect to the Source."

Myra let out a cry of anguish. Blackness edged her vision. The flow of energy that attached her to the Source wasn't there. She extended her fingers and wiggled them. Nothing happened. "Noooo!"

"Come. You can rest with the others here in the Veil." Flayver floated along the path.

Myra stumbled behind. Part of her soul was missing. No longer a witch, she was a Normal in a Realm that survived on magic. She wanted to collapse on the floor and pound her fists, and then break something, anything. But most of all, she wanted to destroy the Veil spell and its guardians. She clenched her fists and followed Flayver. She made a vow: If there was a way to destroy the guardians, she would find it.

Flayver waved a hand at the dense wall in front of them. It parted, forming an arch, and Myra saw mist-covered shapes lying on the ground.

"You can wait here until you recover." Flayver smiled. The entrance closed, putting a wall of mist between her and the guardian. Myra collapsed, and tendrils wrapped around her body again. The blackness expanded in her mind and she sank into it.

The sky had darkened, and the street lamps were lit when she stirred. She bumped against something solid and opened her eyes. She was lying on a bench in the park she recognized as being near Ermentrude's townhouse. She struggled to sit up. How had she gotten here? A tendril of mist unwrapped from her arm and slunk off into the bushes. Flayver had brought her here, but why? She stood and her vision swam. She staggered along the path leading out of the park. Had Flayver left her close to Ermentrude's house on purpose?

She made her way past the other houses on High Flyers Mews until she came to Ermentrude's townhouse. It had escaped damage, but the front yard looked like a meadow in need of mowing. Myra weaved up the garden path and rapped on the front door. It creaked open. Pausing, Myra swallowed the lump that had grown in her throat. Her heart beat faster as she stepped over the threshold.

"Don't hover around in the hall. Come into the kitchen and allow the door to close," Ermentrude called.

Myra entered the kitchen. Wilf, Katryna, and Ermentrude sat around the yellow table drinking cups of brew.

"Sit down," Ermentrude said, gesturing towards the vacant chair. "Want something to drink?"

Myra sat down, nodding her head. This wasn't the welcome she'd expected. She glanced over at Wilf and saw Katryna's restraining hand on his wrist. The muscles corded along in his arm, and he looked ready to pounce.

"What are you doing here?" Wilf asked.

"Looking for Katryna," Myra replied calmly, leaning back in the chair and folding her arms. Inside she was quaking, knowing she didn't have the magic to fight her way out of here.

"To return me to Hywel?" Katryna said.

"He misses you." Myra smiled.

Ermentrude gave a bark of laughter and extended her finger at the steaming kettle. A mug clattered down and a scoop tipped a measure of herbs into it. "I'm sure he does."

Myra glanced from Ermentrude to Wilf. "You gave wizard magic to her as well?"

"Isn't that a fascinating item of news?" Ermentrude said. The mug banged down on the table next to Myra.

"What made you look for Katryna here?" Wilf asked.

"Flayver pointed me in this direction," Myra said.

"That is one busy spell guardian," Ermentrude remarked.

"And now that you've found me, what do you propose?" Katryna said, releasing Wilf's arm and turning slightly to face Myra.

Myra picked up the mug and sipped the steaming liquid, eyeing Wilf over the rim. His wizard ring glowed and she tensed, ready to throw the drink at him before diving for the floor if he made any sudden movements.

"Calm down, Wilf," Ermentrude said. "I won't allow fighting in my kitchen."

"She killed my father and I'm supposed to sit here calmly?"

"For the moment," Ermentrude said, cradling her mug. "Why don't you explain what happened with Reginald?"

"I don't answer to you," Myra said.

"That's true. But you owe Wilf an explanation. He doesn't have a father, thanks to you."

Myra held Wilf's stare, which was one of pure hatred. She had done this to him. He'd been family to her, part of the only actual family she had known. It surprised her how much his hatred hurt her. "It was an accident," she said, her voice little more than a whisper.

"And that makes it all right?" Wilf's ring blazed and sparks flashed from his fingers.

"Wilf," Ermentrude said sharply.

He took a deep breath and the ring's center dimmed.

"No. I panicked when he caught me with his journal. I thought he was attacking me, so I fired on him, but he was casting a protection spell on the book. Honestly, Wilf, I meant to stun Reginald. I don't understand how he came to evaporate." She wanted him to understand. "I admired and respected Reginald. I would never have intentionally killed him."

"I can understand that. You needed him alive. Hywel must have been furious when he found out," Ermentrude said.

Myra glared at Ermentrude. The old crone must love this. Myra's hand shook when she lowered her mug to the table. Her other hand drifted towards her pocket and she caressed the bag holding her remaining vials of elixir.

Ermentrude banged her cup down. "Well, this has been enlightening. Now that we're rested, it's time we departed."

Myra flinched.

"You didn't expect me to hand over my daughter to you and that poor excuse for a wizard, did you?" Ermentrude pushed back her chair and stood.

"Well, we can't let her go," Wilf said.

"What do you suggest we do?" Ermentrude sent the mugs over to the sink. "Leave her here and let the guards arrest her when they arrive? Or do you propose we take her with us as our prisoner? We'd need to watch her, and that might become distracting and dangerous."

Wilf looked at Katryna, but she wouldn't meet his eyes.

"I'm with Mom," she said.

"It's not right," he said.

"I agree, but we have no choice." Ermentrude's bag shrunk and popped into her pocket. The blinds rolled down over the windows.

"Are the guards closing in because you all possess wizard magic?" Myra stood and smiled. "The Witch Council are sending you to Kureyamage, aren't they? That makes sense. The Wizard Council wants Wilf, Hywel wants Katryna, and Ermentrude's an escaped felon."

Katryna held up her ringed hand. "And you're on the Witch Council's Wanted List. We could leave you here tied up with a nice bow on your head and a gift tag."

"I'm not going to debate our current situation. It's not at all helpful," Ermentrude said. "We've stayed here far too long."

"Where are you going?" Myra asked, blocking the exit.

"That's nothing to do with you," Wilf said, pushing past her.

"Hong Kong? You're going to use the warehouse portals? They won't work," Myra said, running after them.

Wilf whirled around and pushed his face into hers. "Really, Myra, stay out of my way."

"If you go to Kureyamage, I know of a portal you could use," she said. There was no chance of her operating a portal without magic, but she'd rather be in Kureyamage than trapped here.

"You expect us to trust you?" Katryna said.

"Before I left Kureyamage, Malik had discovered that the biomes are corrupt."

"Then how…"

"There's a new small portal. Katryna, you came in it with Hywel. It's powered by witch or wizard magic," Myra said. The real question was whether they'd reach Kureyamage with the Veil expanding.

Ermentrude stroked the bristles on her chin and studied Myra. An alarm wailed in the kitchen. "Bat's blood! The guards have entered the Mews." She opened the closet door. "Quick, in here."

Katryna and Wilf exchanged glances but entered the closet. "You, too, if you don't want the guards to find you," she said to Myra.

The coats glided along the rack to allow access to the back wall. Ermentrude pushed on a plaque on the opposite side and a panel slid open. "Quickly," she said, pushing past and entering a corridor. Katryna and Wilf darted through, but Myra hesitated.

"There's no time to wait for you to consider your options. You either come now or I'll shut this wall and you can face the guards."

Myra jumped through just as the panel closed. Without her magic, she had no choice, and at least they had magic at their fingertips.

Chapter Twenty - Ermentrude's House, Mathowytch

Ermentrude led the way down a flight of wooden stairs. Her feet splashed over the muddy floor. A globe bobbed along, illuminating the rough, uneven ground. Roots patterned the dirt walls, and small holes from burrowing animals pitted the surface. A damp, earthen smell filled the air.

"I didn't know this existed," Katryna said, stepping over a large puddle.

"There are few who do. Unfortunately, Degula is one who does know. She had the escape tunnel built for me as a safety precaution. So it won't be long before she informs the patrol of its existence," Ermentrude said.

"Won't she send the patrol to the exit and capture us there?" Wilf asked.

"No. I made a few amendments to the original design," Ermentrude said, leading the way along the tunnel. "I hope the Veil hasn't increased to encompass this far below ground."

"Must we return to Hong Kong via Kureyamage?" Katryna asked. But as they turned a corner, the tunnel ended.

"It's a dead end," Wilf said. They'd stood a better chance blasting their way through the guards.

"Not exactly, but the problem is that we need witch magic." Ermentrude looked at Myra.

"I can't," she said.

"Won't, you mean," Wilf said, turning his back on her. "Katryna, isn't your magic still separate?"

"It's working differently since I spent time with Hywel. I'm not sure what it is any longer," she said, shrugging her shoulders. "I can try."

"What did he do to you?" Wilf said, stepping closer.

"We can discuss all this later. For now, why don't you try reaching out with your magic and see if you can detect a portal?" Ermentrude placed her hand on Katryna's shoulder.

"You have a portal hidden down here?" Myra asked, her eyes widening in surprise.

"We've needed it a few times," Ermentrude said.

Katryna stretched out the fingers of her left hand, but the ring gleamed. "I can't sense anything," she said, panting with the effort. "Myra, can you help?"

"I tell you I can't," Myra said, putting her hands in her pockets.

"What's wrong with you?" Wilf said, grabbing her arm. "You want us to believe you'll help, but the first time we ask you refuse." He dropped her arm. "We should have left you for the guards."

"You don't understand," Myra said. "Flayver did something to my magic. I can't use it."

"I don't believe you," Wilf said. But he started examining the cave. There were no supplies, not even a chair to sit on.

Myra took out a vial of elixir. "I can try one of these." Her hand shook as she uncorked the vial.

"How many of those did you take?" Ermentrude said, brushing Myra's shoulder.

Myra shrugged off the hand and drank the contents. "That's none of your business."

"Great," Wilf said, rolling his eyes. "You're an addict." He used to value her opinions. She was his sister. They'd shared the same apartment for ten years. Now he didn't recognize the person standing in front of him. She was a complete stranger.

Myra extended her fingers. There was a blue tinge to her fingernails. "I can feel something." A smile began to spread across her face.

"Good," Ermentrude said. "Try a reveal spell."

A flow of energy flew from Myra's fingers and the portal appeared.

"Excellent." Ermentrude placed her hand on the panel and a door swung open. "Shall we?"

"Will this take us to Hong Kong?" Wilf asked, entering and finding two bench seats on either side of a globe on a stand.

"Unfortunately, it only goes back and forth to Kureyamage."

"This is the portal that went missing months ago. You stole it from Hywel," Myra said. The laugh she gave had a note of hysteria attached.

"I acquired it when he carelessly lost it and I found it." Ermentrude sat opposite Wilf and Katryna. Myra sat next to Ermentrude.

"Well, go ahead."

"You can't operate it?" Myra asked.

"No. That's why I need you," Ermentrude said.

Flashes of electricity spiked within the glass globe. Myra took a deep breath, but she hesitated to place her hand on its surface.

"What are you waiting for?" Ermentrude forced Myra's hand to make the connection. The energy stabbed into her fingers and she sucked in air. The wall next to them vanished and a tunnel appeared. "The portal's program will return it to Hywel. I hope you can steer it to somewhere other than his tower." Ermentrude released Myra.

"Is that possible?" Wilf asked, turning back from the rectangular window on his right.

"It usually transports to an alley near the market square," Ermentrude said, sitting up straighter and nudging Myra.

The portal chugged forward and climbed before it took a swift nosedive. They lurched left and right with the portal's sudden changes in direction.

"It's like a roller-coaster ride," Wilf said, clinging to the arm of the seat. The portal hurtled around a corner and then climbed again.

"I'm sorry," Myra said. "It's all I can image."

They plunged at breakneck speed into the darkness. Myra's scream was as loud as Katryna's. Ermentrude's face remained calm as she clutched the bench, but it was as gray as a Hong Kong sky. Wilf's fingers cramped around the armrest.

The portal decelerated and crawled the last few feet. When it stopped the window disappeared, and Myra withdrew her hand.

"Where are we?" Wilf asked.

"I was trying for the old safe house, but my mind kept slipping," Myra said, wiping sweat from her forehead.

"Where else were you thinking of?" Wilf asked, catching hold of Myra's arm.

Katryna stepped outside the portal. "The market square in Kureyamage."

Wilf dragged Myra from the portal. "Playing your usual games." He shoved her away from him. "We'd better get out of here."

At least they had made it out of Mathowytch and there didn't seem to be a patrol waiting for them. Wilf noticed the devastation of the square with its collapsed buildings. He remembered stalls covering the center, but now they were crowded together in a corner. The buzz of conversation had been replaced by the quick steps of a few customers.

Ermentrude began walking down an alley. "We might find somewhere to stay until we can portal to Hong Kong." She rounded a corner and stopped. "It would seem the expansion of the Veil is happening in both cities."

Wilf peered around Ermentrude. A gray haze shimmered across the entrance to the street. He shuddered. They were trapped between two opposing teams: the Veil and the patrols. He glanced around. "In here."

He pushed open a gate hanging half off its hinges. Once inside, he swung the gate back into place and put rocks behind it.

"We could have secured it with magic. When will you remember you're a wizard?"

"Never," he said, moving along the garden path towards a house. Only one side still stood upright. "Hopefully we can stay here until we discover how to leave this Realm."

"The way the Veil is advancing, we can't remain here for long," Katryna said, entering the house. She stepped over broken furniture and entered the kitchen. "At least this room is habitable." She dusted a chair before sitting down.

"I'm surprised you're still with us," Wilf said sarcastically as he stepped around Myra.

"Let it go," Ermentrude said.

"If you've forgotten, she murdered my father." Wilf's ring flashed bright red.

"If you continue like this, you'll have the rest of the house brought down," Ermentrude said, wiping another chair. "Besides, I'm not sure she killed Reginald."

"What?" All three stared at her.

"Reginald was a powerful wizard. He knew Myra was searching for the journal — that's why he put the protection spell on it. I can't believe Myra got the upper hand. That's all I'm saying." Ermentrude sat down with a sigh.

Wilf waved his arm at Myra. "She said she killed him."

Myra leaned against a cabinet, putting the table between them.

"She fired at him, that's for sure, but was that the cause of his evaporation?" Ermentrude mused.

"Wait a minute," Wilf said, shaking his head. "What else could have caused it?"

"I don't know. What happened that morning?" Ermentrude stared at Wilf.

Heat rose in his cheeks, but at least his ring was no longer lit up. "We argued about soccer, but that wasn't anything new."

"He received a call," Myra said.

"From whom?" Ermentrude turned to face her.

"I don't know. He was in the middle of telling Wilf not to leave the house when his wrist mirror pinged and he left to answer it."

"How long before you entered the workshop?" Katryna said, leaning forward.

"Soon after Wilf left. Reginald was busy upstairs. It seemed the perfect time to continue my search," Myra said, not meeting anyone's eyes.

They waited in silence for her to continue.

"Go on," Ermentrude said.

"I had to search to find the journal. Reginald had hidden it in amongst the books on the shelves. It took longer than I'd realized. He came silently down the steps. I saw him lift his hand and his ring flash. I thought he was attacking me, and I sent a bolt of blue magic at him. Reginald collapsed, and the journal spun out of my hands and flew across the room to him. I tried to take it, but he smiled. Both he and the journal disappeared."

"He smiled?" Wilf said, dropping into an empty chair. He felt like a punctured ball. He'd been so sure that Myra had killed his father.

"There's more to this," Ermentrude said.

"Looks like our rest period is over if we don't want to reenter the Veil." Katryna pointed at a tendril of mist sliding into the room through a crack in the window.

"How will the Councils dissolve the spell?" Wilf asked.

"That's what they want you for." Malik appeared, sending a stream of magical strands to secure Wilf, Ermentrude, and Katryna. "Guards, take these prisoners to Hywel's Tower." He slung an arm around Myra. "Glad to see you made it back safely. I was worried about you."

The guards pulled Wilf to join Ermentrude and Katryna. "I knew we couldn't trust you," Wilf said, bumping into Myra. "Whatever Ermentrude says, I still believe you murdered my father."

Malik took his arm off Myra. "So you're the troublemaker Wilf Gilvary, Destroyer of Realms. Hywel will be happy, and you'll soon be back under the microscope." He nodded to the guards, and they started out of the building with their prisoners.

Wilf blinked in the sunlight and paused, but the guard pushed him and sent him stumbling along the cobblestone path. He grabbed the alley wall to stop from falling to the ground. The guard sniggered and jerked Wilf back in formation.

They'd allowed Myra to trap them, Wilf thought. She had probably signaled Malik as soon as the portal arrived in Kureyamage and then happily let Ermentrude ramble on, knowing they would be captured soon enough. He tried to summon his magic, but the connection wasn't there. The one time he remembered he was a wizard, it deserted him.

Malik appeared on his right. "There's no use reaching for magic — those cuffs block it."

Wilf looked straight ahead and tried to ignore him.

"I'm sure Hywel will be at the entrance to greet you and his daughter. It should be quite the reunion." He leaned in closer. "Between you and me, I'm not sure he'll be pleased to see Ermentrude, but you never know."

The cuffs tightened and Wilf bit the inside of his cheek as a zap of energy stung his wrists.

"Did I forget to mention that the cuffs are sensitive? They are programmed to deter you from using magic in increasing amounts of severity," Malik said.

Wilf continued to stare straight ahead.

"I've been told you find it difficult to control your magic, so this might be a great teaching aid," he said, laughing.

The cuffs tightened again, and a prolonged burst of energy zapped Wilf. Sweat beaded on his forehead as they started up the hill towards Hywel's Tower.

"I can really see the benefits of keeping you in those bracelets for a while," Malik said, turning his head. "Don't you agree, Myra?"

Wilf glanced at his stepsister. She slouched as they walked. Her arms wrapped around her body.

"Don't tell me you've used up all the elixir Hywel gave you," Malik said.

Myra shook her head.

"I'm glad you're trying to cut down, and that's commendable, but this might not be the best time to suffer withdrawal. I'd suggest a quick fix before we enter the tower. You might need it." Malik draped his arm over her shoulders and pulled her towards him. "I'm only thinking of you, babe."

"Leave her alone!" Wilf shouted.

"See, you're upsetting your stepbrother, and then he'll get angry and reach for his magic..."

Myra looked from Wilf to Malik. She reached into her pocket and pulled out a vial of elixir.

"Don't," Wilf said.

She uncorked the vial and swallowed the contents.

"Here we are," Malik said, putting his hand on the wall plaque. The gate swung open, allowing the patrol and prisoners to enter the courtyard of Hywel's Tower.

"Excellent, Malik," Hywel said, coming out to greet them.

Malik directed the guards to take Wilf, Katryna, and Ermentrude to the basement workshops. "I told you Myra wouldn't fail us. She's one of us."

Chapter Twenty-One - Wakefield Tower, Kureyamage

Katryna shook the broken glass and plaster out of the window seat cushion before sitting down. Sunlight filtering through the window felt like a warm blanket wrapped around her shoulders and back. Hywel had released her from the laboratory and started on Wilf. She hadn't seen him in the last three hours, but she'd seen Malik taking her mother along the corridor when Thiemus had escorted Katryna upstairs to the tower. She'd tried to run after Ermentrude, but Thiemus had grabbed her arm and dragged Katryna up the stairs. She rubbed her arm and winced.

She stared out the window trying not to think about her mother, but the sight of the broken fountain and destroyed trees and bushes in the garden caused a lump in her throat. The garden was a reminder of the earthquakes, a reflection of how broken the Realm seemed to be. She turned back to the room. It wasn't so bad if she kept her eyes from the far corner where a crack ran from floor to ceiling. She didn't want to wonder how stable the tower was, or worry that it might come tumbling down on top of her. How much longer would the earthquakes go on? Would the Realm collapse and disappear into the Thermals, taking them with it? It was best not to let her thoughts run along those lines.

Myra peered around the door and then slouched over to sit beside her. "He released you?"

"Obviously." Katryna sighed, exhaustion draining her. She wanted to be alone, have time to think. Tears blurred her vision.

"There's food in the kitchen." Myra looked around the room. "It's a wonder this place is still standing."

"What do you want from me?" Katryna folded her arms.

"Nothing." Myra sounded hurt.

"Don't lie to me. I've been a lab rat all morning. I've nothing more to give. So tell me who sent you? Hywel, Thiemus, Malik, or all three?"

Myra hung her head. "This isn't my doing. I didn't alert them when we arrived back in Kureyamage. There was a sensor in the portal."

"Whatever. I don't care," Katryna said, standing. Myra could stay here, but she didn't have to. She headed to the kitchen. Her stomach rumbled, but she didn't know if she could force anything down.

Hywel had spent the morning making her try to use her witch magic and wizard magic until her head spun. She had stopped being able to access either separately, which had infuriated Hywel. Malik had accused her of being influenced by the corruption in the Realm. They'd released her and brought Ermentrude in for testing. She wondered how that was going. She was sure her mother would thwart any plan Hywel came up with.

"Katryna," Myra said, but Katryna closed the door on her. At one time she'd sympathized with the other witch, but not anymore. Myra had chosen her path and had to live with it. No one trusted Myra anymore. It was too dangerous to do so.

Malik lounged on a chair in the kitchen. A plate with a half-eaten sandwich sat on the table in front of him.

"We have limited food supplies," Malik said.

Katryna opened the fridge. There didn't seem to be anywhere where she could be alone. There was a bowl of noodles on the top shelf. She sniffed it, then held it at arm's length to recover it and put it back. The past few months in Hong Kong she'd sampled food from India, China, Thailand, Vietnam, and Spain. She'd loved the variety and tastes. With a sigh, she grabbed a container of berries and yogurt, the lack of choice adding to her frustration. She was trapped in Hywel's Tower while chaos and destruction were taking hold of her world. There must be something she could do.

She mixed berries into the yogurt and took a mouthful, expecting sweetness from the fruit and the tang of yogurt. It was tasteless. She looked skeptically at Malik.

"We're forced to use stored nutrition packs and magic. Who knows how long we'll have either," he said, pushing back from the table. "Did you know Wilf's being handed over to the Wizard Council later today?"

Katryna shook her head.

"The Veil won't be here for much longer once your boyfriend is in their hands," he said, walking from the room.

Katryna frowned and pushed aside the bowl. If Wilf was being transferred, this might be her only opportunity to help him. She watched from the window as Malik crossed the courtyard. She ran to the top of the stairs, her mind screaming at her not to go back into the black corridor. She took several deep breaths and then ran back down the stairs.

Malik's globe bobbed along the corridor, lighting the way. He passed the laboratories and then disappeared down another flight of steps.

The air had a musky scent of earth thick enough to choke her. She flattened against the wall when Malik stopped at a door and placed his hand on a panel. The top half slid aside. Katryna squinted, peering into the darkness. Malik sent the globe through the protective shield and the room lit up.

Wilf lay huddled on a bench, his back to the door.

"You can come out, Katryna," Malik said, turning to face her. "I heard you following me."

She stepped out of the shadows and ran to the cell.

"Wilf." At the sound of her voice, he turned around. She gasped. Dried blood crusted around his swollen cheek. "What happened to him?" she said.

"Seems he didn't want to help Hywel with his experiments. Thiemus did a little persuading," Malik said, grinning.

"It's barbaric," she said.

Wilf struggled to his feet. "Are you all right?" he asked.

"I'm fine. What about you?"

"It looks worse than it is." He grimaced.

Katryna shook her head. Wilf's right arm dangled at his side and his left cradled his ribs.

"What has Hywel done to you?"

Wilf coughed, but it turned into a groan. "He's been linking me up to one of his machines. He hopes he can control me enough to take down the Veil spell before it spreads any further."

"Can he do that?" Katryna looked at Malik.

"Which part? He can hook Wilf up and control him. As to taking down the Veil…" Malik shrugged. "In theory, I'd say it's possible."

"Then will he let Wilf go?"

Malik didn't meet her eyes.

"They don't think I'll survive the process. Isn't that right, Malik?" Wilf said, glaring at the other wizard.

"Not my place to say," Malik said, folding his arms and leaning back against the wall. "Any last words for each other? This is your final opportunity. I can't stand around here forever, and I'm not leaving you here with him."

Katryna looked down at her hands and at the wizard ring. She put them behind her back and glanced up. Wilf stared at Malik.

It was strange. Her stomach still fluttered when Wilf's eyes lingered on her, and his smile made her catch her breath. But it wasn't the same consuming hunger the bond had created. Then she'd wanted him touching her, kissing her and… She felt a blush rising in her cheeks. Now it seemed weird being alone with him.

"It's kind of odd," she said.

Wilf made a weak, half-smile. "I know what you mean. The bond. Those feelings weren't real. I like you, but—"

"It's okay. It's the same for me." This was so lame. She must remember that he wanted a Normal's life. Not a girlfriend who was a witch. She had to control her thoughts. "I'm sure we'll find a way out." Did she say that? Who was she kidding?

"That's what I think. We always have before," Wilf said.

"You two are pathetic. Come on, I need to go. Hywel will need me," Malik said, gesturing for Katryna to go ahead.

She glanced from Malik to Wilf. Panic caused her stomach to knot. She had to do something.

Malik grabbed her arm and jerked her forward.

"Stop pulling me!"

He released her, and she fell backwards. He grabbed her again. "I should never have let you follow me down here."

"Let me go!" Rage flooded through her and power built inside her. A roaring filled her ears. She raised her hand and white blasts of energy sizzled across the passage.

Malik put his hands up and deflected the blast. It struck the door of Wilf's cell and the door disappeared.

Wilf's manacles jangled around his wrists as he ran from the cell and joined Katryna.

Malik sent a bolt of energy at Wilf, but Katryna deflected it into the wall. She flung another ball at Malik. It exploded in his face and he dropped to the ground.

"That should delay him. Come on," she said.

Malik tried to send a blast of magic, but it missed Katryna by several feet, ricocheting off the walls and ceiling.

Wilf took a step, but his manacles clanged and Malik sent a bolt of magic in his direction. The smell of sulfur and singed hair showed how close Malik had come to hitting his mark. Wilf pulled the restraints tight and took another step. Malik cocked his head but didn't fire. Wilf crept past Malik until he caught up to Katryna. She wrapped her sweatshirt around the manacles to deaden any noise the chains made.

She ran down the corridor with Wilf trailing behind her. At the corner, she glanced back. Malik was following them, one hand on the wall, groping his way. She ran for the stairs leading to the courtyard. She panted for breath when she reached the top. A pain seared through her and she bent, clutching her side. Wilf stopped next to her. "You okay?"

"Just a stitch! I haven't run in a while," she said.

"What now?" he said.

"How should I know?" She massaged her side.

"Perhaps I can help you," a voice said. Her head snapped up. A ring of guards surrounded them. "You've saved me the trouble of fetching Wizard Gilvary," the Captain continued. "I'm happy to take him off your hands."

Wilf let out a groan as guards seized him.

"I think it might be better if you also accompanied us," added the Captain. Another guard caught hold of Katryna and restrained her arms behind her in handcuffs. Malik emerged from the basement and bumped straight into the Captain, who glanced from Malik's flash-burned face to Katryna. "Yes, you should definitely accompany us," he said.

"Let Wizard Hywel know we've collected the prisoner and this witch," the Captain ordered, signaling to his patrol of guards to march back down the hill towards the Wizard Palace.

"That's his daughter," Malik shouted.

"Then you'd better run and inform him," the Captain said, leaving Malik alone in the courtyard as he took up his position at the rear of his patrol.

A guard pushed Katryna along until she fell in step with the patrol. "Sorry! That must be the worst rescue of all time," she said, marching next to Wilf.

"Not one of your better thought-out plans, I agree, but thanks for trying," he said.

"No talking. Keep moving," the guard said.

They were marched down the hill, across the market square, and into the Palace via a side gate. Katryna looked at the high walls. She remembered escaping the palace with Myra after they'd eluded Thiemus. They had dashed after Wilf and made for the Veil. She didn't think escape would be possible this time.

They were led down a narrow hall until the Captain rapped on an engraved oak door. It swung open, and they were ushered into the grand meeting chamber. Three wizards sat on a dais in large, ornate chairs. Katryna recognized the head judge from Ermentrude's trial. Anger sizzled through her.

"It's about time you apprehended the Gilvary wizard," a slender wizard said. He wore a long dark blue robe, had a long, straight nose and dark shoulder-length hair, and was clean-shaven. "Why is there a witch here?"

"When we arrived at the Tower we discovered that she had assaulted a wizard while attempting to rescue Wilf Gilvary, Your Highness," the Captain said.

Katryna gulped when she recognized Grand Wizard Verger, the head of the Wizard Council.

"Who is she?" Verger asked.

"I'm Katryna Wakefield," she said, holding her head high and meeting the wizard's eyes.

"Hywel's daughter," the Chief Justice said, leaning forward and leering at her. "It would seem Hywel has nothing but trouble with the witches of his household."

"Didn't you sentence his wife—" Verger began.

"Ermentrude. She escaped justice," the Chief Justice said.

"If this young wizard is here, and Hywel's daughter, then I would imagine Witch Ermentrude isn't far behind," Verger said, turning to the Captain. "Where did you apprehend your prisoners?"

"Wakefield Tower, Your Highness."

"Then may I suggest, Chief Justice, that you look there for your witch," Verger said, smoothing out the sleeves of his gown.

"You think..." The Chief Justice's face glowed like a stoplight. "Captain, send more guards to the tower, secure that witch, and bring her here immediately."

The Captain bowed his head and gave instructions to a soldier who left the room.

"How are you proposing we set about destroying the Veil?" the third wizard on the dais asked.

"We will need to coordinate with the Witch Council. That is why you are here, Tyrone. I thought you were negotiating with Akuna," Verger said.

"They are more than agreeable to the Veil spell being taken down; however, they are asking for guarantees for themselves and any witch who resides in Mathowytch." Tyrone thumbed through a pile of papers in front of him.

Katryna had never seen a face turn as vivid a shade of red as the Chief Justice's did. He looked like he was about to explode.

"Guarantees? They stole our city! Attacked the Wizard Palace!" he yelled.

"I'm sure you have an extensive list of charges to bring against them, but at the moment that wouldn't be at all helpful," Tyrone said, polishing his glasses.

"I agree. The time for retribution will come later. The immediate problem is the Veil advancing over the entire Realm. To prevent that from happening, we'll need the cooperation of Akuna and her witches." Verger pointed at Wilf. "We also need to harness the ability of this young wizard, and for that we will need Hywel." A smile crept across the Grand Wizard's face. "It will be our pleasure to reunite him with his daughter."

Chapter Twenty-Two - Wakefield Tower, Kureyamage

Myra's footsteps crunched as if the ground were covered in peanut shells. The smell of ash from an old fire filled her nose and she sneezed. She descended two steps. The floor changed and became soft underfoot. She lit another globe, and the light gradually illuminated the tunnel.

"This is what you wanted to show me?" She wrinkled her nose. With each footstep more clouds of ash rose in the air. She put her hand over her mouth, not wanting to breathe it in.

"Before the fire, it was an underground corridor that led to the Palace," Malik said.

So they weren't nutshells, but rather tiny pieces of bone protruding from the thick layer of white groundcover.

"Witches and wizards died here?" she said. A shiver of revulsion ran down her spine.

Malik nodded. "They'd secured the door into the tower from here."

Myra glanced at the scorched marking running up the walls. "That's…"

"Monstrous," he said.

"Why didn't Hywel open the door?" He was cruel and consumed with his own world and power, but this seemed callous even for him.

"Wilf and the Advancer occupied him at the time of the attack. I doubt he even realized what was happening until it was too late." Malik rubbed his eyes.

"So, while he was torturing Wilf, the witches attacked and caused this?" Myra remembered Seldan and her group planning an assault on the Palace, and this passage connected with Wakefield Tower. Had a fireball run through here and killed everyone trapped underground?

"No one knows how it happened, but a lot of wizards and a

few witches burned down here," Malik said.

Myra turned to leave, but Malik put an arm out, preventing her. Trapping her against the soot-lined wall, he pressed his body against hers. He kissed her, but she turned her head. She put her hands on his shoulders and pushed him back. He resisted at first, but then let her pass. She ran back along the corridor, grimacing with each crunching footstep.

He confused her. One minute he was talking about her being a junkie and how untrustworthy she was becoming; the next, he acted like he was into her.

He caught up to her and slung his arm around her shoulder.

"Why did you show me that?" she said.

"You should know what's been happening. Did you know the Wizard Council has Wilf and Katryna? Which means they'll soon have the Veil down. Then there won't be a Witch Council, and the repercussions for all these deaths will be swift. I'm letting you know so you're on your guard. I'd hate if you got caught on the wrong side," he said.

His eyes seemed hard and calculating when Myra met his gaze. He stopped, putting both hands on her shoulders. He touched her chin and turned her face to him. "What I'm trying to tell you is that I'll look out for you. You can count on me."

"Why?" Part of her wanted to melt with his words and let him be her protector. The other part was gagging and trying to push him away. She wasn't sure he hadn't cast a spell on her, or put a potion in her drink. Maybe she didn't know how to trust. He hadn't given her a reason to doubt him. Except that look in his eyes.

"I like us, and I think you're not averse to the idea," he said.

She shook her head, attempting to clear her thoughts. He took it as affirmation.

"Good." He dropped his hand but kept one arm slung around her as he started walking down the corridor towards the workshops.

Her hands trembled, and it wasn't only because she needed a vial of elixir. She liked Malik, but he seemed to be around her all the time lately. She felt suffocated, but maybe that was her problem. She wasn't used to having someone around. She should be happy he was into her, but a prickling in her subconscious wouldn't let her be. Why couldn't she relax and enjoy being with him?

Hywel appeared in the corridor ahead of them. "There you are. They need us at the Wizard Palace. Malik, collect Ermentrude. Grand Wizard Verger is demanding her presence. Myra, come with me."

"I'll meet you upstairs." Malik squeezed her arm and turned down the adjacent corridor.

Hywel strode off and Myra hurried to catch up with him.

"We're not using the passage?" she said.

"It's blocked," Hywel said, not breaking stride. She jogged up the stairs. He took them two at a time. He seemed barely aware she was there. Should she slip away? He halted, and she banged into his back. He grabbed hold of her arm and pushed up the sleeve.

"Hey!"

He let her go. "Have you been marked the same as Ermentrude and Katryna?"

"No!" Her voice trembled, but she held her ground.

"They both have dual magic and you've been with them. I'm naturally suspicious," Hywel said, heading once more for the front of the tower.

She watched him disappear around the corner, but started walking again at the sound of marching feet. She was helpless without access to any magic. Damn Flayver! At first she'd thought her magic had disappeared, but now she knew that wasn't true. It just lay hidden from her behind some kind of wall. The last time she'd felt this way was when she was a child learning to use magic and couldn't tap into the source. Now she needed time to herself to think and experiment.

"Better look lively," Malik said, coming up alongside her. He and the guard held Ermentrude, her hands secured in handcuffs to prevent her from casting any spells.

Myra gave a deep sigh. She was always being denied alone time.

"It's not that bad," Malik said, nudging her with his arm.

She was slipping if Malik could read her feelings. Falling in step beside him, she kept her eyes away from the guards and Hywel standing in front of the tower's gate.

"Let's get this over with," Hywel said, motioning to the Captain of the palace guard waiting in the street.

They marched down the hill and soon entered the Wizard Palace. The guard proceeded to the central meeting hall after sending an usher to inform the Grand Wizard of their arrival.

"Mom," Katryna said, taking a step before a guard restrained her.

"I'm fine," Ermentrude said, glaring first at the guard, then Hywel, before settling on Grand Wizard Verger as he took his seat on the dais.

"Ermentrude, it's been a long time," Verger said with a smirk.

"It could happily have been longer, but I've been told you're insisting on my joining your meeting," Ermentrude said, shrugging off the guard holding her.

"I hope you don't mind, but it seems you've upset a lot of the members of the Wizard Council," Verger said.

"Excellent," she said, jangling her handcuffs. "Remove these and I'll be more than happy to continue."

The Grand Wizard burst out laughing. The Chief Justice's face flushed bright red as he scrunched up his features and his cheeks expanded. Tyrone leaned back in this chair, a frown creasing his brow as he watched the Grand Wizard.

"The palace hasn't been the same since you left." Verger cleared all mirth from his face. "The Realm is collapsing, and there seems little we can do about it while that Veil spell still exists. It has to come down, Ermentrude."

"I agree," Ermentrude said, looking around. "Do you think I might sit down? I've spent a very tiring morning with my ex-husband."

Verger waved a hand and a chair sprang forward.

Voices echoed in the vast room, which was decorated with black wood panels. Runes and gold lettering adorned most of them. Myra edged closer to the ones by the door and read the names of past council members. Bright globes and pendant lamps hung around the dais, but the rest of the room was largely in shadow. A few small stained-glass windows offered traces of natural light. There were rows of benches, and two podiums were pushed to one side in the space between the benches and the dais.

Ermentrude placed her shackled hands in her lap. "The spell's developed a life of its own. We met a guardian named Flayver whom I suspect has attached to the Realm's source."

Myra brought her attention back to the front of the room with the mention of the guardian who had robbed her of her magic.

"Is that possible?" Tyrone asked, leaning forward.

"That is the same conclusion I reached," Verger said. He pointed at Wilf. "But we should be able to use the boy's connection to this guardian. Don't you agree?"

"We could try, but I'm not sure Wilf has enough control. Flayver used him rather than the other way around," Ermentrude said.

Hywel stroked his beard and glared at Wilf.

"You created this mess, Hywel. What do you think?" Ermentrude said.

"I did no such thing. Training of the boy was inadequate. If you'd left him in my care…" Hywel moved closer to the dais.

"I'd probably be dead," Wilf said, folding his arms.

"Recriminations won't solve the problem," Verger said, leaning one elbow on the armrest. "Dare we risk letting the boy try to nullify the spell?"

Silence fell in the room. Katryna edged closer to Wilf.

"Who do you bet will speak first?" Malik whispered.

Myra jumped. She hadn't heard Malik sneak up to stand next to her.

"We don't have a choice." Tyrone held up his wrist mirror. "The Veil has completely covered the lower section of the city. It will probably encompass the entire city within the next two days."

"Captain, take our guests down to the cells for the night while we discuss this matter further. Tyrone, inform Akuna of the Veil's progress," Verger said, rising from his seat. "I suggest the rest of us retire to the inner chamber."

"You'll warn those witches. They're nothing but a band of saboteurs?" The Chief Justice's face looked ready to explode.

"My Lord Justice, this is not a time for petty squabbles. The Realm is at stake." Verger stepped down from the dais, and the others followed him into the adjacent room.

The guards marched Wilf, Katryna, and Ermentrude from the room. Myra turned to leave, but Malik took hold of her hand and pulled her after him into the chamber. She chewed the skin around her fingers, hardly daring to breathe. She shouldn't be in here. The older wizards took seats at a circular table.

"Hywel, what do you make of this new magic Ermentrude and your daughter possess?" Verger asked, leaning back in the only high-backed chair.

"It seems to be a combination of wizard and witch magic. It's powerful," Hywel said, steepling his fingers.

"Can we control them?" Tyrone asked. "Or will they end up controlling us?"

"What? We can't permit... I mean..." the Chief Justice said.

"Calm yourself. I have no intention of letting those three out of our control until they disperse the Veil," Verger said, pushing a stack of papers to the side.

"With respect. They will be invaluable for research," Hywel said.

Verger turned his attention fully on Hywel. "I don't think we can risk them returning to your custody, if that's what you're suggesting. The last time I believe they all escaped, and we arrived at this situation with the Veil dominating our Realm."

"You can't lay that at my door," Hywel said, dropping his hands.

"We'll see about that. Once this situation stabilizes, I propose we appoint a committee to perform a full investigation into this entire affair and your experimentations," Tyrone said. A smile creased his face.

Myra had the feeling that there was no love lost between

Tyrone and Hywel.

"You question my loyalty?" Hywel smirked.

A flash of lightning lit the room. As the Grand Wizard intended, all the other wizards looked towards him.

Verger clasped his hands together, the ruby in his ring still glowing. "Can we please put these petty squabbles aside?"

Hywel and Tyrone glared at each other, but both nodded.

"Hywel, assemble your team to monitor the Veil. Tyrone, contact Akuna and inform her that I expect her full cooperation in this venture. Agree to whatever you need to. Lord Justice, ensure our prisoners remain contained overnight and ready to perform in the morning. That means housing them well and feeding them." Verger pushed back his chair and walked over to the door. He stopped in front of Myra and took her arm.

She pulled back, but he held her firmly. "You can add this witch to the prisoner count. I'm sure you've noticed that her magic has altered."

"What?" Hywel stepped forward. "She doesn't bear the same markings. I checked."

"You're slipping, Hywel." Verger summoned the Captain over. "Handcuff her."

Myra struggled, but guards fastened her arms behind her back.

"It's not true!" she protested, but the guards were pushing her out of the room and down the corridor. The last look she had of Malik, he was deep in conversation with Hywel. The guards pushed her again, and she jogged several steps to keep from falling. If the Grand Wizard noticed the change in her magic, then why couldn't she access it?

Chapter Twenty-Three - Wizard Palace Dungeons, Kureyamage

A guard placed his hand on a panel and the door slid aside, revealing a steep stone staircase leading down into the dungeons. Wilf went first, followed by Katryna. Ermentrude awkwardly took hold of the handrail and made slow progress down into the dungeon, followed by two guards and the Captain. The dim lighting revealed loose gravel littering the ground. Cracks ran along the walls, and water dripped from the roof.

"Wouldn't it be better if we were above ground?" Ermentrude asked. "If this collapses, who will dispel the Veil?"

The Captain continued until they arrived at a holding cell. "We reinforced this area. You will be safe until morning." He unlocked the door and stood aside.

"That's reassuring," Ermentrude said, stepping over the threshold. "Can you conjure up some chairs and cots?" She rattled the handcuffs. "I'd do it myself, but..."

The Captain hesitated.

"I'm sure you remember Grand Wizard Verger wanting us fed and rested, as the survival of the Realm depends on Wilf's performance tomorrow," she added.

The Captain's wizard ring flashed and four cots with blankets appeared. He marched out of the cell, dismissed the guards, and left without a word.

"That wizard can't count. Let's hope he sends someone with food and drink," Ermentrude said, sitting down.

The door opened again and Myra was pushed inside. She walked over to the farthest cot and collapsed onto it.

"So nice of you to join us," Ermentrude said.

"Why are you here?" Wilf asked, taking a cot.

Myra shrugged.

"Verger noticed something had altered her magic." Ermentrude examined the thin gray blanket covering the cot. "I'm

150

guessing a gift from Flayver when Myra was in the Veil."

Myra hugged her knees and turned to face the wall.

A tray materialized in the center of the room with water and bowls of stew.

"At least the service is prompt." Ermentrude gave a flick of her wrist. The handcuffs sprang open and clattered to the ground. "There are at least some advantages to this new magic," she said, reaching for a spoon.

"Would you like me to pass you food, Myra?" Katryna asked, sitting down next to her mother. Her handcuffs landed with a thump on the floor next to Ermentrude's.

"I'm not hungry," Myra said, wrapping the blanket around herself.

Wilf's handcuffs disappeared, and he stirred the stew. It seemed more liquid than meat or vegetables. "What is this?"

"Whatever you want it to be," Katryna said, swallowing a spoonful. "Mine is coconut chicken curry from that restaurant we enjoyed in Hong Kong."

Wilf stared at the bowl. The contents were mud brown, not creamy yellow.

"It's a nutrition pack. Add magic and it becomes whatever you want to eat. As long as it's some kind of liquid content," she said.

Wilf peeked into her bowl. It looked like curry.

"It can also disappear if you add too much magic," Ermentrude said.

In that case, he'd eat whatever it was. He was too hungry to risk changing it. After the first bite, he decided he was eating beef stew, and that was fine with him. He scraped the bowl clean and placed it back on the tray.

Myra's cot squeaked; her entire body trembled. Wilf glanced over at Ermentrude, but her concerned look didn't reassure him.

"She's suffering," Katryna said, twisting her wizard ring around her finger.

"It's her own fault," Wilf said. The words sounded harsher than he'd meant.

"She's had a tough time," Ermentrude said, wrapping her blanket around her shoulders.

"You believe she didn't kill my father, don't you?" Wilf said, sitting down next to Katryna.

"They used her. First her mother, then Hywel. Even Seldan used her to gain leadership of the spy ring," Ermentrude said.

"What happened to Seldan?" Katryna shuddered.

"Incarceration. She won't be released in a Normal's lifespan," Ermentrude said, yawning. Black shadows spread under her eyes.

"Where is she being held?" Wilf asked.

Ermentrude stroked the hairs on her chin. "I'm not sure. Degula has always taken care of security matters."

Wilf's leg bumped into Katryna's and he let it rest there. He reached for her hand but stopped. He wasn't sure of her reaction.

Ermentrude stifled another yawn. "We should focus on how to escape."

"I don't suppose you have another portal hidden anywhere?" Wilf said, resting his hand on the edge of the cot. He let his little finger touch Katryna's. She didn't move her hand away.

"Unfortunately not, and these guards won't be friendly and find us a secret exit," Ermentrude said.

A sigh came from Myra, and a puff of blue smoke rose from her lips.

The cloud spread out over the ceiling. Wilf sprang up off his cot.

"She's leaking magic!" Katryna said.

The cloud hovered and then disappeared. "She'll need watching through the night," Ermentrude said, rubbing her eyes and rising from the cot.

"I don't understand. Myra's always been in control of her magic," Wilf said.

"That was before she started taking vast quantities of elixir and ran into Flayver."

Katryna sat next to Myra. "I'll monitor her. I owe her for helping me escape this palace when Hywel held us. She could have left me," Katryna said, pulling the blanket over Myra's shoulders.

"You seem to have the best control over magic. I've no objections to you taking the first vigil." Ermentrude lay back down on the cot, and the blanket wrapped itself around her. "I could get used to no more wiggling fingers to perform magic."

Wilf kicked the handcuffs at his feet. "These were supposed to stop us being able to use magic." He concentrated on the shackles. His wizard ring flared and the cuffs vanished. "Our magic is stronger." He stood by the door and placed his ringed hand on the lock, but it remained closed and bolted.

"It was worth a try," Ermentrude said, lying back down. "I suggest you get some sleep instead of wasting energy. You're on the next watch." An eye mask appeared on her face and she turned onto her side, away from them.

Wilf sat down on his cot. "Do you want me to stay up with you?"

Katryna shook her head. "You sleep. I'll wake you in a few hours."

He pulled the blanket up over his chin. He'd no intention of sleeping and leaving Katryna to cope alone. Myra couldn't be trusted. He wouldn't be surprised if they'd placed her in the cell to spy on them and this was all an act.

"Wilf! Wake up." Katryna shook him.

"What?" He opened his eyes and light filled the cell. So much for staying awake. He stumbled out of the blanket and let it fall to the ground. He rubbed his eyes.

"I need help to subdue Myra's magic." Katryna continued to shake him.

"I'm coming," he said, shielding his eyes. The intense light made it difficult to see.

Katryna pulled on his arm.

"All right!" He followed her over to Myra. Her entire body shone with a blue light. "Shouldn't we wake Ermentrude?"

"I know what to do, but I need your help," Katryna said, kneeling next to Myra's cot.

"You've seen another witch in this condition?"

"I've studied it." Katryna grabbed hold of his hand and pulled him down next to her. "We each need to hold one of Myra's hands and then let the magic flow through us in a controlled release."

He shook his head. "Are you insane? I can barely control my magic."

Katryna smiled. "You can do this."

"You've more faith in me than I do," he said, stretching out his arm.

Katryna took Myra's left hand. "Focus the magic on the door. It might blast through it."

Wilf took hold of Myra's right hand, noticing the blue tinge of her skin. He sucked in a breath and allowed the power and heat of Myra's magic to flow into him. It coiled around him, squeezing at his own connection to the Source. He pushed at the stream, forcing it through his body and out of his fingers. He raised his arm and pointed, mimicking Katryna. The prison door and wall glowed red and shimmered.

Ermentrude sat up. "Stop! They will have spells warding the door."

Sparks flew around the cell, bouncing off the walls, ceiling, and floor. Katryna and Wilf tried to drop Myra's hands, but she clung to them. Her eyelids flew open, but only the whites of her eyes were visible. Her head rolled from side to side as she moaned.

"Myra!" Wilf used his other hand in an attempt to free himself.

Ermentrude came over to the bed and shook Myra. "It's no use. Her magic has total control of her." Ermentrude ducked as a massive ball of frizzing magic aimed for her head. "I suggest you both aim at the ceiling, instead of the door."

Wilf and Katryna raised their arms, and a shimmering white blanket of magic appeared across the ceiling. The door and walls kept their original shape and form.

"Doesn't that remind you of the Veil?" Sweat dripped down Wilf's face.

"Do you think Flayver used Myra to carry the spell into the palace?" Katryna asked.

"That would explain why Myra has lost access to her magic." Ermentrude studied the haze now oozing down the walls. It spread out like ivy over bricks, searching for cracks and crevices. "It will soon fill this entire room."

"Then what?" Wilf pulled at his hand , but Myra's fingers clasped tighter. He looked from Katryna to Ermentrude, but both witches continued to stare at the mist. It reached the floor and spread across it. "Ermentrude! You created this spell."

"This isn't the same spell. I could remind you that this is the spell you corrupted, but I won't bring that up because it's not helpful," Ermentrude said, searching in her pocket. "Where is that bag hiding now?" She thrust her arm in up to the elbow and rummaged around. "Ah! There you are." She pulled the red bag out and set it on the cot.

"What are you searching for?" Wilf asked. His knees hurt and Katryna had flopped to her side. "I don't know how much longer I can hold my arm straight up like this."

Ermentrude pulled a box from her bag. An amethyst the size of a blackbird's egg occupied the center. Runes and numbers covered the rest of the lid. Ermentrude placed her hand on the top. The stone flickered several times before it radiated a bright purple glow. "That's a blessing. I thought it wouldn't recognize me." A click and scrape of metal sounded before the lid sprang open. Ermentrude pulled out three talismans.

"I still have…" Wilf patted his chest with his other hand. "When did you take them?"

"I hid them in here after we arrived in Kureyamage. Didn't want them falling into the wrong hands," she said, placing one around her own neck, then Katryna's, and finally Wilf's.

"Do you think these will work? Aren't they linked to witch magic, which you might remember none of us have?" Wilf said, supporting his elbow on the cot.

"I'm willing to hear if you have a better plan," Ermentrude said, closing the box lid with a bang.

Myra uttered a deep sigh and released Wilf and Katryna. She blinked several times and then sat up. "What's going on?"

Wilf eased up and helped Katryna to her feet. He guided her over to a cot and then collapsed down next to her.

"Can you access your magic now?" Ermentrude said, placing the box back in her bag.

Myra's brow furrowed for a minute or two. "Yes," she said.

"That's nice. Can you control the spell?" Ermentrude waved her hand.

Myra glanced around the room. Her face scrunched. "I did this?"

Wilf and Katryna nodded.

"Are you connected to this mist?" Ermentrude spoke in a sharp tone.

Myra jumped and then glared at the older witch.

"I'm serious. Are you in control of this spell?" Ermentrude said, towering over Myra.

"It's nothing to do with me!" Myra edged away.

Katryna trembled, and Wilf took hold of her hand. She moved closer.

"We think Flayver used you to bring the spell into the palace," she told Myra. "That's why you couldn't access your magic."

The mist moved around the room. Tendrils formed and began probing the walls and floor.

"What's it doing?" Katryna asked.

"I think it's searching for cracks," Wilf said. One tendril disappeared into a small hole in the mortar between two bricks. The strand elongated and fed its way into the wall. "I don't think that escape route will work for us," Wilf continued. The mist probed a crack in the wall, then flowed through it until the last strand disappeared.

They sat in silence for several minutes. The only sound was the dripping of water. Ermentrude's feet scraped on the floor as she collected her bag and strode back to her cot. She lay down and pulled the blanket up to her neck. "Good, the excitement's over. I suggest we all get some sleep. I believe tomorrow will be a very interesting day." Her eye mask reappeared and she began to snore.

Wilf realized he was still holding Katryna's hand when she lay down. He stood hovering over her, then bent to kiss her cheek. She smiled, and a slight glow spread through him as he closed his eyes, surrendering to sleep.

Chapter Twenty-Four - Wizard Palace Dungeons, Kureyamage

The clink of keys and the turning of the lock roused Myra from sleep. She'd spent the night tossing and turning after the episode with the Veil spell. Memories of the mist kept startling her awake to stare at the crack where it had disappeared. One minute she was burning hot and she would toss the blanket off the cot; the next, her teeth chattered and she'd search for the blanket again. Now her body ached and her eyes felt as if they were being stuck with pins. She rubbed her eyes.

Malik and the Captain of the guards stood in the doorway.

"Let's go," the Captain said.

Malik took Myra's arm to help her stand. "You look terrible," he said. "I've brought you a gift." He opened his palm to reveal three vials. "These should help."

"Thanks," Myra said, sliding the vials into her pocket. She was happy to see that her hands were no longer blue.

"Don't you want one now?" Malik said, standing in front of her to block anyone else from seeing her.

"No," she said, trying to dodge around him.

He caught hold of her arm and squeezed. "I think it's best if you do. You'll need it."

"Come along, Myra. We shouldn't keep the nice Captain waiting," Ermentrude interrupted, stepping around Malik to Myra's side.

Malik released Myra's arm, frowning. Ermentrude linked arms with Myra and helped her out of the cell.

"Keep these for me," Myra said, slipping the vials into Ermentrude's hand. The other witch nodded and placed them in her pocket.

In the corridor, the guards fell into formation around Wilf, Katryna, and Ermentrude.

"Not you," the Captain said, nodding to Malik.

"Thank you, Captain," Malik said, taking Myra's arm again.

Myra's stomach sank as she watched them march away. She edged away from Malik, not wanting him to touch her. What had she seen in him?

"I've negotiated with Hywel and he's agreed to place you under my protection."

She was only half listening to Malik. Fatigue overcame her, but for the first morning in a long time, she no longer despaired.

"As soon as they take the Veil down, we'll take a portal and escape to Hong Kong." Malik hugged her. Her skin prickled and she had to fight to keep from grimacing.

"I don't understand," she said. Her head buzzed. Perhaps she should take a vial. She shook her head. No. She didn't need the drug messing with her thoughts. Too late anyway, she thought. Ermentrude had disappeared around the corner with the guards.

"We can survive together, away from this Realm." Malik held her shoulders and forced her to look at him. "We'll head back to the workshops. Since the biome magic isn't useable, Hywel set up a system to siphon off magical energy from the Source into the Hong Kong storage tanks." He checked the corridor and then spoke fast. "I'll make sure a tank works with a special code that only I know. One tank of magic should last me years. I'll have a constant source of energy when everyone else's is being rationed. We'll live like supreme beings in a non-magical realm."

"Steal from the Wizard Council?" Myra said. He was talking nonsense.

His eyes were bright enough to light the corridor. Was Malik taking elixir? It was insane to try what he'd proposed. They'd be caught. She wasn't going to risk death because of him. At the first opportunity she'd ditch him.

"Now that your magic's altered, you'll be able to access and use the corrupted magic in the biome. You won't have a problem." He grabbed her hand and set off at a fast pace down the corridor. When they reached the main floor, he produced a pass from his pocket and put it around her neck. She picked up the laminated badge in her other hand. There was a snap and a feeling of cold metal around her wrist. She pulled her hand, but he tightened his hold.

"A bracelet." She yanked her hand harder and freed it.

"I thought you'd be pleased." Malik sounded hurt. "Hywel said you've always wanted one."

She examined the bracelet. The name "Kamder" etched in green letters, glowed. "But how can it have your name on it? We're not bound to each other. There's been no ritual." Her throat tightened, holding in a scream. She was tied to him.

"Hywel is your guardian. Didn't you know? Your mother signed you and Thiemus over to him when you were young. His permission is all that's needed. I can make you happy — you'll have all the magic you need." His eyes searched her face.

"It's a surprise. I wasn't expecting this," she said. How could this be happening to her? She belonged to Malik?

He leaned in to kiss her, but she bent her head, pretending to examine the bracelet once more.

"Let's move," he said, pulling her forward and out of the palace. They walked in silence through the busy streets, back to the Tower, and into the workshops. He'd only briefly let go of her hand when it had been impossible for them to negotiate the narrow staircase.

She sank down into the nearest chair when they entered the workshop, and Malik finally released her.

"What's she doing here?" Thiemus spun around in his chair.

"That's none of your concern," Malik said. "Myra, why don't you stay here and rest while I retrieve something from another workshop. I won't be long."

Myra collected a glass of water, aware that Thiemus hadn't taken his eyes off her.

"What?" she said, returning to her chair.

"He's dangerous," Thiemus said.

Myra let out a bark of laughter. "Thanks for your concern." She held up her arm to display the bracelet. "But your warning is too late. Hywel traded me."

"He gave you to Malik?" Thiemus's chair rocked backwards.

"How long have you known that Hywel is our guardian?" Myra spat the words at her brother.

"After Griselda dumped me here. Hywel showed me the contract so I'd know he was legally in charge of my life." Thiemus was angry, too.

"Yes, well. I had no idea Hywel could give me to whomever he decided," Myra said, slumping back in the chair.

"It's not so bad, unless you've been stupid enough to take part in a bonding ritual with him."

Myra shuddered. "No way."

A ping came from Thiemus's terminal and he swung around.

"But you're my brother and of legal age. Don't you have a say in what happens to me?"

"I'm not eighteen until next week. Then I could have claimed you. If I'd wanted to." Thiemus continued tapping at the keyboard. Dials and charts appeared and disappeared as he flicked through screens. "As Malik has claimed you, I can't help you —

you're under his protection now."

"This is a disaster. I won't spend the rest of my life shackled to Malik." Myra spun the bracelet around her wrist.

"After the witches' demonstrations caused problems in Kureyamage, the Council decided bracelets were the best form of control. You can blame this on Ermentrude and her friends."

The door swung open and Malik entered carrying a box of cables.

"What are those for?" Thiemus asked.

"I need to make a few adjustments," Malik said, dumping the box next to his terminal. "Don't you have some potions to brew?"

"Hywel told me to monitor the flow of magical energy in the storage tanks. It'll be the only uncorrupted magic in the Real World." Thiemus rolled his chair to another screen.

"But now that I'm here you don't have to, do you?" Malik said.

Thiemus looked as if he'd argue, but then he stood. "I suppose not." He didn't sound convinced, but he left the room.

Malik waved his hand, and the door slammed shut. "Here, you can help me," he said, holding out a cable to her. She pushed out of the chair and grasped the end. "What am I supposed to do with this?"

"Plug it into that terminal. The third port from the right." Malik reached around the back of his own terminal and plugged in the other end. He pulled up a chair and started punching keys. "Excellent. There's one storage tank at full capacity. Now I just need to release this code into the live system." An install bar's progression flashed across the screen. "The program will take about an hour to install, but we don't have to babysit it. Once it's uploaded, the system will reboot and the program will self-start." He came over to her and wrapped his arms around her waist, pulling her in for a hug. He kissed her and she hid her revulsion. She couldn't let him know how she really felt, not yet.

"I think it's time we left here. I can secure the door so that idiot brother of yours can't interfere. I think we should watch your stepbrother's performance."

"We're going back to the palace?" Myra couldn't believe he'd drag her back there. She swallowed her panic.

"There's a portal in the palace we can use as soon as the Veil releases its hold on the Thermals. Then we're out of here," Malik said, kissing her again.

She couldn't breathe. Everything was happening too quickly. She took a step backwards when he released her. She would pretend she was still into him until she could escape.

"Let's go," he said, grabbing her hand and rushing them up the stairs and back down the hill. Before she had time to recover her senses, they were back at the palace.

"We can go up to the gallery," Malik said, opening a door within the paneling.

"When did you find this?" Myra said.

"I saw Hywel use it a few times," he said, producing a light globe. "We need to be silent, as they can hear every sound we make in the council chamber. It should be quite the show watching Wilf dissolve the Veil spell."

Malik led the way along the dark, dusty space. Cross struts blocked the way and Myra had to climb over them. Cobwebs hung low, and she cringed whenever a strand touched her face or neck. Visions of the Veil seeping into the wall kept invading her thoughts. Her hands and legs shook as they crept along.

She had her magic again, but did she trust she could use it? There was a nagging suspicion that if the time came when she needed to defend herself, it might refuse to obey her commands. Lost in her own thoughts, she didn't notice when Malik stopped until she bumped into him.

"Careful," Malik whispered. He indicated a grate overhead. "We can see and hear from there." He floated up and beckoned Myra to follow.

Would her magic work? She felt a surge of energy as she pointed her fingers at the ground and floated up to join him. Malik smiled when she stopped beside him.

Myra peered into the council chamber. Wilf, Katryna, and Ermentrude stood on a raised platform, linked by long cables to a terminal.

"What are we waiting for?" Grand Wizard Verger asked.

"Malik should be here any minute. I need him to work the machine," Hywel said, turning his head towards the door.

Myra glanced at Malik.

"Frog's entrails! I'd better go. You stay here," Malik said, floating back to the ground. He took the globe and hurried back down the passage, plunging Myra into darkness except for a slit of light coming from the grate. She tried not to think of spiders or the Veil. She returned her focus back to the chamber.

"Why didn't you bring your technician with you?" Tyrone leaned forward in his chair and glared at Hywel.

"Sorry I'm late," Malik said, bursting through the door. He marched over to the terminal and turned it on.

"Can we now proceed?" Verger asked.

"As soon as it completes the boot-up sequence," Malik said, typing furiously.

"This should have commenced before you called us to the chamber. I'm not used to being kept waiting by junior wizards," the Chief Justice said.

C. B. Lyall

Malik bent his head over the keyboard. "All ready," he said.

The cable from the terminal to Wilf pulsed with red light. Myra watched as Wilf braced and sucked in a breath. He turned to Katryna and gave her a weak smile. Then Katryna gasped as her cable pulsed. Myra was glad that Ermentrude's glare hadn't been sent in her direction.

There was a sudden pounding on the door and the Captain burst in.

"Explain the meaning of this interruption, Captain!" Verger said.

"The Veil has surrounded the palace, Your Highness!" the Captain said, his voice trembling. "Head Witch Akuna messaged to say the Veil has enclosed their council building, too."

"We'll soon have that down," the Chief Justice said, shaking his fist.

Myra felt an icy chill sliding up her leg and dropped to the floor.

"What was that?" Tyrone said. "There's someone in the wall, Captain."

The Veil continued to climb up from the floor. Myra's knees were now completely shrouded in mist. A light shone into the corridor from an opening several feet away. The Captain's head appeared, and a globe bobbed towards her.

"Come out of there!" he shouted.

Myra glanced down the corridor towards the other door, but a shadow stood in the opening. They'd surrounded her. The Veil shrank away. She sighed and stumbled along the corridor to the Captain.

He grabbed hold of her arm and dragged her into the chamber. "You!" he said. "It's the other prisoner, Your Highness."

Myra glanced over at Malik, but he ignored her and kept monitoring the screen.

"Glad you could join us. Put her with the others," Verger said.

Myra struggled, but a guard pulled her over to stand next to Ermentrude. She tripped, bumping into the older witch. "The walls have more than spiders in them," she whispered.

Ermentrude gave a slight nod.

The guard jerked Myra away and picked up a cable. He attached the five prongs to the ends of her fingers. The cable pulsed and Myra gasped as sharp needles extended into her fingertips.

"They're all connected to the controller," Malik said.

Hywel stepped in front of Ermentrude. "Use the boy and bring down the spell."

Ermentrude gave a bark of laughter. "Not a chance."

"Increase the flow to Katryna," Hywel said, staring straight at Ermentrude.

Katryna gave a cry and tried to pull her hand away.

"That's your own daughter!" Ermentrude said, narrowing her eyes.

"Then stop her suffering. It's within your power," Hywel said, taking a step closer. "This is all your fault. You brought this on when you turned traitor and created that spell."

"You don't need Ermentrude. I can do it alone. Only stop hurting Katryna," Wilf said. Sweat stood out on his forehead and the muscles bulged on his forearms.

"Reduce the flow to Katryna," Hywel said. "You have two minutes to prove you have the control."

Wilf closed his eyes, and a silence fell on the chamber.

Chapter Twenty-Five - Wizard Palace, Council Chamber, Kureyamage

Wilf let his mind go blank and inhaled. He reached out through his magic, searching for the connection to the Source. A wave of calm spread through him and he opened his eyes.

"I've made the connection," he said.

"Start collapsing the spell. Reduce the flow of power to it," Hywel said, waving his arms.

"He's absorbing a lot of power," Malik said, looking up from his screen. "I don't know how he can hold that much."

Grand Wizard Verger strode across the room until he could peer at the terminal. "Malik's right, Wilf is absorbing the magic."

Hywel stepped over. "That's not possible."

"I'd suggest lowering the feed," Verger said, holding onto the back of Malik's chair.

"I'm trying to, but the terminal isn't responding," Malik said, pressing keys. The dial in the corner of the screen continued to rise.

"Get out of my way," Hywel said, pushing Malik from the chair and punching some keys. It was futile. "Remove the cable," he ordered.

Malik yanked the cable out of the terminal. Katryna staggered and Ermentrude ripped the needles out of her fingertips and ran to support her daughter. The needles floated out of Wilf's fingers and flew across the room at Hywel.

The wizard deflected them at the last minute. "That shouldn't be possible."

"Stop him!" the Chief Justice said, letting his chair crash to the floor as he stood.

Malik helped Myra remove the needles from her hands. "Look," he said, his voice trembling. Mist seeped into the room, covering the walls and creeping along the floor and ceiling.

"Guards, form a shield around us!" Verger shouted.

The Veil pushed towards Wilf.

"Do something." The Chief Justice glared at Hywel.

"What do you suggest?" Hywel said, moving closer to Wilf.

"I'm not sure it's such an excellent idea being this close to Wilf," Ermentrude said. She took Katryna's arm. "See if you can reach him."

"You broke the bond, remember," Katryna said.

"This isn't the time for recriminations. Try it!" Ermentrude ordered.

Katryna laid her hand on Wilf's arm. The golden vein running up her arm pulsed. "Wilf, can you hear me?"

He nodded.

"You're pulling too much power from the Source." She pulled at her arm. "Wilf, please let me go." She held her wrist with her other hand and pulled harder. "I'm stuck."

Hywel grabbed her waist and pulled.

Wilf closed his eyes. When he opened them again, he could see Katryna. "The energy is draining away." Tears appeared in his eyes. "This Realm is dying."

"Don't be ridiculous. Release your connection and the drain will stop," Tyrone said, not taking his eyes off the advancing mist.

"Wilf, can you sense the Veil?" Verger asked.

"It is part of the Source," Wilf said, sounding like he was still in a trance.

"Then stop it," Hywel said.

The Veil held its position outside a ten-foot circle surrounding the group. Wilf took hold of Katryna's hand and lifted it off his arm. "I could connect with you again briefly," he said, smiling.

She gasped. "How is that possible?"

"I don't know," Wilf said.

"That's enough. If you can control the Veil, you can take it down. What are you waiting for?" the Chief Justice asked.

"I'm not sure it's as simple as that," Ermentrude said, moving closer to Wilf and Katryna.

"The Veil is part of the Source," Wilf repeated. He had to make Ermentrude understand, but he didn't know how to explain it. When he closed his eyes, there was a swirling mass of energy coming to him from his attachment to the Source, but he could hear an off-pitch whine sounding from outside. The second he opened his eyes the noise disappeared, but he sensed that it came from the Veil.

Flayver appeared, her black gown remaining half submerged and combined with the Veil. "You mustn't try to break the spell. It's not yet time," she said. Her hair streamed behind her as if blown by a breeze.

"Another witch. Where are they all coming from?" The Chief Justice poked the Captain in the chest. "You'll have a lot to answer for. The security around the palace is substandard. When this is over I'll demand a full investigation."

"She's a guardian," Ermentrude said. "Nice of you to join us, Flayver."

"The time isn't right. You must stop the connection," Flayver said.

"That's what we're attempting to do!" Hywel told her.

A second guardian materialized on the room's opposite side. "Don't listen to Flayver. She's corrupt. She killed my sister and took her place," Betrine said, wringing her hands. A wail filled the room.

"The Source created me because of the imbalance in the Realm," Flayver said.

"You kill wizards and witches with your tendrils. I'm the true guardian. You are corruption." Betrine waved her hand towards Flayver. The wailing became louder.

"The Veil belongs to the Source. It is you who is rogue magic," Flayver said, extending her hand. Tendrils wrapped around Betrine's body, pulling her down into the mist.

"Don't let her do this to me!" Betrine screamed, but the Veil dragged her inside.

"What are you going to do with Betrine?" Ermentrude said, wrapping a protective arm around Katryna.

"She is no longer. Her duty has ended," Flayver said. Tendrils broke free and pushed against the edges of the circle. A hissing sound came from them and sparks flew, but the mist couldn't advance.

"You formed a barrier?" Katryna said. She went to touch Wilf, but stopped before she made contact.

"I'm not sure how long I can maintain it," Wilf said. His voice shook.

"It's all right. You are the link to the Source," Flayver said, smiling.

"What is she talking about?" the Chief Justice said.

"It might not have been a splendid idea linking Wilf up to that machine of yours," Ermentrude said, looking at Hywel.

Wilf let their voices fade. He found it hard to concentrate on holding back the Veil with all this bickering and extending theories. He pushed against the spell and for the first time its resistance faltered. He sent a stream of energy at Flayver. She brought up her hands and blocked the blast. He increased the flow and sent a surge of power. Flayver staggered back several steps. The mist yielded more ground, circling the guardian and the edges of the room.

"Stop. It joins us," Flayver said, pushing back against his power. "You need me."

"It's working," Katryna said, her voice breaking through Wilf's concentration.

Flayver's knees buckled under the attack, and she slumped to the ground. The mist covered the lower portion of her body. Wilf sent a barrage of power at the guardian.

"It's not time," she whimpered, sinking lower until only her fingertips were visible. Then she disappeared. A high-pitched whine pierced the room. The mist retreated back into the walls, leaving the room free from the Veil spell.

Wilf collapsed to the ground. Trickles of blood ran down his fingers. His vision blurred and then cleared.

Katryna dropped to the floor next to him. "Are you all right?"

"I think so," he said. His chest heaved. He felt euphoric, as if he'd scored the winning goal of the championship.

He'd controlled his magic.

The Captain ran to the chamber door and threw it open. "The spell has pulled back out of the palace!"

"Check the rest of the city," Verger said, helping Wilf to his feet. "That was an impressive display of power."

The building shook and the floor trembled.

"Take cover!" the Captain shouted.

Everyone dove under tables and benches. There was a rumble, followed by a tear and popping. The ceiling came crashing down, smashing the terminal and platforms. A cloud of dust rose into the air.

Myra and Katryna huddled on either side of Wilf. Malik crawled his way across the room.

"We should leave," he said, pulling roughly on Myra's arm.

"That's an excellent idea. We should all get out of this building," Wilf said, helping Katryna to her feet.

Ermentrude brushed dust off her shirt and came out from under the desk she'd shared with Grand Wizard Verger. "It's safer to remain here until the tremors cease," she said.

"I agree," Verger said.

The floor rippled under Wilf when the building shook again. Katryna's body trembled next to him. He put his arm around her and she snuggled into him.

Paneling clattered and fell from the walls. A large thud reverberated from behind the dais. The door hiding the secret passage buckled in and the doorframe collapsed.

"How long should we wait?" Katryna asked.

"You can stay here as long as you want, but I won't be buried here." The Chief Justice clambered over the dais and stumbled across the room. As he pulled open the Council Chamber's door there was a deafening crack. The door splintered and fell. The Chief Justice's scream died when he disappeared under the broken wooden door.

"Dig him out," Tyrone shouted at the soldiers. They pointed their fingers, but nothing happened. They ran forward, tearing at the plaster and wood with their hands.

"The magic doesn't appear to be working," the Captain said, staring at the dull stone in his ring.

"He's right," Verger said. He turned to Wilf. "Can you connect with the Source?"

"There's no magic," Hywel, Tyrone, and Malik said, almost together. They stared at Wilf.

"I have contact, but it's very faint," Ermentrude said. "Wilf?"

"It's the same for me," he said.

Katryna nodded. "I couldn't light a globe with the amount I can hold."

The soldiers pulled the Chief Justice's body out of the rubble and placed it on a table.

"We should leave now," Ermentrude said, stepping around a broken chair. "The tremors seem to have ceased."

Wilf helped Katryna clamber over the broken debris and out of the room. An eerie silence filled the deserted hall, though he'd expected the place to be full of panicked witches and wizards.

The Captain and his soldiers formed a protective detail around the group as they made their way out of the palace.

"Where is everyone?" Wilf asked. It wasn't only that the palace was devoid of anyone. The streets were abandoned, too. Were they the only survivors? He shivered. It was too horrible to contemplate. They must have escaped.

"We should head for the bunker. We'll be able to monitor the scale of the earthquake and also any traces of the Veil," Tyrone said, sidling up to Grand Wizard Verger.

Verger nodded and trudged towards a steel door in the hillside.

Wilf walked next to Ermentrude. "Doesn't it strike you as strange that everywhere seems deserted?"

"Once we're inside the bunker, I'm hoping we can discover where everyone is hiding," Ermentrude answered, striding up the hill.

Hywel placed his hand on a panel, and then Verger stepped forward, pulling out a seal on a chain around his neck. He placed it on the panel and the door lowered into a ramp.

Verger and Councilman Tyrone entered. Hywel stood in the entrance and blocked the way. "Captain, it isn't appropriate that we allow the Witch Wakefield to enter."

"Allow everyone, Hywel," Verger called from within the bunker.

Clenching his fists, Hywel stomped down the corridor after the Grand Wizard.

Ermentrude smiled and stepped into the bunker. "This was a well-kept secret until now."

They filed down a sloping corridor until they reached a large room filled with screens and desks at one end and a wizard's workshop at the other. Five wizards stopped working and bowed to the Grand Wizard.

"How much backup magic is there?" Verger asked.

"Two cylinders. A three-day supply," a technician said.

"Quite the setup you have here," Ermentrude said, settling down at a desk.

"Touch nothing," Hywel said.

Ermentrude spread her fingers on the desk and smiled.

"Do we have damage reports?" Tyrone asked, walking over to a wizard.

The operator brought up several screens for him to look at.

"Seems bad," Tyrone said. "Half the city has fallen, but the Veil has left Kureyamage. In fact, we have no reported sightings of it. The road into Mathowytch is open."

"Captain, advise the guard to proceed into Mathowytch and secure the city, but be careful in case there are any more earthquakes," Verger said.

The Captain started barking orders into a communication mirror.

"Congratulations. You've destroyed the Veil," Malik said, slapping Wilf on the back. "Although I'm not sure the outcome will be the best for the Realm."

"What do you mean?" Wilf said.

Malik grinned and walked away.

"I don't like that wizard," Katryna said, gripping the back of her mother's chair.

"My apologies, Your Highness, but I can't raise the outside guards," the Captain said. His cheeks were flushed.

Malik caught hold of Myra's arm and pulled her to one side. He bent in close.

"That's impossible," Verger said, coming to stand next to the communication mirror.

"Malik seems very keen on Myra. He hardly lets her out of his sight," Wilf said, pushing his hands deep into his pockets.

"Your Highness, we seem to be the only occupants of the Realm," the Captain said, tapping combinations of runes.

"Myra is wearing Malik's bracelet," Ermentrude said, rolling her chair closer.

"What?" Wilf and Katryna said together.

"When did that happen?" Katryna said.

"Must have been recent. She wasn't wearing it in the cell," Ermentrude said, sliding open a drawer and peering in.

"Wasn't he supplying her with elixir?" Wilf asked.

"He brought her some to the cell, but she gave it to me," Ermentrude said, closing one drawer and opening another. "We'd better watch him. He seemed very pleased that we were brought down here."

"Captain, that is a ridiculous assumption," Tyrone shouted as he joined the Grand Wizard at the communications mirror.

Katryna's hand brushed Wilf's, and he felt an electrical charge shoot up his arm. "Did you feel that?"

She nodded. "This is weird." She rolled up her sleeve. The golden vein had disappeared.

Malik was drawing Myra towards a corridor at the end of the room.

"I think we should follow Myra," Wilf said, nudging Katryna.

"I'll stay here and monitor Hywel," Ermentrude said. She grabbed hold of Wilf's arm. "Don't take any risks."

"Of course not," Wilf said, hurrying along the edge of the room. He and Katryna ran into the corridor.

C. B. Lyall

Chapter Twenty-Six - The Command
Bunker, Kureyamage

A pinprick of light from Malik's globe sent elongated
shadows flickering on the tunnel's concrete walls.
The floor sloped downward. Wilf jogged after Malik
and Myra, with Katryna keeping pace at his side.

The light vanished, and he stumbled over a rock. "We'll have
to chance some light," he said.

A globe appeared in Katryna's hand, its dim light only bright
enough to warn of hazards on the floor. Wilf sped on and
Katryna followed. She bent over, sucking in air when he stopped.
He peered around the corner. A wooden portal stood at the end
of the corridor.

"They're leaving," he said, stepping out. Katryna tried to grab
his sleeve, but he pulled his arm out of reach. He walked down
the slope.

"Were you hoping to join us?" Malik asked, coming around
the side of the portal. He placed his hand on a panel. The door
slid open and he pushed Myra inside. "Sorry, but we're not taking
passengers."

"Where are you going?" Katryna asked.

"That's none of your concern," Malik said, blocking the
entrance.

"What about Myra? Does she want to go with you?" Wilf
said, taking several steps closer.

"Of course she does," Malik said, his eyes flicking from Wilf
to Katryna.

"I need to hear her say it," Wilf said.

Wilf knew that Myra had always wanted to return and live in
the Magical Realm. He'd had to sit through numerous lectures
about why they should move to Kureyamage. She wouldn't
abandon her dream so easily. This seemed more about what Malik
wanted.

170

"I want to go," Myra said, peering around Malik.

"There, you heard her. Now step aside." Malik gave Wilf a shove. Wilf raised his hand, pointing his fingers at the other wizard.

"Are you going to blast me?" Malik said, sneering at Wilf. "Try it!"

Wilf reached for his magic, but the ring remained dull. It reminded him of how it felt wearing the handcuffs in the palace dungeon. Then he'd redirected the flow, pushed through the barrier. It had taken him some time to solve that puzzle. Time he now didn't have.

"What's happening?" Katryna said. She had her own hand extended, but no ball of energy materialized.

"There's a force field in the bunker preventing large surges of energy. You can't fire inside here, whatever magic you possess." Malik reached inside the portal and pulled out a shotgun. "Unless you have one of these. An invention I've being longing for the opportunity to use."

Wilf stepped in front of Katryna. "How are you going to use the portal if there's no surge of magic allowed?"

Malik pulled out an access card on a chain. "I have one of these. A pass to use the portal." He jerked the barrel of the gun at them. "Now, move away from here. This uses cartridges filled with energy blasts."

Katryna pulled on Wilf's arm, urging him backwards. He resisted at first, but then took several steps.

"That's right. Myra, connect with the portal," Malik said, inching towards the door.

Katryna kept her hold on Wilf. He braced, ready to jump forward when he saw an opening.

"I can't. The Source isn't responding," Myra called from inside the portal.

A smile slid across Malik's face, but his eyes remained cold. "We have room for passengers after all." He waved the gun at them, inviting them in.

"No way I'm helping you," Wilf said, crossing his arms. He'd been prepared to fight Malik, but relief that he didn't have to flooded through him.

"I'm offering to bring Katryna along for you. I could leave her here. So either you play nice and get inside, or I'll set this to stun and take you anyway," Malik said.

"You won't. You need me conscious to connect to the portal," Wilf said. If he kept Malik talking perhaps the Captain would wonder what had happened to them and come looking.

Malik sneered. "I can shoot her. She's not needed." He pointed the gun at Katryna and moved a switch on the side.

"And risk shooting me," Wilf said, stepping in front of Katryna.

"This is no Normal's gun. The cartridges are deadly accurate," Malik said, leveling the gun at Katryna's head.

"Do as he says!" Katryna bent close to whisper, "If Malik takes us with him, then at least we might rescue Myra later. She can't be going willingly."

Wilf sighed. "All right." He took her hand in his and walked to the portal. Malik stepped aside but kept the gun trained on them until they were inside.

Myra was curled up on a bench. Malik waved for Wilf and Katryna to sit on the other side. The portal door slammed shut.

"Make the connection," Malik said, placing a hand on Myra's knee.

Wilf hesitated, then spread his fingers over the globe. He sucked in air as the spikes of energy connected with his fingertips. "Where are we going?"

"Your home city, Hong Kong," Malik said, placing the keycard into a slot on the globe's pedestal.

"Myra, are you sure you want to return?" Wilf asked.

"We're together. She goes where I go," Malik said, patting her knee. "Don't you, babe?"

Myra nodded and turned her head to the blank wall.

"The Thermals aren't letting anyone in or out. How are we supposed to get to Hong Kong?" Wilf said. Energy flowed through his fingers. He wasn't sure how much magic he still possessed after taking down the Veil.

"We'll get through with the Veil gone," Malik said. An alarm sounded inside the portal. "Envisage the route and get us out of here."

The wall became a window. Outside, a single track appeared before them. The portal gave a shudder and then lurched forward.

"Speed it up," Malik snapped.

The portal accelerated as if Wilf had hit the gas pedal, and it sped along the horizontal track.

Myra hunched further into the corner. Malik handed her a vial. "Here, you'll need this," he said.

"Don't," Katryna said, reaching out, trying to touch Myra's arm.

Myra twisted away. "Don't tell me what to do," she said, taking the vial. She turned into the corner and uncorked it.

"See, babe, I'll always be here to take care of you," Malik said, holding out his arm for her to lean into him. She shuffled along the bench and he rested his arm around her shoulders.

The portal tipped. "Keep your mind on the route." Malik snapped his fingers at Wilf. "Tell him where we should land,

Myra."

"At the end of Tai Wang Street, next to the temple," she said.

Wilf glanced at Katryna. He'd never seen his stepsister like this, meek and subservient. What had Malik done to her? Or was this a role she was playing until she could break free?

"Won't there be a bunch of angry witches around there?" Malik asked Myra.

"They'll all be inside the store, freaking about the loss of the Veil," Myra said, sitting straighter.

Wilf focused on the track. Streaks of neon light streamed past. He was envisioning an MTA train going from one stop to the next. As they rattled along, his thoughts wandered. What was happening to Ermentrude and the wizards they'd left behind? The Veil had covered the Realm except for the Wizard Council chamber. Where was everyone? Flayver couldn't have killed all those witches and wizards. Panic stirred in his stomach. The portal tipped. Wilf gritted his teeth and straightened it again. He kept his eyes on the window, and Katryna put her hand on his arm. He smiled, needing the reassurance of contact with her.

A sigh of relief escaped Katryna when a glimmer of light appeared in the distance. The light grew to form a fissure, and they glided down out of the sky. Trees and foliage surrounded them as the track continued on for several feet along the ground. The portal bumped to a stop under an archway.

"Don't break your connection yet," Malik said as Wilf went to lift his hand. Malik jumped up and opened the door.

The sweet smell of vanilla and musk from the incense burner wafted through the opening. Wilf had landed the portal inside the courtyard of the Hung Shing Taoist Temple.

"I told you to stay outside the temple. It's a historic landmark. We can't leave the portal here, people will bump into it," Myra said. The elixir must have revived her, Wilf thought. She sounded more like herself.

Katryna leaned over, straining her neck to see past Malik.

"I did my best," Wilf said, a trickle of sweat running down his forehead. He ached to flex his fingers. He could sleep for a week, after consuming several bowls of noodles. He was that tired.

"Just move it closer to the store and stop whining," Myra said, leaning forward.

"It's not a taxi. You can't put it in gear and slowly reverse," Wilf said, wiping his forehead with his sleeve.

"Do as Myra says and move it," Malik said, sitting back down.

Wilf glared at them, but switched focused back to his connection with the portal. It crept through the arch, bumping into the sidewalls as it went, until it was on Tai Wang Street.

"Be careful!" Myra said.

"That's what I'm doing," Wilf yelled. "If it's so easy you take over."

Malik slammed his hand on top of Wilf's, preventing him from breaking the connection. The portal tilted before straightening again. It juddered forward and then came to a halt halfway down the street against the granite rocks.

"That's as far as I go," Wilf said, pulling his hand from under Malik's and breaking the connection. The window morphed back into a wall.

Malik glared at Wilf, but stood and opened the door. They stumbled out.

"It should be fine here," Malik said, slinging his arm around Myra and pulling her closer.

Katryna and Wilf started for the store. Shouts grew from the crowd outside the entrance.

"Not so fast," Malik said, overtaking them and blocking the way. "We need to stay together."

"We should find out what's happening in the Magical Realm," Wilf said.

"Who cares?" Malik wasn't interested.

"I care. My mother is there," Katryna said, placing her hands on her hips.

"Well, why did we come here if we're not entering the store?" Wilf wanted to know.

"It made it easy for you to visualize the way." Myra stared at the store. "I suppose it won't hurt to find out what's happening."

They pushed through the crowd. The noise was deafening when they stepped inside the store. Witches shouted, wailed, and screamed over each other.

"Guess they know that Mathowytch has fallen." Malik elbowed his way through the crush.

Katryna led the way down the stairs to the workshop. The sense of panic in the store was nothing compared to the pandemonium below ground. The noise may have been less, but the sense of trauma and shock was thick enough to cut.

"What are you doing here?" Degula said. She waved her hand at the Executrix guards, who stepped aside, allowing them to enter.

"We escaped, and I thought you could use my help with the biomes," Malik said, crossing over to the witch and the main bank of terminals in front of her. He peered over her shoulder, reading the charts and symbols flashing across the screen. His forehead became more creased as the data reloaded.

"What's his game?" Wilf whispered to Myra. "One minute he doesn't care about anyone but himself, and now he's sucking up to Degula."

"He's checking on the biome magic that he needs," Myra said.

Degula urged them into a corner. "What is happening in the Magical Realm? We've lost contact with the Witch Council."

"The Veil covered almost the entire Realm before Wilf extinguished the spell," Malik said, coming over to join them. "Now it's disappeared along with most of the Realm's citizens."

"I expect you've been in contact with the Wizard Council?" Katryna strained her neck trying to read the screen next to her, while still keeping a wary eye on the gun slung over Malik's shoulder.

"Why would they contact us?" Degula said.

"Because you work for them." Wilf folded his arms.

Degula's eyes flashed with anger. "I've had no contact with either Council," she said.

"There were major earthquakes before we left. We should assume that the Realm is lost." Malik surveyed the workshop.

Degula's face paled. "That can't be true. What will we do for magic?"

"There's a portal appearing outside," another witch said.

"A portal?" Degula marched across the workshop and up the stairs. They ran to keep up with her.

A large black dome occupied the space next to the store. An entrance appeared and the metal door lowered like a drawbridge. Ermentrude and Grand Wizard Verger stepped out into the street.

"There you all are," Ermentrude said, coming over to hug Katryna. "That saves us having to hunt you down. Come along inside." She blocked Degula's way. "What games have you been playing?"

"I did what was best for the witch community," Degula said.

"You handed over my daughter and, from what I heard in Mathowytch, other daughters, too." Ermentrude glared.

"Katryna held the key to balancing the Realm. It seemed foolish to hide her here," Degula said, trying to step around Ermentrude. "Besides, I don't answer to you."

Ermentrude raised her hand. "As a member of the witch community you do, but more importantly, as Katryna's mother and your friend, you certainly answer to me for your actions."

Degula folded her arms. "I command the Executrix Squad. You should consider that before you threaten me."

Ermentrude laughed and sent a blast towards Degula's feet. "But I have magic!" Ermentrude said.

Degula took a step backwards. "How?"

Ermentrude leaned forward. "Remember, I'm the witch wielding power around here." She turned and entered the portal. "Degula, I believe you're acquainted with Grand Wizard Verger. We've decided it will be best to run operations from here. The workshop and store are overcrowded."

Malik seized Myra's arm and pulled her aside. "We need to leave now," he said.

Wilf paused to listen.

"Don't you think we should find out what they're planning?" Myra said.

Malik shook his head. "We need to secure the tank I isolated before they find out we've tampered with it."

Myra glanced at the mob of witches moving from the storefront to crowd around the black portal's entrance. "Let's go," she said.

Wilf tried to push through the witches to reach them. The portal's door clanked and began to rise. He sighed and then jumped inside the black portal before the door closed.

"Where's Myra?" Katryna asked.

"She left with Malik. They were talking about securing a tank." He followed Katryna in the command center. Myra had wanted to go with Malik. What was she up to?

Chapter Twenty-Seven - Wilf's Store, Hong Kong

They walked down Tai Wang Street towards the temple.
"How do we get to the biome from here?" Malik asked

"We can take public transportation." Myra let him take hold of her hand.

"There has to be a better way, surely?" Malik said, stopping outside the wooden portal. "Do you think you can connect with the portal now?"

She held her breath. Did he suspect that she'd lied to him before about having trouble accessing her magic? It had been one way to ensure Wilf and Katryna came with them. He didn't seem to have noticed that she hadn't drunk the elixir he'd given her in the portal. She opened her hand and a bubble of energy grew in her palm. Power surged through her, enough to make her shimmer. She grinned at him. "It's there. I can connect with it." She didn't need the elixir anymore. After the Veil had left her in the prison cell she'd felt sick, but by the time they'd dragged her into the council chamber she was cleansed of the drug's effects. The mustiness was gone from her head.

Malik placed his hand on the portal's panel and the door slid open. They rushed inside, Myra collapsing on the bench. She held out her hand over the globe but hesitated, knowing the pain of connection. Malik pushed her hand down, and she gave a yelp when the spikes attached to her fingertips.

"Good!" he said. "You've still got magic. Let's get out of here before anyone notices we're missing." He placed his card in the reader.

Myra let the image of Wilf's track develop in her mind as the wall disappeared from the portal.

"You don't want to image a route. That would bounce us into the Thermals. This portal will travel to the biome if you develop an image of the warehouse portals in Sha Tin. You've been there, so it shouldn't be a problem." Malik sat back on the bench. "It works by locking on to your mind's image of the destination."

"Oh! I don't need a track like Wilf created?" She started to lift up her hand but stopped, not wanting to go through the connection pain again.

"Don't do that. Who knows where we'll end up?"

Myra closed her eyes, letting a picture form of the warehouses in Sha Tin. The portal shook and lifted from the ground.

"You need to cloak it," Malik said.

Myra nodded. She imaged the portal being wrapped in an invisible blanket of magic. Opening her eyes she stared through the window as they floated up into the sky, across Victoria Harbour to Kowloon. The portal picked up speed. It was amazing. She recognized places as they flew in and out of the clouds. There was Mong Kok, Kowloon City, Sz Tuz Shan, and then Sha Tin. The portal descended onto Shing Wan Road.

"You need to slow down," Malik said, gripping the edge of the bench.

She'd forgotten he was there, she'd been so wrapped up with the magic and the flight. Hong Kong was so different up here. Loosening her connection to her magic, she took a deep breath, and the portal slowed as it bumped to the ground.

"Well done!" Malik said, taking her hand off the globe.

She smiled.

"Although it might have been better if you hadn't put us in the middle of the street for anyone to drive into," he said.

"I'm sorry. I didn't..."

"Think? You don't seem to do that a lot lately," Malik said, ruffling her hair before stepping through the opening door. "Come on. Move the portal from out here."

She staggered into the daylight, feeling drained. He'd taken all the joy out of her achievement. She extended her fingers and grunted with the effort of moving the portal into the corner of a parking lot.

"You don't need all that finger display anymore. Use your mind," Malik said, walking towards the biome.

"Sorry!" she said. Why was she apologizing again? This was ridiculous. He needed her. He should be the one apologizing. Is this what it meant to wear a bracelet? It was making her subservient. That couldn't last. She had to snap out of it, she thought, running to catch up.

Malik spun around as she reached his side and captured her wrist. He jerked her to him. "Don't think you can use your connection to the biome like your own personal elixir bubble. It's not an endless supply. Do you understand?"

She nodded.

"I need to hear you say it."

"I understand. I wouldn't." Her voice quivered.

He stared at her.

"I won't," she said.

"Good," he said, releasing her and continuing towards the biome. He entered a concrete building with a flat roof.

Myra straggled behind, rubbing her wrist. Magic coursed through her. Malik was right. She no longer needed to wiggle her fingers. The energy was there. She let a tiny ball of energy move between her fingers. The door opened and she dismissed the magic.

"What are you waiting out here for?" Malik said.

"Nothing." She would play the role of dutiful girlfriend until she found a way to remove the bracelet. Then she'd ditch him. He acted like he owned her, but she didn't need his possessiveness. She had a source of magic, and freedom seemed within her grasp.

He glared at her before crossing the room to several terminals. Taking a compact mirror out of his pocket, he connected it to a computer. "This upload shouldn't take long, and then you won't be the only one with access to magic here."

"Are the storage tanks only wizard magic?" she asked.

"The witches panicked because they can't connect to the Source any longer. Hywel reserved a storage tank for witch magic, but with the number of witches here that will deplete soon," Malik said, tapping the keyboard.

Myra rolled her chair away from the terminal. Where would she go when she escaped Malik? A house in the New Territories? Or perhaps she'd keep the portal and travel? The name Kamder glittered on the bracelet. Until she removed the foul thing she was stuck in Hong Kong with Malik.

He bent his head over the keyboard. His hair flopped over his eyes and he pushed it behind his ears. She was beginning to loathe him. She had to be careful not to cringe when he placed his arm around her.

"Hey, I need you to log into that terminal," Malik said, pointing to a flickering screen.

"I know nothing about this technology," she said.

Malik woke up the system. He punched in the login sequence. "When I tell you, hit enter. I'm sure you can do that," he said, walking back to his chair.

"Shouldn't be too hard," she said.

He continued typing after a brief glance in her direction.

"Press enter," he said.

She hit the key and the screen in front of her went blank.

"I did what you said, but nothing's happening." She waited for him to explode and braced. But "Give it a few seconds," was all he said.

The screen burst into life, and a gauge appeared showing the tank to be full.

"It's working," she said, letting out a breath.

He came over and stood behind her. "It'll take a few hours before my access program is fully up and running." He spun her chair around until she faced him, took hold of her arms, and pulled her up. "What shall we do while we wait?" He kissed her.

She pulled back. "Won't Hywel send someone here?"

"Who can he send? I'm with you and Thiemus was in the tower when the Veil wiped the Realm."

She'd forgotten about Thiemus, but Malik was right. The Veil must have caught him.

"You don't think he's dead?" She might not have been her brother's biggest fan, but she didn't wish him gone.

Malik released her. "I'm not sure what's happened. I can't believe the Veil eradicated the entire Realm. It wasn't a malicious spell."

"What if it transported them to the Real World?"

Malik shook his head. "I'm sure we would have seen a larger number of wailing witches in Wan Chai or here if that were the case."

She looked at the gauge showing the progress of the installation. "Would the biomes be able to support the population of the Magical Realm?"

"Not even a tenth," Malik said.

Two more terminals switched on and gauges appeared on their screens. "Hywel has begun the calibration. He's about to find out that one of his storage tanks is offline," Malik said.

She pulled against his arm. "You're sure that won't bring him here?"

"We'll have left by then. Remember, we have the only working small portal here. He'll be forced to take your public transportation." Malik laughed. "I'd love to see his reaction to that."

Myra wasn't sure she would find it a laughing matter if she was in close range to Hywel.

"Where are we going?"

Malik grasped her hand and led her across the room. A sofa, armchair, and table were pushed up against the wall. He dropped onto the sofa and pulled her onto his lap. He kissed the tip of her nose and then her cheek.

"It's a surprise. Every visit I made here over the past few months, I've been preparing to leave Hywel's employment." He kissed her lips and the tip of his tongue ran along her lower lip.

She wanted to push him away. Her stomach churned as she opened her mouth, deepening the kiss. She had to make him think she still liked him. His hand slid under her T-shirt and his fingers spread across her stomach. She sighed, trying not to recoil.

He lifted his head and his mouth extended into a slow smile. "I've wanted to hold you without interruption for a long time. It's great that we're here, together."

Myra wrapped her fingers around the back of his neck and pulled him towards her. She kissed Malik, but caught his hand and pulled it back out from under her shirt. How long must she keep this up? Wouldn't he notice her responses weren't real?

Red lights and a siren sounded inside the room. Malik pushed Myra off his knee onto the sofa and raced across the room to the terminal.

"No! That's not possible."

"What?" Myra said, rushing to join him.

"The program has stalled." He pounded on the keyboard. "It's not responding." He ran to another terminal. "Same here. The corrupted biome is pumping magic into the storage tanks." He tried each terminal before returning to the first. "I can't stop it, but if this keeps up there won't be any magic. Some fool has started the biome collection program instead of keeping it closed off." He slumped into his chair and looked at her. "What the hell can we do now?"

"Hywel perhaps thought he was releasing access to the storage tanks, but instead he gave the biomes access. After all, you're the one who's been running the system."

Malik ran his hands through his hair. "It's possible, I suppose." He looked towards the door. "We need to leave. The Council will know. They must be on their way." He collapsed, holding his head in his hands. "Where can I go? I won't have magic. I'll be a Normal if I leave." He sprang up and grabbed both of her arms. "Are you working for the Council? You're a spy, aren't you? Are you playing both sides to get what you want? Hywel warned me about you when I asked for the bracelet." He shook her until her teeth rattled and her neck hurt.

"I wouldn't betray you. Remember, we're in this together," she said, repeating his words back to him.

"Are we?" He pushed her away and she staggered, catching hold of a desk. "You didn't seem grateful or excited this morning."

"I'd spent the night in the cells. I was exhausted and surprised. That's all." She cradled the bracelet in her hand. "I'm flattered you've given me your name."

He took a step towards her and she braced, but he enfolded her in a hug.

"I forgive you." He kissed the top of her head, then let her go. He wandered over to the terminal. "We'll need to invent a story as to why we're here."

She released the magic she was holding. She couldn't keep doing this. What if she blasted him now and made a dash for it? The bracelet seemed to tighten on her arm.

He moved from one screen to another, bringing up different charts and data, shaking his head as he read.

Knowledge and secrets had been her entire life. It had kept her alive. Self-preservation ran deep in her. But she knew this would be her toughest role yet, the doting girlfriend.

The door banged open and Hywel, followed by Degula, Ermentrude, Grand Wizard Verger, Councilman Tyrone, Katryna, and Wilf stormed into the room. Executrix guards seized hold of Malik and Myra, dragging them away from the terminals.

"Sabotage!" Hywel stood almost nose to nose with Malik. "You'll pay for this."

"Me? Why would I contaminate the storage tanks? I need them. We came to monitor the equipment and just discovered this disaster," Malik said. He struggled against the guard holding him.

Hywel turned to Myra. "But your junkie girlfriend has full access."

Malik turned to look at Myra. "She wouldn't." His hurt look turned to rage. "You did this so you'd possess all the magic? Has your addiction become so bad that you only care about the next fix?"

Each accusation hit her like a blow to the stomach. The real Malik on full display. There had been no genuine affection, only the desire to possess her. She shook her head. "I didn't do this." Everyone in the room turned a hostile look in her direction, except Ermentrude. She expressed no interest in Myra's drama.

"She's not the only one with access to magic," Wilf said. "We do, too."

Hywel turned to face Wilf, Katryna, and Ermentrude.

Ermentrude folded her arms. "It's true. I can connect to the biome magic."

"How is that possible?" Degula asked, signaling to her guards to surround them.

"That's a lengthy story and one I'm not sure I fully understand. Something about the Veil, Flayver, Wilf, and the Source." Ermentrude sat down on the chair next to the terminal.

"For now, why don't you release Malik and Myra? The corruption is clearly not their fault, although I suspect their plan involved the theft of magical energy and a storage tank. But we've no proof."

"Why should we take any notice of you?" Hywel said, pushing through the guards.

"Because I have a biome and several storage tanks full of magic at my disposal," Ermentrude said, smiling at her ex-husband.

Wilf pointed at Myra. "You can't release that witch. She still has to answer to murder charges."

Myra held up her head and returned his glare. She needed to be free to find out what Malik's plans were and how to break his hold over her. That wouldn't be possible if she was locked away in some cell.

"Given her involvement in the death of Reginald, a scheme to steal magic, and that she is dangerous, I agree with Wilf," Grand Wizard Verger said, nodding at the guards. "She has access to magic and can't be allowed to disappear. Confine her until a trial date can be arranged."

Handcuffs appeared on Myra's wrists.

Malik whispered in her ear as he walked over to a terminal. "It was me who killed Reginald." His voice was so soft, like a gentle breeze across her ear.

"What?" Myra said, jerking her head away.

He leaned in again so no one else could hear. "Reginald had been poking his nose into the workings of the biome and learned about Hywel's extra storage tank. He threatened to report what he'd discovered to the Wizard Council. I couldn't let him do that. It would leave me locked in the Magical Realm at the beck and call of Hywel and the Council. I wanted what Reginald had. Freedom from them. I used the portal to enter his workshop. I saw you raise your fingers to fire on him. I sent a killing energy burst at almost the same time."

Myra pulled at the restraints, but they held her.

"Sorry, babe, that you had to be the fall guy for that one, but it was before I knew you." He smiled at her.

"I'll make you pay for this," Myra said, but the Executrix Squad marched her from the room. Degula fell in behind them.

"Where shall we hold her?" the guard asked.

"Take her to one of the upstairs rooms," Degula said. Her gaze followed Malik.

"But it was Malik — he killed Reginald," Myra said, trying to summon magic.

"While the Council needs his expertise, he will be immune to prosecution." Degula waved the guard away. "Also, you're a witch. It will be your word against a wizard's."

"That's unfair," Myra said.

"It's life," Degula said. She stepped out of the guards' hearing, and Myra followed her. "I don't think those handcuffs will hold you for long. If I were you I'd disappear, but let me know how to contact you. I have a proposition for you."

"To work for you?" Myra said.

"I'll discover evidence of Malik's guilt and clear your name," Degula said.

"In return for what?" Degula was the slipperiest witch Myra had ever met. Her word wasn't worth a bat's fart, but what choice did she have?

"Just a few magical tasks every so often," Degula said.

Myra nodded. If anyone could find evidence on Malik, it would be Degula and her guards.

The guards marched Myra up a flight of metal stairs into a small office and left her alone.

She sat down and sent a trickle of magic into the lock. The handcuffs fell to the ground.

Chapter Twenty-Eight - The Biome's Data Center, Sha Tin, Hong Kong

Wilf laid a hand on Katryna's arm. "Did you see Myra's reaction to Malik? It looked as if she wanted to hurt him, rather than kiss him. I wonder what he said that upset her."

"I'm not sure she even likes him," Katryna said.

"Degula was quick to take control of the situation. Do we trust her with Myra?" Wilf continued. Was his hatred of Degula clouding his judgment?

"The same thought is repeating through my mind," Ermentrude said, keeping her voice low. "I'm presuming you can both sense the magic in the biome?"

They nodded. "It responds differently. Harder to control," Katryna said.

"Seems the same to me," Wilf said.

"The ratio of witch to wizard magic might be the problem," Ermentrude said.

"What are you three planning?" Hywel asked, standing in front of them with Tyrone and Verger listening in.

"We're discussing the consistency of the biome magic. How are you finding it?" Ermentrude snorted. "Oh! I forgot. You're powerless... to have an opinion on this subject."

Hywel's face went red and he puffed out his cheeks.

"And what have you deduced?" Verger said. His eyes creased with amusement.

"There seems a greater amount of wizard magic than witch. Similar to how the Magical Realm was before it collapsed," Ermentrude said. "Katryna and I are having difficulty molding it to our spells."

"Wilf, what about you?" Hywel said.

"It's always been difficult for me to control," he said, shrugging his shoulders. He didn't see why it mattered.

"Hywel, did you find out anything in your recent experiments? Weren't you trying to discover how Katryna has both magics?" Tyrone asked.

Wilf didn't like the councilman, especially when he was eyeing Katryna as if she were a laboratory experiment.

"We were still in the early stages," Hywel said, busying himself at a terminal.

"We're doomed to a life without magic," Tyrone said. "Your Advancer made the boy able to use any magic. Can't you create another machine?"

"I made it using magic. How do you expect me to reproduce that achievement?" Hywel demanded.

"Instruct Wilf," Tyrone said.

"It wouldn't work for several reasons. The environment isn't the same. I don't have my notes or tools. You're asking the impossible. There has to be another way."

Wilf slinked off to sit on the sofa, and Katryna dropped next to him.

"They'll talk for hours and do nothing," she said.

"We could take the portal that's outside and head back to the apartment," Wilf said, pushing his hands into his pockets.

"Mom will want to stay and find out what the wizards decide," Katryna said, curling her legs up next to her.

"She can stay as long as she likes. Let's get out of here before someone decides we're dangerous and imprisons us," Wilf said.

Katryna glanced over at Ermentrude. "I don't want to be Hywel's lab rat again."

"They seem engrossed in the screens. We can leave," Wilf said, standing up.

He took hold of Katryna's hand and led her towards the door, but his heart thudded. He expected to hear his name called with each step as they came closer to the door. He eased the door open and squeezed through.

"Made it," he said, grinning.

"Where are you two heading?" Degula shouted from the top of the stairs.

"Run!" Wilf yelled. They bolted down the street towards the portal. He placed his hand on the panel, but nothing happened.

"You try," he said.

Katryna tried, but the door didn't appear.

The Executrix Squad's footsteps pounded on the street. Wilf grabbed Katryna's hand. "Leave it. Come on." They sped around the corner. A green taxi stood with its light on.

"Get in," Wilf said, running around and jumping inside.

"MTA," he said to the driver. He watched the guards out of the back window as the taxi pulled away from the curb. "That was close," he said.

"How do we pay?" Katryna said.

Wilf reached into his pocket, pulled out his billfold, and waved his Octopus Card. "I wouldn't leave the apartment without this."

Soon they were at the MTA station and aboard a train to Wan Chai. The journey back to the apartment was uneventful until they entered Tai Wang Street.

"How do we sneak into the apartment without being mobbed by angry witches?" Wilf asked.

Katryna shook her head. "We'll never get past them."

Wilf looked down Queens Road East. "I know, let's head to the Football Club. No one will look for us there."

Katryna folded her arms. "That's the first place anyone would search for you."

"Only you," he said, taking her hand and tugging on it until she uncrossed her arms. "I work out problems by kicking a ball around. I always have. Do you have any other suggestions?"

"It's worth a try," she said, letting him lead her along the streets to the Football Club. "I only hope your girlfriend won't be there."

"Amy will be in school," he said, allowing her to enter. "Why don't you wait for me in the stands. I'll collect my cleats and ball from the locker room." He didn't wait for a reply but jogged through the club.

Enzo was changing when he entered.

"What are you doing here?" Enzo said, pulling on his practice shirt.

"I needed to play. It feels like a part of me is missing when I'm not kicking a ball," Wilf said.

Enzo held his gaze. "You and your witch aren't welcome here."

"I understand you're upset, and I won't interfere with the team."

Enzo bent over to finish tying his soccer cleats. "I hope not," he said, leaving the room.

Wilf opened his locker and took out his kit. He silenced the voice inside questioning if he should be here when the Magical Realm and most of its inhabitants had disappeared. They were out of ideas. He found it ironic that he still had magic and would have been happy to lose it, while its loss devastated everyone else. He laced up his cleats and headed for the soccer field. Katryna sat in the stands, and he clambered up to her.

"What are you doing? When you said you needed to kick a ball around, I didn't imagine you playing with the team," she said, her hands balled into fists.

"Enzo was in the locker room. He's still mad at me. I have to play," he said.

"Give me a break. You want to play is the actual reason." She raised the pitch of her voice.

"I've always used practice to work through problems. It works for me, promise." He kissed her cheek before running down the stairs to join the team. They stood in a circle, passing the ball between them. He allowed his mind to roam. This was muscle memory, and he didn't need to be fully engaged.

"Five laps of the field," Coach said.

Wilf jogged next to Enzo. He glanced over at Katryna. It had felt normal to kiss her. He wanted her here with him. He turned back to the track — his fondness for Katryna wasn't the problem he was here to deal with. He listened to the rhythm of his feet as he ran. It cleared his mind for a lap. Then he turned to the problem of magic. What was he missing? The biomes. Storage tanks of corrupted magic. Malik and Myra. He shook his head, but his thoughts seemed shrouded and out of reach.

"You using magic to make us all look slow in front of Coach? It's not a race," Enzo said, coming up on his right.

"What?"

"We're jogging and you're sprinting," Enzo said.

Wilf slowed down. "Give it a rest, Enzo. I know you're pissed at me, but I don't need this right now. I've other problems to solve than how upset you are."

"You cheat and could cause the team to be banned from the championship and you act like it's nothing?" Enzo stopped running. "Watch it!" he yelled as another team member ran into him, sending him forward.

"Enzo, get moving! This isn't a water break!" Coach yelled.

Wilf glanced back as his friend came panting up beside him. Coming here hadn't been the right thing to do. Enzo's animosity was preventing him from working on his problems. He glanced over at the bleachers. Amy climbed the stairs and paused next to Katryna.

"It's time you and that girl got the message and moved on," Enzo said, catching him up.

"I've got your message loud and clear. You're welcome to try with Amy," Wilf said, matching strides.

"Oh no, man. That is also your mess to clear up," Enzo said, pulling ahead.

"Okay gents, get some water," Coach ordered.

Wilf picked up a water bottle. Katryna hadn't regained her full ugliness, but standing next to Amy's stunning beauty the contrast was striking. Life was original with Katryna around. He was glad that learning magic had allowed him to save her. His father's formula had turned out to be lifesaving. If only it hadn't been locked in the journal by that ridiculous spell.

"The journal!" Wilf ran up the stairs to Katryna.

"We need to look in the journal. There were pages and pages of Dad's notes about the biomes. Something there might help."

"Hi, Wilf. Nice to see you too," Amy said, flicking her ponytail.

"Oh! Hi, Amy." He reached for Katryna's hand. "Come on. It's in the locker room." He jerked Katryna out of the seat and down the stairs, only releasing her hand outside the locker room.

Enzo blocked their way. "Are you running out on us again!"

Wilf glanced from Enzo, to Coach, and then back to Katryna. As much as he wanted to stay, he couldn't. He reached out to Enzo, but his friend stepped back.

"I have to go. I'm sorry." He edged around Enzo and down the players tunnel.

"Don't come back," Enzo shouted after him.

"Wait here!" he said to Katryna in the entrance as he bolted for the locker room. He pulled out his shorts and rummaged in both pockets. He couldn't find it. Magic! He should call for it. He held out his hand. A speck of dust landed on his palm and expanded into the journal.

Throwing on his street clothes, he ran out to meet Katryna, letting the locker room door bang shut behind him. He waved the journal in the air. "I've got it." He ran up the steps to a seating area and Katryna perched down next to him.

"Show us the biome section," he said, placing the journal on the table. He placed his ringed finger on the cover and the ruby flashed. The locks snapped open. Pages flicked over until words formed.

"Biomes: There are several situated around the Real World. The following pages explain how the process works." Diagrams and mathematical symbols covered several pages.

"It looks very complex," Wilf said. "Do you understand the symbols?"

Katryna shook her head. "I think we need to ask specific questions."

"Okay. What do we do if the magic has combined and you need to separate it back into witch and wizard magic?" Wilf asked.

The writing disappeared from the journal page.

"It doesn't have an answer for that one," Katryna said.

Without warning, words scrolled across the empty page.

"It is impossible to separate combined magic."

"That's not helpful. What are witches and wizards supposed to do if they can no longer access magic?" Wilf asked.

"Witches and wizards will need reeducating on how to use Traditional Magic."

"We should return to the store and show Ermentrude. Although I'm not sure how much use this is," Wilf said, closing the book.

Katryna jumped to her feet. "Come on. Let's hope she's back from Sha Tin."

Wilf put the journal back into his pocket.

He led Katryna out of the Football Club and back to Tai Wang Street. Guards stood outside the black portal. "I think Grand Wizard Verger and Ermentrude have arrived back," Wilf said, pushing his way through the witches clustered around the entrance.

"I need to speak to my mother," Katryna said to the guards.

One pulled out her contact mirror and then shook her head.

"Seems the guards are getting used to being Normals," Wilf said, smirking.

The guard glared at Wilf, replaced the mirror in her pocket, and went inside. Degula appeared.

"Where have you two been?" she asked.

"We need to speak to Ermentrude," Wilf said.

"Tell me, and I'll decide if I should disturb a senior witch," Degula said, blocking the entrance.

"Nice try," Katryna said. Her ring flashed and Degula moved sideways.

"That witch has magic," one of the crowd shouted.

"Her mother's part of the Council. They're keeping it for themselves," another yelled.

"I think we'd better get inside," Wilf said as the crowd surged forward.

They ran up the gangplank and into the portal. The guards and Degula retreated inside. The portal door slammed shut.

"Maybe using magic in front of an angry, magic-starved crowd wasn't my best idea," Katryna said, following Wilf into the control room.

"You think!" he said, shaking his head.

"There you are." Ermentrude welcomed them, holding a mug.

"Mom, Wilf's journal says Traditional is the name for combined magic," Katryna said. "It suggested we reeducate witches and wizards to use it."

Ermentrude pondered this. "If the information proves useful, then it will be even harder to live with that book. It'll behave like it's the font of all knowledge." She put down her mug and tapped the desk. "Well, let's see."

Wilf opened his palm, and the book materialized. The locks popped open when he placed his ring on the cover's surface. Words once again materialized on a blank page.

Chapter Twenty-Nine - Wizard
Command Portal outside Wilf's Store, Hong Kong

Hywel held Wilf's journal. "Could the biome magic be Traditional? What do you think, Malik?"

"I'm into technology and science, not history," Malik said, keeping his eyes fixed on his screen.

Katryna saw a slight movement of his head towards the journal when Hywel wasn't looking. Her throat tickled, but she didn't want to cough and draw any more attention to herself.

"But that was generations ago. Before the population migrated to the Magical Realm," Grand Wizard Verger said. Hywel handed him the journal.

"We have to do something. Only those three…" He waved his hand towards Wilf, Katryna, and Ermentrude. "I don't even know what to call them. They're not wizards or witches, but an amalgamation." Hywel wrinkled his nose.

"In Mulkulth, the name was Mage for users of Traditional magic," Verger said. Pages flipped in the journal. "Yes, the book confirms it."

"That explains why my father's crystal is called the Mages Crystal?" Wilf said.

"I'm a witch. No matter what magic I'm capable of using," Ermentrude said, glaring at Hywel and Verger.

The Grand Wizard held up his hands. "Your title is your prerogative to choose. I have no problem in your continuing to be addressed as Witch Wakefield."

"I'm glad that's settled. Now, can we get back to the matter at hand?" Creases formed across Ermentrude's forehead. "I propose that Wilf start the process for reeducating wizards. He's more used to this magic. Katryna and I will assist where we can."

"Me?" Wilf shook his head.

"Wilf isn't qualified for this," Hywel said.

The journal jumped out of the Grand Wizard's hands and

back into Wilf's pocket.

"Even the book seems skeptical," Malik said.

"It should be a team effort," Verger said, leaning forward in his chair. "Wilf, aided by Ermentrude and Katryna, can follow the instructions in the journal. Captain, select a volunteer to be the first Mage." The Grand Wizard went into the kitchen, signaling the end of discussions.

"I'm tired of that wizard thinking he's in control," Ermentrude said, walking over to Degula. "We'll need your guards to get to the other portal, and we'll need an access card."

"Where are we going?" Katryna said.

"Sha Tin. We should be near the biome when we try the first conversion." Ermentrude gestured towards the blank screens. "This doesn't work without wizard magic."

"Where's Myra?" Wilf asked

"There isn't anywhere to hold her here, so I left her locked in an office at the biome site." Degula folded her arms. "I hope you approve."

Wilf snorted. Malik picked up his backpack and fell in behind the guards. The Captain sent some of his soldiers to join the Executrix Squad, and a path cleared through the crowd of witches blocking the street. Malik placed his hand on the panel and the portal's door swung open.

"Who's the pilot?" Malik asked, sliding along a bench and taking out his access card.

"Wilf, you know Hong Kong best. Take us straight to the biome," Ermentrude said, gesturing for him to sit down opposite Malik. She sat next to him.

The soldier sat between Katryna and Malik.

"As I told Myra, you don't have to image a route. We don't have to go through the Thermals. Picture the landing site instead," Malik said.

Wilf's hand hovered over the globe. Ermentrude pushed it down. "Ouch! That wasn't necessary."

"Looked to me like you needed help, and that's what I'm here for." Ermentrude smiled.

"Shall we get this portal off the ground? I'm tired of looking at this stone wall," Malik said.

Wilf closed his eyes, and the portal lifted off the ground and floated over Hong Kong.

Katryna watched the city spread out below. Could they do this? Reeducate an entire population? Beads of sweat stood out on the soldier's forehead. His knuckles were white as he clasped his hands in his lap. If they converted every magical person, what then? How much magic did the biome have? Was it renewable? There were too many unanswered questions. And what about the Magical Realm and its inhabitants? They couldn't have all evaporated. That was too terrible to imagine.

The portal bumped down on the ground and Wilf lifted his hand, flexing his fingers.

"I'll check on Myra," he said.

"You're being a little obsessed," Katryna said, exiting the portal.

Wilf spun around to face her. "She killed my father. I promised she would pay for it." He ran on ahead and entered the warehouse. Ermentrude, Katryna, and Malik followed him inside.

"I'm still not convinced it was her," Ermentrude said, crossing towards the terminals. "However, that will keep. We've more important tasks at present."

"Does the energy renew?" Katryna said, sitting next to Malik.

He pulled out a keyboard. "It does, but that's if we don't allow the biome to become more than a third empty at any one time. I can't imagine how they'll control the flow if every magic person draws on the biome at once. And there are a lot of desperate witches."

Wilf ran into the room. "She's gone! Myra's not here. They left her unguarded. Degula meant for her to escape."

"You're sure?" Malik had half risen from his seat, but at a glare from Ermentrude he sat back down.

"I checked all the rooms. She's not here," Wilf said.

"You're focusing on the wrong activity." Ermentrude waved her hand in the direction of a small kitchen area. Water poured into the kettle.

"Were you involved in her escape?" Wilf demanded.

"No, but I'm not surprised, since Degula left the room with her," Ermentrude said. A mug banged onto the counter next to the boiling kettle.

"You knew they'd allow her to escape and did nothing!" Wilf shouted.

"I didn't know. I said it wasn't a surprise. Can you please remember why we are here?" Ermentrude said.

Wilf held her gaze for several seconds before walking over to a terminal and collapsing into a chair.

"The journal," Ermentrude said.

The book appeared in Wilf's palm and sprang open. Malik grabbed the book and it snapped shut, almost trapping his fingers.

"It's temperamental," Katryna said, biting her lip not to laugh. "It needs Wilf's consent before it behaves."

Malik threw the journal back to Wilf. He snatched it out of the air and placed his ring on the cover. The lock sprang open and pages turned.

"Here," he said, offering the book back to Malik.

"I'll rig some extra cabling to the storage tanks since they'll only be holding one kind of magic," he said, poring over the journal before handing it back to Wilf. He left, taking some cables and screwdrivers from his backpack.

"Do we trust him?" Katryna asked.

"He's a wizard who wants magic. That should motivate him," Ermentrude said, wandering over to the whistling kettle. "A brew, anyone?"

"Why don't you sit down?" Katryna said to the soldier. The poor guy was shaking.

"Thanks," he said.

"What's your name?" Katryna said, accepting a mug from Ermentrude.

"Jayden," the soldier said.

Ermentrude sent a mug towards Jayden and another to Wilf.

"You'll need to reeducate yourself on what you use magic for. It will be in short supply — you shouldn't use it to float mugs around," Wilf said.

"Witches and wizards think magic. It's who they are," Katryna said, lifting her mug.

"What does this process entail?" Ermentrude asked before taking a sip of brew. "Will the entire population end up with a vein running up their arm like mine?"

Katryna rolled up her sleeve. "Mine's gone."

Ermentrude pushed up her sleeve. "So's mine. Well, that's a blessing. It was only temporary." She smiled and Wilf winced.

"My tattoo is gone," Jayden said. "Will it come back?"

Wilf glanced at his hand. "Mine disappeared a while ago. I don't think they return."

"No more wizard classifications! That should give the ruling class an anxiety attack." Ermentrude chuckled.

"All set," Malik said, letting the door bang shut behind him.

"What's first?" Ermentrude said.

"Connect with the Source within the biome, and then to the energy receptors within Jayden," Wilf said.

"A direct connection with the Source is dangerous. It was one of the first lessons — never connect with the Source directly," Katryna said, stopping as the reasons swirled around in her head. "There's too much energy for a single witch to control. It will overpower anyone who attempts to tap into the Source. You may never break the connection at the end," she recited.

"The biome's source won't be as powerful as the actual Source," Ermentrude said, twirling the hairs on her chin.

"Will we all connect at once?" Katryna said, peering over Wilf's shoulder at the journal.

"I think Wilf should try first. Malik can monitor the drain on the biome. If it looks too much, we can assist," Ermentrude said, picking her mug back up.

A classic mum move, Katryna thought, to hide behind a mug of brew whenever she didn't want to appear less than confident.

"Malik, is the magic stable?" Ermentrude asked.

"Yes, there's no drain on it. I ended all collections to the storage tanks," Malik said.

"No need to delay then," Ermentrude said, rolling her chair next to Malik.

Katryna laid her hand on Wilf's arm. "You'll be fine."

"I wish I had your confidence," he said. "Jayden, you'd better move next to me."

The soldier glided his chair over to Wilf.

Katryna picked up Wilf's mug and took it to the kitchen. Then she sat next to her mother, but kept her eyes on Wilf and Jayden. This had to work. Wilf would be fine — he'd survived the Advancer machine. She felt sure he could survive this. She crossed her fingers, hidden in her pockets.

Wilf took a deep breath and closed his eyes.

"He's made contact." The gauge on Malik's screen flickered.

Wilf straightened his arms and spread his fingers. The gauge dipped a few degrees but settled.

"Good, he seems in control of the connection," Ermentrude said, twirling the hairs on her chin again.

The fingertips on Wilf's right hand glowed blue and his wizard ring burned a deep red.

"Is that supposed to happen?" Katryna asked, picking up the journal. The book snapped shut. "Seriously! We can't access the journal without Wilf." She resisted the urge to throw the book against the wall. When this was over she would enjoy helping Wilf discipline his journal.

"We should have expected that," Ermentrude said, shaking her head.

"He's starting to draw energy," Malik reported. The gauge took another dip.

"Isn't that rather a lot for him to hold?" Katryna said, watching the needle move into the red.

A flash of energy spiked across the room from Wilf's hand.

A scorch mark spread across the wall as the energy pierced the sheetrock.

Malik's fingers sped across the keyboard. "He's not the only one drawing from the Source."

"Myra!" Katryna said, looking towards the door.

"We need to find her," Ermentrude said. "Malik, stay here with Wilf. Katryna, help me track Myra. She has to be around here."

Katryna ran after her mother.

"You search upstairs. I'll look around outside." Ermentrude pushed open the door.

After running up the stairs, Katryna burst into the first office. Myra must have hidden when she heard Wilf come looking for her earlier. Katryna checked under the desk and in a large cupboard before running to the next office. This room had an oval table with chairs around it. She checked behind the door — nothing. She entered the bathroom at the end of the corridor.

A groan came from the end cubicle. Katryna tried the locked door and then looked underneath.

"Myra, open the door." She pounded on the door.

The sound from Myra grew louder and then her legs appeared under the door.

"I'll get help," Katryna said, running from the bathroom and heading outside.

"Mom," she shouted. "I've found her, but she's collapsed."

Ermentrude appeared from behind the biome.

"A whole biome of magic must have been too hard for her to resist," Katryna said, retracing her steps back to the bathroom.

"That witch is nothing but trouble," Ermentrude said, taking her bag out of her pocket. She set it down on the bathroom floor and rummaged inside. "There it is," she said, producing a screwdriver and unlocking the door.

Myra sat in a crumpled heap. Katryna and Ermentrude each took one of her shoulders.

"We'll take her downstairs. Hopefully she released her hold on the biome's magic when she passed out," Ermentrude said.

They edged into the monitoring room. Sparks fizzled from Wilf's fingers, but the energy beam had disappeared.

"What's happening?" Ermentrude asked, helping Myra to the sofa, then sitting down next to Malik.

"The level has stopped plunging, but it's about half. I don't know if Wilf's holding his own or if his mind is being controlled by the biome," Malik said.

Katryna hesitated to touch Myra. She didn't want to join the battle with the biome's magic. If only she could reach Wilf. But again she hesitated. There was a new connection between them. It wasn't the same as the bond they'd shared last time, true. She couldn't feel his pain or instantly know where he was, and she didn't experience the consuming desire to touch him. But she'd become used to him being around. She liked him holding her hand and smiling at her. She rubbed her cheek where he'd kissed her and blushed.

She couldn't imagine him not being in her life. If he pulled through — and he had to — she promised she wouldn't object to him playing soccer, which was quite the most ridiculous way for anyone to spend their time. Well, she'd try.

Chapter Thirty - The Biome's Data Center, Sha Tin, Hong Kong

Myra was vaguely aware of being carried down the stairs and into the Data Center. Pain surged through her body, and a gray mist floated at the edges of her thoughts. What was happening? She'd been wondering when it would be safe to leave the bathroom.

Magic! She'd been thinking that she possessed magic in a Realm that didn't use it. Malik had said they would live like rulers. Was that true? Could she use a deception spell and buy a house in the New Territories? Reginald had restricted her use of magic in Hong Kong, but now she could decide how or when to use it. She had access to the biome magic and wouldn't have to worry about supply.

She remembered creating a tiny ball of energy and rolling it between her fingers. She'd been elated. She could finally live her dream — freedom and magic. But the bracelet on her wrist was a reminder that she only had freedom as long as Malik couldn't access magic. Once he did, he would be able to trace her.

That was when she had closed her eyes and connected with the biome's source. There had been a silent warning in her mind, a memory, but she ignored it. The energy had flowed, and she'd drawn a little more, expanding the ball of magic in her fist. The biome was there for her to connect to whenever she wanted. She didn't need to hide. She should blast her way out and deal with Malik.

She'd drawn more energy from the biome's source. It had surged through her. She couldn't control it. She'd tried to release the connection, but it had forged a stronger hold, searing through her. Power had coursed through her until she'd felt her skin glowing. When she'd extended her fingertips, they'd pulsed and a flashing blue spike of energy had sizzled from the ends. She remembered opening her mouth to scream and nothing coming out. She floated in the bathroom cubicle. Magic oozing from her — her mind was merging with the biome's magic.

She sank deeper into the blazing mass of power. But a voice swam in her head. "Myra, don't let go."

It wasn't possible. "Wilf? How?" Darkness surrounded her. She clung to the sound of his voice.

"We're both trapped by the biome's source, but if we work together I think I can break you free."

"I didn't kill Reginald. It was Malik."

"I'm glad, but that isn't a priority now," Wilf said.

"Why would you help me?"

"You're my sister. Do you want my help or not?"

"Will I still have magic?"

"Isn't your mind more important? How great will a connection to the biome be if your brain is fried?" Wilf asked.

Another surge of pain ripped through her body. "Get me out of this!" she screamed.

"I'm going to sever your connection, but it shouldn't be permanent. Trust me."

"Do it," she said. Pain rippled through her head and she gasped. An emptiness feathered at the edges of her mind and pressed deeper. She spiraled down into a void.

"Her eyelids flickered." Katryna's voice floated through the fog in Myra's head. She attempted to lift her hand, but it felt weighed down.

"Get her some water," Ermentrude said.

Hands pulled at her until she sat propped up and water dampened her lips. She slowly opened her eyes, and the room came into focus. Katryna was sitting next to her, and Ermentrude hovered over her shoulder.

"How is she?" Malik's voice sent a chill through her body.

"He did it," Myra said.

"Who did what?" Ermentrude leaned closer.

"Malik... killed Reginald... It wasn't me." Sharp pains stabbed her throat as she spoke.

"Don't talk," Katryna said.

"Wilf..."

"Yes?" Ermentrude said.

"He's attached to the biome's source. I spoke to him."

"Is he okay?" Katryna said, grabbing hold of Myra's arm.

"I'm not sure, but he helped me break the connection with the biome," Myra said, taking the glass from Katryna and drinking.

"How is she?" Malik repeated as he moved next to them.

"She'll survive," Ermentrude said, turning to look at Wilf. "I only hope he will."

Wilf lowered his hands, but his eyes stared out, unfocused.

The sparks of energy no longer flared across the room. His fingers had lost their blue color, but his face had a bluish tinge.

"What happened to you, Myra?" Katryna asked.

"I drew magic from the biome. It felt wonderful being connected to its source, but I couldn't handle it. It overpowered me. Then a ripple flowed through the connection and Wilf spoke to me. He broke my connection, and I woke up here," Myra said, easing her throat with another sip of water.

Ermentrude and Katryna stood over Wilf, and Malik slid next to Myra.

"We can escape. I've still got the codes to one storage tank. Once Wilf's converted my magic, we can be off," Malik whispered, squeezing her arm.

"I'm not going anywhere with you," Myra said. "I'm just a scapegoat, remember."

"You've misunderstood. I would always rescue you. Babe, I'd never leave you here alone," Malik said, stroking her hair.

"I don't believe you," Myra said.

Malik picked up her hand with the bracelet on. "I amended this so it's also a tracking device. I can always find you." He smiled. "I would have rescued you." He leaned in and kissed her. She tried to turn her head, but he held her. "Once Wilf gives access to everyone, they still won't notice one tank is offline because I've put in a feedback loop. We'll make our escape during the celebration. I told you. I've a place close to here that I've been equipping on every trip. We'll be our own masters," Malik said, glancing over at Ermentrude and Katryna.

"What if I don't have magic?" Myra said, narrowing her eyes.

"Did Wilf cut you off?"

Myra nodded and watched his expression. She hoped he'd cast her aside.

"I'll have enough magic for the two of us. Besides, it might only be a temporary loss. Besides, I don't care. I want you to be with me," Malik said, hugging her and kissing her forehead. "Myra, I love you."

"For real?" There wasn't an ounce of her that trusted him, but if he had somewhere for them to go, why not take advantage until she could persuade him to remove the bracelet? Or set herself free?

"Babe, it's you and me together." He grinned and squeezed her arm again.

"What are you two planning?" Ermentrude said.

Malik ignored her. "How are the gauges?" He strolled over to the terminal.

"They seem volatile," Katryna reported, watching the gauge bounce around the amber section.

Myra swung her legs off the sofa and eased upright. Her head felt as heavy as a sack of rice. She shuffled across the room to sit next to Wilf.

"You can do this," she whispered in his ear.

Wilf's eyes snapped open and he caught hold of her hand. A tingling ran up her arm and into the base of her skull. She tried to pull back, but he held her in a viselike grip.

"Wilf, let go," Myra said, pulling her arm.

When he dropped her hand, the chair she sat on went careening across the room and crashed into the wall. Her arm and head throbbed, but it was as if he'd turned on a faucet. The magic in the biome called to her. "I can sense magic again!" she said

Malik gave her a thumbs up before turning back to the screen. "There doesn't seem to be a significant difference in the output. I think he's stabilized the magic."

"Wilf, can you hear me?" Ermentrude said, standing in front of him.

Wilf nodded.

"Are you ready to connect with Jayden?" She signaled for the soldier to move closer.

Wilf stared at the soldier and held out his hands. Jayden hesitated and then extended his arms. Wilf clamped his hands onto Jayden's wrists. His eyes rolled back until the pupils disappeared. Jayden's jaw clamped as he gritted his teeth. Veins stood out on his muscular arms. Sweat dripped down his face, but he didn't utter a word.

Wilf's fingertips turned purple and became transparent, with only Jayden's wrists showing. Jayden's eyes widened. His lips parted and a wail penetrated the room like the keening of a wounded animal. He collapsed to the ground as Wilf released his hold.

Wilf shuddered and examined his hands. They'd returned to normal. "He'll be fine," Wilf said, his voice shaking. "There has to be another way. I don't have the strength to keep doing this."

"Perhaps we can connect to the magic in groups. Isn't that how they created the Veil?" Katryna asked.

Ermentrude twirled the hairs on her chin. "That could work. Wilf can focus on a group. We might have to help him."

"Lead a group? How much do I have to discipline my magic to pull that off?" Wilf said, taking a glass of water from Katryna.

"Do you have a better idea?"

Jayden staggered to his feet.

"How are you?" Katryna asked, rushing over to help him.

"Can you connect to the biome's source?" Ermentrude said.

Jayden stretched out his hand and a ball of energy grew. He

grinned and then laughed. Wilf, Ermentrude, and Katryna joined in.

Malik stood next to Myra. "We should leave as soon as I persuade Wilf to connect me next," he said in a low voice. Myra went to stop him, but it was too late — he'd walked to stand in front of her stepbrother.

"I'm willing to be your next test case," Malik said.

"Never," Wilf declared.

"What?"

"You heard me. It was you who killed my father. I can't prove it yet, but I will. At the moment, leaving you without magic seems to be a fitting punishment since you used it to kill him." Wilf struggled to his feet and faced Malik.

Malik glanced in Myra's direction. "I don't know who told you that, but it's not true. I've never met your father. How could I? Until recently I spent all my time in Kureyamage working on the biome project."

It was as Degula had predicted, Myra thought. Who would take her word over Malik's without evidence? The magical world would always blame her. She was a known spy, turncoat, and addict. Who would trust her word over a wizard's?

"We should get back to the store. The Council will want to test Jayden's magic," Ermentrude said.

"But…" Wilf began.

She held the door open. "This mess will take time to unravel. We've got an angry mob of witches that need magic. I suggest we focus on that first."

"Who can we trust to guard the biome?" Wilf asked. "We can't leave those two alone here."

"We'll reset the passcode on the warehouse lock so they won't have access. I'll dispatch the Executrix to guard the facility," Ermentrude said.

"I don't like it, but I can't think of a better solution," Wilf said, marching across the room.

"Jayden, will you escort Malik and Myra out of the building?" Ermentrude asked.

Wilf took Myra's arm when she stepped outside and pulled her to one side. "Is it true what you said in the Source?"

"Do you believe me?" She met his gaze, willing him to accept her version of events.

"Yes, but I don't know if that's because I don't want you to have killed our father," he said, not meeting her eyes.

She laid a hand on his arm. "All I can tell you is that I didn't send a killing blast at Reginald. It surprised and horrified me when he evaporated."

He nodded.

A tear rolled down her cheek. "I'll miss you," she said, hugging him.

He wrapped his arms around her. "You don't have to go with Malik. I don't trust him."

"Until I find a way to remove this bracelet, I need to be with him. But I'll be careful. Once this is over I'll find you. You're my family." She kissed his cheek and walked away from the building. Malik ran to catch her.

"Let's get out of here," he said, placing an arm around her shoulders and pulling her towards him. He released her at the end of the street. "They forgot I've an access key to the portal," he said, glancing back at the warehouse. "Can you transport us with your magic?" He placed his hand on the panel and the door opened.

Myra connected with the sphere. "Where are we going? I need to visualize the destination."

"Take us anywhere for now. We can move the portal to my base later," Malik said, settling on the bench in front of her.

Myra built a picture of a remote location she knew in the Shing Mun Country Park. The wall next to her disappeared, and the portal floated away from Sha Tin.

Chapter Thirty-One - Wizard Command Center outside Wilf's Store, Hong Kong

Wilf, Katryna, and Jayden returned to the Wizard Council's portal headquarters.

"What took you so long?" Hywel asked.

"First, Malik, your assistant, stole the portal and disappeared with it. Next, it took us some time to make our way through the crowd outside," Ermentrude said, squaring up to her ex-husband.

"Did you connect with the Source?" Grand Wizard Verger asked, pushing past Ermentrude.

Jayden produced a tiny ball of energy. A cheer rang through the room.

"How?" Verger said.

"I had to connect to the biome's source. Katryna thinks we can set up coven rings and link the witches," Wilf said.

"It could work. What do you think, Hywel?" Verger said, stopping the other wizard from bickering with Ermentrude.

"I agree that could work for witches, but not for wizards," Hywel said, shaking his head.

"The magic is the same," Ermentrude said. "No difference between witches or wizards."

"Ermentrude is correct. We'll all be Mages," Verger said, smiling at Ermentrude. She let out a snort.

Mages! Wilf glanced towards the store. "The Mages Crystal," he said, staring at the senior wizards.

"What do you mean?" Hywel said, rubbing the back of his neck.

"My family used it to determine our wizard classification when we reached thirteen years of age. If I can infuse the crystal, we might use it as a conduit for both wizards and witches to connect to the biome's source."

"It's broken. Defective. Who knows what might happen if you try to connect that relic to the Source? Don't you agree, Grand Wizard?" Hywel said.

"It's worth a try," Ermentrude interrupted before Verger could answer. "You can't expect Wilf to link to every wizard." Hywel glared at her.

"Captain, take your men and go with Wilf to secure the crystal." Verger turned to Wilf. "Let's see what's left." The soldiers cleared a path from the black portal to the store.

"Everyone outside," the Captain commanded, directing his men to form a blockade around the remains of the crystal.

"See, I told you! It's fractured, and I suspect useless," Hywel said, puffing out his chest.

Verger walked around the crystal and shook his head. "I'm not sure this will work."

"I'd forgotten how little remained," Katryna whispered to Wilf.

"Let's hope there's enough," Wilf said, placing his hand on top. Katryna took hold of his other hand.

"I'm here if you need me," she said.

"Thanks. It helps to know you have my back." He dropped her hand and placed both of his hands on top of the crystal. The shards reflected his image, only this time his eyes were bright, alert, and full of purpose. All traces of guilt were gone.

Growing up, the crystal had reminded Wilf of a rotten hard boiled egg, with the gray albumen holding the black yolk at its center. The difference now was that jagged half-crystals surrounded the center. Throbbing bands of color pulsed from the ends of Wilf's fingers into the crystal. The black center turned to mirrored glass and a pinprick of light spread out, covering the surface in a red glow.

"It's working." Wilf heard the Grand Wizard's voice as he closed his eyes and focused on his connection to the biome's source.

The swirling mass of energy welcomed him in and surrounded him. A high-pitched hum wrapped around him. Visions of flames played behind his eyes. He pushed the thought aside. It was a memory of being in Hywel's Advancer. He'd made it through that ordeal using rage after Hywel had admitted to killing Wilf's mother. Wilf wrestled those thoughts aside, needing to remain in control of his emotions and magic. Revenge could wait. He needed all his strength to forge a powerful connection between the crystal and the biome's source.

He recalled the elation of scoring the winning goal at the qualifier, and he clung to that sensation. The feeling of winning despite overwhelming odds. This felt like a similar battle. This time it was him against the untamed magic of the biome's source.

He mentally created an interface between the crystal and the Source, seeing it grow link by link. A chain of source magic attached to the crystal.

Wilf pulled back and lifted his hands from the crystal. A throbbing pulse of pink light covered its surface.

"It's done," he said, bending over and catching his breath.

The Captain stepped forward. "What do I need to do?"

"Place your hand on the crystal. There will be a sharp pain when you connect. I'm not sure how it will affect you after that, but don't break the connection until you can feel the Source with your mind," Wilf said.

The Captain nodded and placed his hand on it. He grunted at the connection and scrunched his eyes. Sweat collected on his forehead, and his jaw tightened as the crystal pulsed a deep red and hummed. Everyone watching held their breath, willing the connection to work.

The Captain gasped and opened his eyes. The crystal's surface returned to a pale pink. He pulled his hand off and staggered back. Every soldier, senior wizard, and witch stared at the Captain. The silence in the room became deafening while they waited for him to speak. He pulled back his shoulder and stood tall, then extended his hand and produced a minute ball of energy. A grin spread across his face.

"Well done," he said, extinguishing the ball and shaking Wilf's hand. "Thank you."

"I'm glad it worked," Wilf said. "We'll leave you to organize your men."

Verger and Hywel had their heads together as Wilf approached.

"After the soldiers, would you like to go next Grand Wizard, or should I?" Hywel asked, turning his back on Wilf.

"I believe the Grand Wizard and I should go before you," Tyrone said.

"I think we should allow the Executrix Squad to go next. Then senior wizards," Verger said, wrapping his cloak around his body.

Wilf shook his head at the squabble and wandered over to Katryna.

The Captain was talking to his sergeant. "You can be the focal point. Organize the troop into groups of ten. Have the soldiers place a hand on the right shoulder of the man in front of him. Let's get this done."

"Yes, sir," the sergeant said, saluting.

"Witches next," Katryna said, looking at the faces pressed against the store's windows when Wilf joined her. He opened the door.

"Why are the wizards always first?" someone shouted from the crowd.

"When are you going to help us?" another yelled.

Angry muttering ran through the crowd.

"We're organizing the return of magic for all," Katryna yelled back. She linked her arm through Wilf's and asked him, "How do you want to organize this?"

"How large was the coven that produced the Veil?" he asked.

"Ten," Katryna said.

He groaned. There had to be several hundred witches outside the store. "This will take a long time. Let's hope the crystal can keep its connection," he said.

She kissed his cheek. "You'll be a hero. They'll erect a statue of you right here." She laughed. Wilf rolled his eyes, but grinned.

Ermentrude and Degula came over to join them. "The Executrix Squad first, then we'll be able to control the crowd," Degula said.

"I agree," Ermentrude said. Katryna took her mother's arm and drew her to one side.

"Why are we giving magic to Degula? She handed me to Hywel and now you're rewarding her?"

"She's in charge of the squad for now. If there were a choice, I'd agree with you, but those witches under her command would demand it. They're extremely loyal."

"It's a mistake." Katryna watched as Degula rounded up the squad and marched them into the store. The Captain and his men came marching out to form a blockade around the entrance after allowing Wilf, Katryna, and Ermentrude to enter.

"Do we need one of you to lead us?" Degula asked.

"You should be able to connect. But be careful, the Source might fight the connection."

She gave a brief nod.

Wilf stood by the door as the squad positioned itself around Degula. Each guard placed a hand on the shoulder next to her in an arrowhead formation. The guard at the front placed her hand on Degula's shoulder. When she made contact with the crystal, Degula's eyes rolled until only the whites appeared. She rocked from side to side.

"Stop!" The Captain came running into the store. "My sergeant and his men evaporated!"

Ermentrude grabbed the Captain and drew him to the side. "It's too dangerous to stop."

A groan came from the squad connected to the crystal. Degula's arm pulsed red as if her veins were trying to break free from her body. The guard next to her screamed. Soon all the Executrix Squad were moaning and wailing. A vein pulsed up their arms and into the back of their necks.

Degula pulled her hand off the crystal and staggered away from the coven. "What's happening?" she gasped.

"I don't know," Wilf said. The crystal continued to pulse, its surface turning from red to purple. The witches in the Executrix Squad dropped their arms from each other's shoulders. They flickered. Their bodies kept losing substance until finally it was possible to see through them. A shriek filled the air, then there was nothing. The squad and Degula simply disappeared.

"What have you done?" Hywel said, coming to stand next to Wilf and Katryna.

"The patrol I commanded has also vanished," the Captain said.

"How's that possible?" Wilf said.

"You did this!" Hywel said, pointing at Wilf.

"No. You created a virus that unbalanced the Realm," Wilf said. "YOU did this." He extended his hand and a web of magic wrapped around Hywel's hands.

Hywel shook his bound hands. "How dare you! Release me!"

"What's this?" Grand Wizard Verger said.

"He killed my mother," Wilf said.

"Hywel, is this true? Were you involved in the death of Yan Shuai?" Verger demanded, glancing from Wilf to Hywel.

"She was a necessary casualty. Reginald was proving difficult to control." Hywel waved his bound hands.

"So you murdered his wife?" Verger said, widening his eyes.

"I put the needs of the Council and the Realm before any individual," Hywel said, straightening to his full height.

"The question of your loyalty is not in dispute. It's your morality that's being called into judgment," Verger said, shaking his head. "The Council would never have sanctioned a witch being killed under any circumstances."

Hywel sneered. "You forget that the Council ordered the release of the Pulch Virus. How many witches died then?"

The Grand Wizard sucked in a deep breath and let his arms drop to his sides. "You assured us that no witch would evaporate."

"None did," Hywel said.

"Because the virus took all their magic and made them incapable of evaporation!" Wilf shouted.

Verger shook his head defiantly. "I'll have you stripped of your title and position. If we restore magic" — he stood toe-to-toe with Hywel — "I will guarantee that you will never perform another spell in your life."

Hywel bumped into Katryna, sending her sprawling towards the crystal. She put out her hands and connected to its surface. Hywel fell on top of her. He encircled her in his bound arms and laid his hands on the crystal, trapping her against it. His ring flared as the connection formed. Katryna struggled, trying to pull her hands from the crystal. She expelled a high-pitched scream.

"Wilf! Mom!" Her body and Hywel's flickered.

Wilf could see through them both. He reached out, trying to catch hold of Hywel, but Ermentrude pulled him back.

"The Source…" Katryna gasped, and then disappeared.

Silence fell. The light in the center of the crystal grew brighter and Wilf covered his eyes.

"Everyone outside!" he shouted.

A low, vibrating hum emanated from the crystal. It increased in pitch and volume. Wilf's ears buzzed. He ran outside and secured the door to the empty store before backing away. A groan rumbled through the air, and then the crystal exploded.

A tremor ripped open the sidewalk. Windows shattered, shards flying into the street. Witches turned to run, but the crystal daggers pierced their skin. Screams and groans came from the witches writhing on the ground. A flash of green light blinded Wilf, and then silence fell again. A cloud of dust descended on the silent forms scattered across the broken street. It whipped into a tornado and then rose into the sky.

Ermentrude staggered up from her crouched position next to Wilf and he caught her elbow. She shook him off. Tears were running down her face. "This is bad." Her ashen face lifted to the sky. A rift opened and the dust cloud entered. "They can't have all evaporated."

Wilf stared at the empty street. He ran through the black portal's entrance and into the control room. It was empty.

Ermentrude shuffled behind him and collapsed into a chair.

"Seems you have your wish," she said.

"What do you mean? I never asked for this." His fighting strength had faded. A hollowness filled him.

"You wanted to return to Hong Kong without magic. We don't know how to support the biome environment. It will die and then magic will cease to exist."

"I cannot believe we are the only ones from the Realm who survived," Wilf said. He stared at the blank screens. They had to keep the biome working. "There's Malik and Myra. We can find them. Malik will want to keep the biome running."

Footsteps sounded in the hall, and the Captain entered with Jayden.

"Where is everyone?" the Captain said.

"Vanished. How did you survive?" Wilf said.

"I came looking for Jayden." The Captain ran his hand over his head. "That entire crowd of witches — gone."

Wilf nodded and picked up his backpack. "Collect whatever you need. We have to search for Myra and Malik."

The communication mirror flickered, and a shrouded image appeared. "Wilf? Mom?" A voice crackled through heavy static.

Wilf ran to the mirror. "We're here."

"I'm…" Crackles and hisses stole Katryna's voice.

"Say again." Ermentrude grasped the edge of the table next to Wilf.

"The crystal connected to the Source." The static grew, then silence.

Ermentrude and Wilf stared at each other. "What do you think she meant? And where is she?" Wilf said.

"I don't know, but she's alive," Ermentrude said.

"Then perhaps others are, too," Wilf said.

"Captain, can we move this portal to Sha Tin?" Ermentrude asked.

"We don't have enough personnel to run it."

Ermentrude sighed. "I guess we're using public transportation."

Wilf slung his backpack over his shoulder. "Malik won't be far from the biome."

"How will we trace them?" Ermentrude asked, following Wilf out of the portal.

"We'll cut the feed from the biomes to the storage tank. That should bring Malik to us." Wilf headed into the store.

"What are we doing in here? I thought we were heading to Sha Tin," Ermentrude said.

Wilf climbed down into the basement. He had hoped never to see or deal with Malik again. Now he'd have to bargain with him, but he would do whatever it took to find Katryna and the other witches and wizards. He'd thought he had connected to the biome, but Katryna had said he'd connected to the Source. This was his fault.

He tapped on the bookcase in the basement, and his ring flared. A book tipped forward, and a door appeared. It swung open, revealing his father's portal. If they hadn't evaporated, then where would a Realm of magical people disappear to? It was a mystery he intended to solve.

Ermentrude took a seat next to Wilf, the Captain and Jayden opposite. Wilf connected with the sphere and pictured the warehouses in Sha Tin.

The wall disappeared next to him. The portal shuddered. A shaft of light appeared running from the basement into the street, and the portal ascended. It navigated through the sky over Hong Kong. Wilf looked down at the Football Club.

A knot tightened in his stomach. There was just one week before the championship, and he had every intention of making that match. He could do this. He would convince Malik to help them, find Katryna, repair his friendship with Enzo, and then make the championship. Piece of cake.

CB Lyall is in full possession of her English accent, even after spending half her life living in exotic locations - New York, India, Belgium and Hong Kong. Despite her undiagnosed childhood dyslexia she finally developed a deep love of books and writing. She has published two novels in The Virus of Beauty Series and numerous short stories.

She currently resides in Westchester, New York, but who knows how long that will remain true. Her passions are her husband, three sons, her grandchildren and golf.

To learn when her next book will be released, or to get updates on other magical things in the works and life, sign up for her newsletter at cblyall.com.

If you enjoyed this book, please write a one- or two-line review on-line. Thank you

You might also enjoy the other books in the Series:
The Virus of Beauty – Book 1
The Veil of Corruption – Book 2
The Vassal of Magic – Book 3